TREBLE

AT THE

JAM FEST

A FOOD LOVERS' VILLAGE MYSTERY

LESLIE BUDEWITZ

D0089775

MIDNIGHT INK
WOODBURY, MINNESOTA

FIRST EDITION
First Printing, 2017

Book format by Bob Gaul
Cover design by Lisa Novak
Cover Illustration by Ben Perini
Editing by Nicole Nugent

Midnight Ink, an imprint of Llewellyn Worldwide Ltd.

Library of Congress Cataloging-in-Publication Data
Names: Budewitz, Leslie, author.
Title: Treble at the jam fest / by Leslie Budewitz.
Description: First edition. | Woodbury, Minnesota: Midnight Ink, [2017] |
    Series: A Food Lovers' Village mystery; 4
Identifiers: LCCN 2016047686 (print) | LCCN 2016055162 (ebook) | ISBN
    9780738752402 | ISBN 9780738752655
Subjects: LCSH: Women detectives—Fiction. | Murder—Investigation—Fiction.
    | GSAFD: Mystery fiction.
Classification: LCC PS3602.U334 T74 2017 (print) | LCC PS3602.U334 (ebook) |
    DDC 813/.6—dc23
LC record available at https://lccn.loc.gov/2016047686

Midnight Ink
Llewellyn Worldwide Ltd.
2143 Wooddale Drive
Woodbury, MN 55125-2989
www.midnightinkbooks.com

Printed in the United States of America

For the musicians,
who give our lives a soundtrack,
and the retail ladies,
who make our towns and villages hum.

Acknowledgments

Over the last few years, I've watched the development of the Crown of the Continent Guitar Festival and Workshop, in the village I call home, as concertgoer, student's wife, auction contributor, and friend to the organizers, students, and teachers. Although the festival created on these pages is much different, I've drawn on my own experiences and observations of "the Crown." Thanks to David and Judy Feffer, Diane Kautzman, guitarist Doug Smith, Doug Averill, and many others for their stories—and for their contributions to our community. Special thanks to Donna Lawson for buying a character name at a fundraiser— you're the perfect cozy character!

And in a case of life imitating art, I must say that I wrote this book before learning that the Crown planned to bring Gypsy jazz to our fair village.

As always, thanks to Derek Vandeberg, who gets a new name on these pages, at Frame of Reference; Marlys Anderson-Hisaw and crew at Roma's Gourmet Kitchen Store; and Cathi Spence of Think Local, for putting the books in the hands of local readers and sharing stories of retail life.

Readers who cook will be as grateful as I am to Lita Artis for her red chile sauce, aka Ray's enchilada sauce. *Grazie* to Brian Mahoney, bartender at the Marina Cay in Bigfork, for his champagne cocktail recipe, a drink to die for.

Our buddy Dave Snyder christened the closing event, and my friend Brin Jackson chose Erin's new accessory. Mark Langlois once again lent me his bar.

Thanks to Paige Wheeler of Creative Media Agency, Inc., who found the villagers and me a new home at Midnight Ink, where Terri Bischoff, Nicole Nugent, Katie Mickschl, and the crew welcomed us. Thank you all. I am deeply grateful to Ramona DeFelice Long, whose sharp insights made this book stronger.

And as always, thanks to my husband, Don Beans, for testing recipes, blocking out fight scenes, and enduring other challenges of the writer's life.

There's no such thing as a wrong note.
It all depends on how you resolve it.
—Jazz pianist Art Tatum

If music be the food of love, play on.
—William Shakespeare, *Twelfth Night*

The Cast

The Murphy Clan:

Erin Murphy, manager of Glacier Mercantile, aka the Merc

Francesca "Fresca" Conti Murphy, Erin's mother,
the Merc's manager emeritus

Molly Murphy, Erin's cousin, a budding real estate agent

Chiara Murphy Phillips, Erin's sister and co-owner of
Snowberry Gallery

Landon Phillips, Chiara's son, age six

At the Merc:

Tracy McCann, sales clerk and chocolatier

Lou Mary Williams Crawford Vogel, veteran retail clerk

The Jazz Lovers:

Grant and Ann Drake, fundraisers and festival champions

Rebecca Whitman, gallery owner and festival director

Marv Alden, festival board member

The Musicians:

Gabrielle Drake, the voice of a new generation

Dave Barber, barber by day, guitarist by night

Sam Kraus, winemaker, guitarist, drummer

Jennifer Kraus, winemaker and bass player

Gerry Martin, prodigy turned headliner

Jackson Mississippi Boyd, mentor to musicians young and old

Villagers and Friends:

Adam Zimmerman, Erin's boyfriend, wilderness camp director

Ned Redaway, long-time owner of Red's Bar

Tanner Lundquist, Adam's childhood best friend

Michelle, the barista

The Law:

Kim Caldwell, sheriff's detective, on leave

Ike Hoover, undersheriff

Deputy Oakland, new on the beat

Erin's Housemates:

Mr. Sandburg, a sable Burmese, king of the roost

Pumpkin, a full-figured orange tabby, challenger for the throne

One

Blame it on the rhubarb. That's as logical a start to the story as jazz or love—or greed, jealousy, or any of the thousand other notes the human heart can play.

Nothing says "slow down, girl" like letting a jar of strawberry-rhubarb jam slip through your fingers and smash on your shop's wood floor. Worse—the jam splashed a customer. A customer wearing white ankle skimmers.

"Not my pants!" she said, stepping back nimbly.

"I am soooo sorry. Stay right there." My palms covered in pinky-red goo, I grabbed a damp rag and sped back to the scene of my crime.

The customer stuck out her leg and we both leaned in for inspection. She took the rag and dabbed at one gold-sandaled foot, the jam nearly the same tint as her nail polish. "Just that one speck."

Thank God for small favors.

The floor, on the other hand, looked like a finger-painting gone wrong. Tracy, my sales clerk, appeared with a bucket and mop and began the cleanup. I swiped a bit of jam off my shin, glad that my flouncy blue skirt had been spared.

I plucked another jar off the display, careful to get a good grip, and held it out. "Courtesy of the Merc, with my apologies."

"That's generous. Thank you." The woman took the jar in one manicured hand, a diamond the size of my first apartment catching the morning light. "Strawberry-rhubarb. My husband will love it." She slipped the jar in to her matte black leather bag, a designer logo plainly visible. Genuine, or a knock-off? Around here, you never know. Especially as tourist season kicks in. Some of Jewel Bay's wealthiest residents and visitors dress like they haven't updated their closets since 1965, while others flash designer labels more suited to Manhattan than Montana.

She tucked a highlighted golden strand behind one ear, exposing a diamond stud. "I'm Ann Drake, by the way. We're part of the festival crowd."

"Erin Murphy, proprietor." I held my damp hand palm up, in a gesture that said *pardon me for not shaking*.

"Mom, what about this pottery? You said you wanted rustic-but-classic." A bright-eyed young woman stepped into view, maybe ten years younger than me, in her early twenties. She peered at the bottom of a large hand-thrown bowl, her shiny black hair swinging. "R R inside an almond?"

"Not an almond—a football," I said. "Reg Robbins. Long-time NFL all-star. Took up throwing pots for stress relief and found a new career." I dried my fingers, realizing why the girl looked familiar. Hers was one of half a dozen tiny photos on the poster advertising tonight's pre-festival concert. "You must be Gabrielle Drake. Your picture's in our window. And the earrings give you away."

Ann took the bowl and her daughter reached up reflexively to finger one earring—a red, white, and blue guitar pick on a wire. "Call me Gabby. And yes, I'm playing with Gerry Martin tonight—can you believe the luck?"

"It's hard work, darling, not luck. You've earned this opportunity. And the shot at a tour." Ann returned the bowl to the display, a brittle edge to her words. "I'll lend you a pair of good earrings for tonight."

Daughter ignored mother. "I'm hoping for a recording session, too," she told me. "He's building his own studio."

"That's great. The courtyard where you'll be playing should be ready—let's take a peek." I led the women through the back hall, first tossing the rag over the stainless steel counter that divides the Merc's commercial kitchen from the retail shop floor. The rag landed in the sink with a soft thud. *Bingo.*

"Oh." Gabby Drake clapped her hands together a minute later. "It's magical."

"It will be," I said, "when the lights are twinkling in the trees and the wine is flowing."

Since I took over the Merc a year ago, I'd worked hard to make the courtyard functional. It was more than that now—a bit of paradise, a microcosm of the village and its heavenly setting. We'd feng shui'd the cozy space and upgraded the wooden fence—another rustic-but-classic touch—that separates our yard from Red's larger patio next door.

To throw a party for a crowd, all we need to do is unlock the gate, slide the wheeled fence out of sight, and voilá! A Jewel Bay institution as venerable as the Merc, Red's boasts a stage perfect for a musical evening under the stars. Now that my mother owns both properties, there's a lot less grease and grime, but Red's is still a cowboy bar deeply rooted in the Montana tradition of cowboy bars.

The annual Jazz Festival and Workshop didn't officially begin until Sunday, but Gerry Martin, a regular guest artist, had agreed to jump-start the fun with a Friday night concert. Openers included a local trio, a sax player, and young Gabby, his protégée.

A gaggle of volunteers had spent hours decorating, leaving Tracy and me free to mind our own business. The last volunteer, Rebecca Whitman, left off precisely positioning chairs that would soon be jostled any old which way to greet the Drakes.

"Ann!" The two women touched their manicured hands to each other's shoulders, feather-light, and kissed the air along side each other's cheeks.

"I was shocked to hear—" Ann said, her voice low. Rebecca shook her head. Ann nodded slightly, then directed her attention to Gabby, who'd climbed the short steps to the stage and now stood in the center.

"As if she owned it," went the phrase, and it fit. But I was curious what had shocked Ann.

"Every year," Rebecca said, "more confident and more beautiful. You have a star on your hands."

A satisfied smile played on Ann Drake's perfect pink lips, her dramatic cheekbones flushing under her careful makeup. "When I think how far we've come, from that overcrowded orphanage. Those first years trying to get her to talk, then all the lessons and outfits and tears …"

Rebecca slipped her arm around the other woman's waist.

"Erin, Adam's on the line." Tracy appeared at my elbow and I hurried inside, anticipation mingling with worry. I follow my rule against staff carrying cell phones on the shop floor, to avoid distractions. So while I call or text my sweetie when I'm in my office, I sensed trouble when he called me on the Merc's landline.

"Hey, there," I said into the receiver. "What's up?"

"Tanner missed the flight—some meeting ran long. They rebooked him, so we'll make the concert, I promise." Adam's apologetic tone did little to soothe my nerves. I'd been eager to meet his best friend, but pile Tanner Lundquist's arrival on top of hosting our first big do in the redone courtyard and welcoming the annual flock of musicians and music lovers, followed in a week by the surge of Memorial Day tourists...

It was a wonder I'd only dropped one jar of jam. Jam I hadn't entirely scrubbed off. I licked a red dot off the back of my hand. "Not a problem. We'll have plenty of food and plenty of beer."

"Just save me a kiss." His voice dropped a notch.

"That's easy," I said with a laugh, almost feeling his lips on mine.

We clicked off, and I dropped the phone into its cradle, next to the brass cash register that had been here since the first Murphy in Jewel Bay rang up the first purchase in Murphy's Mercantile in 1910. Classy, but no longer practical except as a cash drawer and a stand to hold the iPad, our modern substitute.

"Rhubarb pickles? Who ever heard of such a thing?" The customer, a plump woman in a navy T-shirt and striped capris, peered at the label through reading glasses perched low on her nose. "And rhubarb chutney."

"The pickles are done with ginger, mustard, and a hint of orange. The chutney's made with raisins and onions, and a touch of spice." I crossed the shop floor to the counter, opened a jar, and spread a sample on a water cracker for her.

"Oh, my word." She called to her companion, obviously her sister, "You have got to try this chutney."

"Come try these chocolates," the sister called, a sample bite in hand. "They'd make a dead man drool."

"Tracy makes the best truffles in the state," I said, gesturing to my beaming employee. For the first time, I noticed her earrings, miniature red-and-black electric guitars. The in-house chocolateria—a shop within the shop—had been a late-night brainstorm when I feared she'd decamp and start her own business. Freeing her up for more hours in the Merc's commercial kitchen meant I needed another employee. So far no luck, no matter how often I rubbed the trio of colored stars tattooed inside my left wrist.

"Rhubarb mustard sauce, rhubarb cherry sauce, rhubarb halapeny sauce—somebody's got a heck of an imagination," one of the sisters said.

The jalapeño combination had been Adam's idea, sparked by the memory of a jam eaten at a childhood friend's house. His own mother's idea of gourmet cooking had been to toss frozen vegetables in with the boxed mac and cheese. My family's obsession with good, fresh food—the more local, the better—had baffled him when we first got together late last summer.

The rhubarb, local though it was, had presented a challenge. Blessed with an overzealous crop, a friend of the shop had left three crates of gleaming red stalks at the Merc's back gate, with a promise of more to come. Our jam maker had filled the shop with sweet and spicy scents, and my mother had created a divine rhubarb sauce she'd tested over lamb for last Sunday's family dinner. A bumper year in one garden suggested similar bounty in other yards, so we printed up recipe cards. The sole holdout had been Jennifer Kraus, co-owner of Monte Verde Winery, who pronounced rhubarb wine quaint but undrinkable.

What's a food lovers' village without a food snob or two?

The customer licked her pudgy fingers. "If I worked here, I'd be a workaholic."

"If you lived here, I'd hire you. Where are you visiting from?"

The sisters chatted about their travels with their husbands and two other couples in a caravan of RVs wandering the West. "We never expected so charming a town. Mountains, fishing, yes, but your art and music took us by surprise. And the food—what a treat."

In addition to the truffles, they chose honey, cheese, and several varieties of my mother's pastas and sauces. And for good measure, rhubarb pickles and early produce from Rainbow Lake Garden. I rang up their purchases and sent them on their way.

"Why does everyone want green tea truffles one day and double chocolate cherry the next?" Tracy asked as she refilled the display case. "I wish I could tell what will sell and what will be a dud."

"You and every retailer. At least we can eat your overstock. One year at SavClub, they overbought this chopper-sealer-grinder thingamajiggy, and after Christmas, management gave one to every employee. I bet half ended up at Goodwill, next to mine." I scanned the jam and jelly cabinet, then headed for the basement to bring up another case of strawberry-rhubarb trouble.

Five minutes later I huffed up the last step to the back hallway. The sound of heels rapping on the plank floor signaled Ann and Gabby Drake's return from the courtyard, and the rise and fall of voices told me Rebecca Whitman was with them.

The front door chimed, signaling a new arrival. The footsteps slowed, and I sent the women a mental message to hurry up—I hate to keep a customer waiting, and the box was getting heavier by the second.

The chatter continued as I stepped into the hall behind them. I stretched up as tall as I could with the heavy carton in my arms and peered over Ann Drake's shoulder to spot the customer.

Not a customer. Dave Barber—who is a barber, and a musician and festival board chair—in his tan Stetson.

And the look on his face was as deadly as any old-fashioned razor blade.

Two

f tables could groan ...

Rebecca and her crew, with help from the bar staff, had lined one wall of the courtyard with buffet tables, now covered with red gingham in washable vinyl. On each café and picnic table sat blue canning jars filled with red and white flowers, a tiny American flag waving from each.

"If music be the food of love, what's the food of music?"

"Ned, you're quoting Shakespeare. Sort of," I said.

"I've learned a line or two in my life, girlie." Old Ned Redaway, Red's founder and namesake, winked and reached for a fig-and-goat cheese bruschetta. Wendy and Max, whose bakery and bistro are the stomach of the village, had provided several varieties of their trademark toasts, while my mother had whipped up trays of her grilled Caprese kabobs and stuffed dates, and Ray Ramirez of the Bayside Grille made Reuben bites, using his famous beer-soaked sauerkraut. His recipe, canned in our basement, was available only at the Merc and the Grille. It might not help my hips, but it was boosting the Merc's bottom line considerably.

"Pigs in a blanket?" I leaned forward to inspect a platter. Decidedly retro—not a bad thing, but unusual. Jewel Bay calls itself the Food Lovers' Village for a reason, and that reason includes food that is adventuresome without being weird.

"The tea shop guy made them." Wendy balanced a tray of fresh fruit skewers on a cake stand. "Local sausage, nice springy dough. They're good."

So good I ate two.

On stage, Sam Kraus and Dave Barber hoisted a speaker on to a tall stand. I still had no idea why Barber had glared at me so bitterly earlier. A customer had trailed in behind him and Tracy had been busy at the chocolate counter, so I hadn't had a chance to confront him before he pushed past me and out my back door.

But I was going to make the chance now.

"Dave? A word?"

Barber's boot heels made hollow sounds as he strode to the front of the wooden stage. He crouched and pushed his hat back with one finger. "Everything under control?"

"You tell me," I said. "The way you came stomping into my shop, glaring and glowering, then charged on through like I wasn't there? What was that about?"

Barber lifted his chin, his jaw tightening. "It's got nothing to do with you, Erin."

I squinted, confused, then remembered the women who'd come in from the courtyard at the same time as Barber arrived. "Well, whatever beef you have with Rebecca Whitman or Ann Drake, you keep it out of my shop. And don't let it spill into tonight, either. Too much work has gone into putting on this concert."

"Yes, ma'am," he said, the teasing tone contradicted by the flinty eyes.

"Barber, you working or BS'ing? I could use a hand," Sam called. Barber studied me another long moment, then pushed himself up and followed Sam down the stage steps. They went out Red's gate to the alley, also known as Back Street, where Sam's van idled.

Heaven help the woman who gets between a man and his gear.

On our side of the courtyard, water flowed down the metal wall-mounted fountain. I strode over to unplug it before I forgot. We didn't need one more sound to interfere with tonight's music. My hand shook as I reached for the cord, still irked by Barber's behavior.

I had not imagined his ire this morning, or his dismissiveness now. Few things irritate me more than being treated rudely, then told it was nothing.

In the corner stood a giant propane torch, and I leaned in to check the gauge on the tank. I didn't anticipate much of a chill tonight, but in mountain valleys like this one, any kind of weather can happen almost any time of year.

"Erin, you seen Gerry Martin yet?"

I straightened. "Wow. Look at you, all spiffed up."

Jennifer and Sam Kraus had come to town for the first jazz workshop and stayed, buying an old cherry orchard with a few rows of grape vines that they built into Monte Verde Winery, co-sponsors with the Merc of tonight's event. They played a lot of local gigs, but I'd never seen her in anything fancier than a sundress.

"Tracy took me shopping." Jennifer plucked at the waistline of her turquoise lace dress, a close-fitting bodice over a full skirt that swung when she moved. She looked lovely and awkward at the same time, a tomboy-turned-homecoming princess. Tracy may have helped her scour thrift shops for the perfect dress, but the thick-soled black rubber flip-flops reminded me that Jennifer's fine taste ran only to her palate.

"You'll outshine the rest of us," I said. "Martin should be here any minute. Can you believe what Rebecca did with the courtyard? Her volunteer spirit is amazing."

Jennifer sucked in her cheeks. "She spends more time telling the rest of us what to do than running her own business."

Her catty tone surprised me. Pre-performance jitters? "Speaking of business, that reminds me. I got an e-mail from the orchard and winery supplier in Walla Walla. They took some used bottlers in trade. Might be what you guys are looking for."

Her face brightened. "Yeah." Behind her, Sam tested the cymbals. The left side of her face twitched. "That's my cue." She slipped a finger under the shoulder strap of her sleeveless dress to adjust something and sped toward the stage.

Nerves hit us each a little differently.

Next thing I knew, the courtyard was packed, the noise level rising. J.D., Ned's grandson and bartender, had enlisted help from Michelle, a barista at Wendy's bakery, and the two of them were busy pouring Monte Verde wines. The fairy lights gave the courtyard sparkle, and the jazz trio's soft sounds filled the air as music-loving villagers and visitors ate, drank, and made merry.

I still hadn't seen Gerry Martin, our headliner, or Gabby Drake. Or Adam and Tanner. I hoped this flight wasn't delayed, too, though the jet from Minneapolis could easily have flown overhead without my noticing. Adam had promised they'd be here, and he keeps his promises, but when airlines are involved ... I ran a thumb across my stars.

Despite all my planning, I'd forgotten to change my own clothes. The blue skirt and white top would do, but my workday flats had to go. I dashed inside and up to my office, where I checked my phone. No messages from Adam—a good sign.

Then I tugged on my red cowboy boots. Stuck out a foot to admire them.

Let the good times roll.

∞

"What's the difference between a bass player and a pizza?" Dave Barber stood at the microphone, one hand cradling the neck of his guitar. Sam made a low drum roll. "A pizza can feed a family of four."

He showed no traces of the earlier nastiness. The crowd laughed, except for me. And Jennifer, clutching her electric bass.

"Why does a banjo player always lock his car when he leaves his banjo inside?" We waited. "If he didn't, when he came back, there would be two."

The audience groaned. Barber nodded to the others and they began a jazzy piece I didn't recognize, but many around me bobbed their heads as if they did. I leaned against the wall near the Merc's back door. Happily, Barber had taken my advice to leave the argument—whatever it was—for another time. The trio appeared to be in good form. A few minutes later, a sax player from across the valley joined them.

Say what you want about Jewel Bay, we know how to party.

"Erin, aren't we selling CDs?" Michelle spoke in my ear. "People are asking."

"What? Oh, heck." I dug around under the buffet table and hauled out the box of Martin's CDs, the one detail Rebecca and her crew had missed. "Let's say twelve bucks, a Friday-night special. I'll make a sign."

I dashed inside and made magic with card stock and a Sharpie, returning in time to hear Barber wrapping up his introduction.

"Please welcome back to Jewel Bay the master of contemporary jazz guitar, your friend and mine, Mr. Gerry Martin."

Behind him, Sam gave another drum roll, all but drowned out by the applause as Martin bounded up the steps and took center stage, swinging his guitar into place. The gesture forced Barber out of the way. For the second time in a few hours, I saw Barber's face darken, but the hat hid his features as he fiddled with the tuners on his guitar.

Until today I'd thought him the picture of the people-loving barber-shop personality. Had I misread the situation earlier? Was the source of tension not Rebecca or Ann, but Martin?

Martin swung into action, setting the rhythm. Once the mood and melody were established, he cut loose on a lead. The first piece was all him, all-star, all spot-on, a clinic of control and stage presence. Proof of what hours alone in a room with a guitar can produce. This valley is blessed with more than its share of creativity and some pretty talented musicians, but when the big kids come to town, sit back and enjoy.

Slim and intense, dressed all in black, Martin poured his energy through his fingers into the strings. He clearly relished the spotlight—even when that spotlight was a bulb in a rusted coffee can, shining on a worn wooden stage, its walls hung with signs from businesses long gone.

The piece ended, and Martin acknowledged the applause, guitar up, poised for the next tune. He muttered signals, counting off like a quarterback in church. Though I'm no jazz whiz, I thought the intricate rhythms sounded a hair off, and judging by the furrowed glance Martin shot Sam, he seemed to think so, too. Whose fault, I couldn't tell. Then the rhythm evened out, and Martin pivoted toward the crowd. But his head was bowed, eyes on the frets, as if by concentrating, he could force the trio of backup musicians to his will. As if we weren't there.

A few minutes later, he threw a phrase to Barber, who threw it back, and they bounced off each other in a long counterplay, Martin keeping time with one black-booted foot. Then Barber stepped forward and took the lead, but Martin didn't step back. If that was supposed to be Barber's cue to keep it short, he ignored it, going off on an extended riff that I quite enjoyed. So did my neighbors, judging by the swaying shoulders and tapping toes. Martin played along, but his shoulders had stiffened and the animation had left his face.

Barber built to a climax, then wound down, signaled Martin, and stepped back, fingering a quiet pattern.

"Hey, sunshine." The voice I'd been waiting to hear broke through the applause, and a familiar scent enveloped me as Adam's lips brushed my cheek.

I stretched up for a kiss, then stood to hug Tanner. "Welcome to Jewel Bay. I can't believe it took us so long to meet."

Adam and Tanner had been best friends since the first day of the first grade, more than twenty-five years ago, but since Adam and I had gotten together last August, we'd been too busy for a visit. The timing wasn't great now, either, but that's life. A shiver of delight sped through me, to see them reunited. They were two sides of a coin, both tall and slender, Tanner's close-cropped hair dark blond, Adam's brown curls permanently tangled by the wind. They were even dressed alike, in cargo pants and hikers.

"Facebook doesn't do you justice," Tanner replied, a twinkle in his blue eyes.

The music started up with a dramatic "take charge" chord that led directly into a fierce lead. I didn't have to look at the stage to know Martin was reclaiming the focus after Barber's solo. Adam handed Tanner a beer and they sat on either side of me. I reached for Adam's hand.

No way was I going to let a little disharmony on stage mess up my world.

When the piece ended, Barber tromped down the steps without a word, and Martin took the microphone from the stand.

"Once in a generation," he said, "a voice comes along that redefines music as we know it. Somehow, in a magic lost to us mere mortals, the singer creates a new sound not bound by any labels. That, my friends, is the gift this beautiful young woman is sharing with us tonight. I'm proud to have discovered her here two years ago, in a beginning jazz workshop, and to present, in her festival debut, a voice you will never forget, Miss Gabrielle Drake."

This wasn't actually a festival event, but no point quibbling over genius.

The stage lights turned Gabby's black hair into gleaming ebony. Her sound truly was a marvel, her guitar almost as big as she was. She started with a sultry Norah Jones cover. Adam pressed his leg against mine. Then the young singer and her mentor shared a duet, a love song he'd written for two pop stars who'd since divorced. I'd heard the pop version on the radio endlessly a few years back, but the jazz rendition sounded fresh and lively. Gabby's soulful notes slipped around Martin's, then swung back to the light side, as bright as the hot pink dress that barely covered her bottom.

I leaned forward, searching for Ann. She and a white-haired man in his late sixties sat at one of Red's weathered picnic tables, eyes on their daughter, faces glowing.

I glanced at Tanner. He, too, stared intently at the stage, arms crossed, face expressionless. He vibrated with nervous energy, though I didn't think it came from the music. I hoped his nerves weren't over meeting me.

As if he felt my gaze, he turned and smiled, sweet and slow.

Then Gabby began another piece and I focused on the stage. She was clearly taking the lead, and if I read the rapid shifts on Martin's face right, she'd caught him off-guard. They couldn't have had much time to rehearse, and the impression he gave was of surprise—not the irritation he'd shown at Dave Barber's stage bravado. Like a true professional, he settled into the background, letting the young phenom shine.

All too soon, the set ended and so did the music. It had been a short concert—all we could hope to wheedle out of Martin for a freebie in the backyard of a retail shop and a village hangout.

I excused myself and hustled across the courtyard to thank the musicians.

"Amazing," Donna Lawson, the liquor store queen, said. "If this is what we can expect all week—"

"You bet it is." I wriggled past her and ran smack into Reg Robbins.

"Starting out on the right note," Reg said, his trademark Hawaiian shirt so big that his girlfriend, Heidi Hunter, could have worn it as a bathrobe.

Heidi's diamond-and-sapphire tennis bracelet gleamed as she reached out to give me a hug. "Erin, this was wonderful. I've loved his music for decades. To finally hear him in person … "

"It's going to be a fabulous festival," I said. I wound between friends and neighbors and reached the foot of the stage. Gabby unplugged a cord and I heard Martin speaking, his back to the audience, his tone ugly.

"Don't ever show me up again like that. They came to hear a five-time Grammy winner, not some upstart music school brat who barely knows her way around the fret board."

"They'll get to hear you all week," Gabby replied, her voice rushed. "This was my chance to show people what I can do. If you think I'm a star in the making—"

Martin's back stiffened. "I'll show you—"

"Hand me your guitar, sweetheart." The man I presumed to be Mr. Drake materialized beside me. "Then we'll find you a bite and a drink."

Gabby spun away from her mentor and handed her big guitar to her father. "Erin—hi! What a great night! I hope it sounded as good out there as it felt up here."

Give the girl credit, she could turn on the shine in a flash. Her bright eyes and high color betrayed not one hint of conflict.

What was going on?

"This is my father, Grant Drake," she said, jumping off the stage. "Daddy, Erin runs the cute shop with all the local food and pottery we told you about."

"Ah, yes." He gave me a courtly nod. He had to have heard Martin's sharp tone, if not the actual words. But instead of rising to his daughter's defense, he'd ignored the matter. Or was he following her lead, singing a happy tune? "Thank you for the jam. From what I hear, it was hardly necessary."

"I try never to make a mess without making amends. Come over to our side of the courtyard. We've got plenty of food left."

"We'll be there as soon as we get this guitar safely tucked away." He draped his arm around his daughter—she barely reached his shoulder—and led her away.

In need of something cold and wet—Red's serves a surprisingly good Pinot Grigio, far more to my taste than Monte Verde's offerings—I headed for the outside bar. Part of the charm of the place is the two giant spruce trees growing in the middle of the courtyard, so big their branches shade our side as well. One wide trunk shielded the man on the other side from view, but after listening to his singing and commentary for forty-five minutes, I recognized Gerry Martin's angry tones in a heartbeat. This time they were aimed at Rebecca Whitman.

"I don't know what ever made me think making plans with you was a good idea. Your plans were nothing but false pretenses. And you better believe I'm going to tell everyone who's anyone in Austin and Nashville what this town is really like." Martin stepped into view and spotted me. "I suppose you want something too. Everybody in this town wants something."

He stalked out the back gate, ignoring a small cluster of fans with their phones ready for selfies with him, CDs in hand for his autograph.

"What did we do?" I asked Rebecca.

Neck taut, jaw stiff, she gave a slight shake of the head. "I have no idea."

A flash of turquoise flew by us.

"Gerry, wait," Jennifer Kraus called. But even a runner can't move quickly in flip-flops, and he was out of sight before she reached the gate. She kept going, and I heard her calling his name again. I appreciated her attempt to smooth things over but feared the cause was lost.

Rebecca looped her arm through mine. "I need a drink."

"You read my mind."

J.D. and Michelle were efficient bartenders, pouring drinks with two hands, and Old Ned had the beer taps under control. But the few minutes it took to snare a glass of wine and weave my way back to the table where I'd left Adam and Tanner were long enough for me to realize that the crowd had been oblivious to the musical missteps and harsh tones. If Martin thought that the other musicians had made him look bad in front of the public, he was mistaken. The public had not noticed.

Which I suspected would only make him angrier.

Three

I love the Merc in the morning. I love it in the evening, too, though it sometimes tries my patience midday.

I let myself in the back gate Saturday morning, grateful that the volunteers who'd dolled the place up, to borrow Old Ned's phrase, would swing by soon with brooms and garbage bags. Wendy was catering a bridal shower in the space this afternoon—she and Michelle could carry the food out their back door and into the courtyard, and the bride and her pals could party for hours without interfering with business at the bakery, the bistro, or the Merc.

That's the kind of partnership that makes this village special.

Inside, I switched on the milkglass schoolhouse lights that hang from the painted tin ceiling. They were original, like most of the fittings, though I'd had to replace one of the big display windows last summer after—

Well, that was water under the bridge.

Upstairs in my tiny loft office, I tossed my blue leather tote under the desk. A score from the sale rack at a pricey boutique in Seattle, when I'd been a grocery buyer for SavClub, the international warehouse chain, it had seen better days. Better years.

On the wall hung a painting by my dear friend Christine. My dear, dead friend. Letters stenciled on a paint-spattered background read:

DREAM
CREATE
SNICKER
DOODLE

Pretty good philosophy, if you ask me.

Downstairs, I set up the till, started our Cowboy Roast coffee, and poured a bag of Jewel Bay Critter Crunch into one of Reg's serving bowls. As a product sample, it was far less risky than strawberry-rhubarb jam, as long as we swept twice to catch all the stray popcorn kernels.

Tracy arrived minutes before opening, Diet Coke in one hand, a white paper bag with her morning maple bar in the other. "Sorry I missed the fun last night. Rick got stuck on a sales call, and I didn't want to come back downtown by myself. Bozo and I hung out, and I made a batch of gluten-free dog cookies."

I clicked on the iPad and made sure the POS—point-of-sale—software was up and running. "Oh, good. They're almost as popular as your double dark chocolate truffles."

"A man at the gas station said Gabby Drake knocked his socks off."

"She was great. I don't know whether to call her sound jazz, or pop, or what. She mixes it up, which I love."

Tracy put a stray bag of Montana Gold biscuit mix back where it belonged. "Sounds like this will be a killer week."

Oh, good. If no one but me and the musicians—and Grant Drake—had noticed the tensions on stage, *good, good, good.* And there was no reason for me to be nervous—my part in the festivities was done.

When I co-host a party, I like things to run smoothly. I like the food to be tasty, the drinks yummy, and everyone happy. But no matter how much you plan, when you bring together a crowd of people, each with their own goals and worries, you never know what will happen.

Kinda like retail.

"So, tell me about Tanner."

I looked up with a start, then smiled, remembering the evening. "I like him a lot. I knew I would. They went kayaking this morning, on the Wild Mile. You and Rick should sit with us at the concert in the park tomorrow night. Oh, let's be sure we have enough picnic baskets."

One of my brainstorms after I took over last summer had been ready-made Breakfast Baskets, featuring a pair of coffee mugs, Cowboy Roast coffee or one of our new herbal teas, and Montana Gold pancake mix with Creamery butter and a choice of huckleberry or chokecherry syrup. Eggs and sausage were extra. Our Lakeside Picnic baskets ("Just Add Water") feature champagne and plastic flutes, crackers, cheese, and other tasty treats. This year, we were offering baskets for the Sunday-evening concerts in the park, adding my mother's tortellini salad and other carry-out options. Plus, customers could reuse the baskets, trimmed with our signature yellow and blue ribbon, all summer long.

"I filled a few yesterday when we hit a lull. We'll need more baskets soon."

"Thanks. I'll check the inventory." One more item, and my mental to do list would be longer than Front Street. We'd met the women who run the Helena Handbasket Company at last summer's street fair. Affordable and Montana-made—a match made in heaven.

I flipped the sign to OPEN and unlocked the door. Within minutes, the Merc buzzed like a bee on caffeine. Over and over, Tracy greeted customers with our motto— "If it's made in Montana, it must be good." I heard it so often, I was almost sorry I'd come up with it.

A few minutes later, Ann and Gabby Drake came in, Gabby sipping a go-cup. I called out "Hello" as Ann, elegant as the day before, made straight for the pottery display. I went back to answering a customer's questions about our organic beef and pork. We'd worked hard to establish reliable supplies of meat, cheese, produce, and eggs. The Merc's days as a full-scale grocery were long gone, but I was determined that we be more than a high-end specialty shop carrying luxury foods.

I rang up the customer's purchase of Italian sausage and an elk roast, then found Gabby testing Luci's Lavender Valley lotion. "Gabby, you were wonderful last night. I can hardly wait to hear you again later this week."

"Thanks." She looked younger in daylight, in her blue denim short-shorts and midriff top.

"If you don't mind my asking, what was the problem with you and Martin?"

She flicked her eyes toward her mother, then dropped her voice. "I thought he'd be thrilled to hear me do one of my own compositions. We worked on it by Skype and he raved. I'm supposed to play with him during the final concert, but now I'm not so sure. What if he tosses me off the bill?"

"Can he do that?" Young as she looked, surely she was old enough to realize you can't go changing other people's plans.

She made a face and hunched a shoulder. She didn't know.

"Your mom and Rebecca Whitman are friends, right? From working on the festival? If you're worried, ask her to talk to him."

Gabby's eyes widened. "Didn't you hear—"

"Erin, are other pieces available in this pattern?" Ann's question broke in from across the shop. "The craftsmanship and design are superb."

"I'm so glad you like it." *Please, please, please*, I told myself. *Let me start the season with a big sale.* "We haven't restocked for summer yet, but I'll call Reg and see what he has on hand. I'm sure he'd be happy to make more. Meanwhile, take a bowl home—try it out."

"That's generous. Thank you. We can return it anytime," she said. Her daughter stifled a yawn. "*I* can, anyway. I can't vouch for Gabby— I well remember how keyed up one gets after a performance, even if the hour doesn't seem late."

"Oh? Were—are you a musician, too?" The Jazz Festival began in my years away from Jewel Bay, and I was just getting to know the new crop of regulars it had brought.

"Soprano with the Metropolitan Opera. No major roles, but I worked steadily, in New York and in the traveling company. I retired when I became a mother." Chin lowered, lips together but curved, she gave her daughter a fond look. If Gabby were inches closer, Ann would have stroked her hair.

The door chimed and Sally Grimes marched in, grabbed a bag of chai mix, and plopped it on the counter. I excused myself and went to help her.

"My daughter's coming up today, and she loves this stuff. It's too spicy for me."

"How is Sage? And the baby?" I broke open a new roll of nickels to make her change. Sally runs the children's clothing store and had almost lost her nickname of Sally Sourpuss since reconciling with her daughter.

Sally's face lit up. "She's such a good mother. And Olivia is the most beautiful little girl. I've got to run—town is hopping. Since when do we have a parking problem at ten thirty in the morning? Doesn't help to have all those fire engines and ambulances blocking the River Road."

My hands froze above the change drawer. "What's going on?"

"Oh, who knows—some idiot in trouble on the river, I suppose."

"The river? Oh my God, no." I threw her change on the counter and slammed the cash drawer shut. "I've got to find out."

I ran out the door. Ran up Front Street to Hill, a block and a half from the shop, and made the turn. Part way up the hill, my Mary Jane clogs not meant for running, I slowed to keep myself upright. A red fire engine crept toward me. No lights, no rush, no need. The engine was headed home.

I squeezed past the moving truck and made for the trailhead. Half a dozen walkers, some with strollers and dogs, stood by. The River Road hasn't been a road in decades—it's officially the Jewel River Nature Trail, but no one who's been in town longer than five minutes calls it that. It's a gem, for walking, running, and sight-seeing, high above the river. The sometimes-treacherous Jewel River, with its stretch of Class IV rapids known as the Wild Mile. It draws kayakers from all over the world during whitewater season.

Which we were smack in the middle of.

I grabbed the arm of the EMT standing guard by the gate, now unlocked, meant to keep out all but emergency vehicles. "What's going on?"

"Body on the rocks. Our guys have already checked him." He shook his head. "We're waiting for the sheriff."

I took off, pounding up the dirt trail.

"Hey!" he called. "You can't go in there."

But when a Murphy girl is on a mission, there's no stopping her.

Four

Around the bend, a quarter mile from the trailhead, stood a square white ambulance. Beside it, on a lichen-stained boulder, sat Tanner Lundquist, clad in a black wetsuit, one long leg outstretched, his head in his hands.

The world went gray. It spun, the giant evergreens suddenly spiking downward in front of me, the sun's rays shooting up. I reached out a hand to steady myself, but grasped thin air.

What's going on? Was he—

"Erin! Erin, what are you doing here?" An electric hand touched my shoulder and the shock spun me toward the voice I loved, the voice I'd feared never hearing again.

"Adam. Oh my God, Adam. You're okay. You're all right. You're …"

His arms enveloped me and the world steadied itself. I held on. And then he stepped back, his hands on my upper arms. "Of course I'm all right. We're fine, both of us. Did you think—?"

"All I knew was that there was a body and that you two were out on the river and …"

He held me tight, and Tanner wrapped his arms around us. I kissed him, too. They were safe. *They were safe.*

So who—?

I pulled back. "What happened? Why are you two up here? And who's down there?"

Derek D'Orazi, a picture framer and EMT, rose into view. He climbed from the hillside on to the trail, breathing hard, his navy uniform smudged with soft, red-brown dirt. He wiped his hands on his pants, though they were too filthy to help.

"That musician," Adam said, and a hot, sour taste bubbled up in my throat. "Not the local guys. The guest artist."

Oh my God. "Gerry Martin? He played with the trio, and with Gabby Drake."

"Yeah. We'd just shot out the last rapid, and Tanner got ahead of me."

Tanner broke in. "I let the current push me sideways, so I could take in the view. I looked up and couldn't believe what I was seeing. Two figures, standing close, then all of a sudden—" His eyes and mouth went wide, and he traced one hand through the air, demonstrating what happened next. "The other person reached out and shoved him. He came flying down the cliff, arms and legs flailing. He hit a small tree, and crashed right past it. Nothing could break his fall. He hit a rock, bounced, and landed on another rock. I signaled to Adam. We paddled over and he climbed up to see if ..." His voice cracked. "But no one survives a fall like that. Not the way his neck was bent."

Adam runs outdoor camps for kids. He's a search and rescue expert with years of experience in wilderness medicine. He races rapids and climbs ice cliffs for fun. Naturally he'd been the one to paddle to shore and scramble up the rocks to check for signs of life. Now he pressed his lips together, eyes downcast.

"Somebody pushed him? Who?" I asked.

Tanner pressed his lips together. "I couldn't see well enough to tell. Not from that distance and angle, with the trees and shrubs in the way, and the current moving me. I don't know who anybody is here, anyway."

"I was on the other side of the big rapid," Adam said. "I didn't see a thing."

I blew out a noisy breath. Footprints and witnesses gave the best chance at identifying the killer, but there was no one else around.

The River Road is heavily lined with brush and trees, except in a few spots like this one, where about ten feet of the edge stood open, unobscured and unprotected. "This is where you think he went over? Where did you come up?"

"Best I can tell. We followed a game trail, upstream a ways. Crazy-steep, but we made it. We'd left our phones in the car, so Adam sprinted to the nearest house to call 911 while I stayed here to mark the spot."

The EMTs had scuffed up the ground, but their footprints were easy to identify—heavy tread in a distinct pattern.

I silently cursed my own rules. My phone was back at the Merc, in my bag in the tiny upstairs office.

Derek stood by the back of the open ambulance, not far from a yellow sawhorse that meant no access. Farther east, another sawhorse blocked traffic from the other direction. He frowned when I approached. "There's no reason for you to be here, Erin."

"I need your phone."

His eyes narrowed. "Why?"

I wriggled my fingers. "Because none of us has one. C'mon, Derek, help me out."

He glanced down the trail, then handed me the phone. "Make it quick. The sheriff will be here any minute."

I snapped several shots of the ground near his feet, for the footprints, then two more shots of the soft marks made by the gripper-soled water shoes Adam and Tanner wore. They must be part goat to have climbed the steep, rocky slope in those. No doubt adrenaline helped.

I didn't want to mess up the scene any more than I wanted the sheriff's deputies to yell at me when they arrived, so I crossed to the far side of the trail and circled around the other barricade. I hopped back on the rock ledge, a few feet east of the gap where Martin had gone over, roughly where the guys had come up. Heights rarely bother me, and my balance is decent, but I didn't want to look down the steep slope. Didn't want to see what Adam and Tanner had seen.

Near the edge, the ground was badly scuffed. Tanner had seen a second person, but from this angle, I could not pick out their tracks.

I crouched. The ground below the cliff's edge was undisturbed. I saw no indication of impact—no scuffed dirt, no broken branches where Martin had reached out, grabbing for anything to break or slow his fall.

In other words, the scene and Tanner told the same story.

I took a deep breath, then wrapped my left hand around the trunk of a scrub pine, its pungent scent striking my nostrils. I steadied myself, and peered over.

The cliff was about three hundred feet high. Gerry Martin had tumbled down nearly the full length, over sharp rocks and round ones, past stubby spruce, tall pines, and birch beginning to leaf. He'd landed, finally, on a flat sandstone ledge. Farther upstream, larger outcroppings serve as viewing platforms and picnic spots. During the annual Whitewater Festival, held a couple of weeks earlier, thousands of kids and adults had clustered on the big rock ledges to watch kayakers from all over the country race the river.

I shivered in the slowly warming air and drew back. Took another deep breath and leaned forward, still clutching the pine. For reassurance as much as safety.

Last night, on stage, Gerry Martin had worn black from head to toe. The distance and angle made it hard to tell, but he appeared to be in black now as well.

Had he taken a solo stroll along the River Road to calm himself before the day's activities, only to encounter someone with a gripe?

Or had he walked up here with his killer?

Male voices interrupted my internal chatter, and I glanced up to see an SUV marked with the sheriff's shield. Undersheriff Ike Hoover jumped out of the passenger side, the uniformed driver emerging more slowly. The EMT I'd seen at the gate climbed out of the back. I took several more quick shots, then e-mailed the photos to myself. I handed Derek his phone and stood beside Adam and Tanner, rubbing pine pitch off my palm.

If Central Casting sent out a rural Montana sheriff, it might be Ike Hoover, except that his version of a work uniform is khakis and a polo shirt, biceps straining the short sleeves. When the weather requires, he adds a fleece pullover. He's second in command, but I'd heard talk that the sheriff might retire—the rumor mill said cancer, though the rumor mill often says that, true or not. Ike was the obvious choice as successor after thirty years on the job, and I knew he had the ambition.

He stopped at the yellow sawhorse. Hands on his hips, he surveyed the scene, his dark eyes pausing briefly on me. He exchanged a few words with Derek, who pointed at Adam and Tanner.

"Erin, I didn't expect to see you. Adam," Ike said. They shook hands. I'm five-five, but I felt like a shrimp, surrounded by men six feet or better. Adam introduced Tanner, who described what he'd seen. Ike listened intently, then, when Tanner had finished, asked a few questions. I admired Tanner's composure, though his voice trembled at the part about the body hitting the rocks, and I shivered involuntarily. Adam wrapped an arm around me.

"You're sure the other person shoved him?" Ike said.

"Absolutely," Tanner said. "But height, gender—no idea. Sorry."

"Keep that to yourselves, if you wouldn't mind." Ike's face gave away nothing. "All three of you."

We nodded, and Ike trained his attention on the trail, as I had done, careful of his footsteps. Deputy Oakland took the same shots I'd taken, using a ruler and a big camera on a tripod. Ike directed him to get a few close-ups at the trail's edge. I wondered if they could see prints or scuff marks that had not been visible from my rock perch.

Ike conferred with the EMTs, then came back over to us. "We'll need to make a water approach, to get the body. It's too steep to safely bring him up this way—I won't put anyone else at risk. We can come up from the bay and skirt the last rapids, but the water's too shallow for our power boat."

"I can borrow a motorized raft from an outfitter in town," Adam said. "No reason to wait for Search and Rescue to truck theirs over."

"Good idea." To his deputy, Ike said, "Coordinate with Dispatch to commandeer that raft. D'Orazi, can you take the ambulance around to the bay, then bring a stretcher up with the raft? I'm going down to check the scene."

Deputy Oakland opened his mouth, but at a look from Ike, he closed it and handed his boss a smaller camera, which Ike hung around his neck before heading down the game trail the guys had used. Never begrudge a law enforcement department its in-house exercise gym and weight room.

We watched him go over the edge, then he disappeared from sight and Oakland started muttering. "He's too old for that. If Deputy Caldwell were here—"

He caught himself and broke off, glancing at me sharply, then radioed Dispatch with an update and to request a call for the raft.

I'd been at more than my share of crime scenes in the last year, each unique, but what made this one different was the absence of Deputy Kim Caldwell, my BFF from the sixth grade to the middle of senior year. When my father was killed in a hit-and-run that February, I'd lost my best friend, too, and hadn't learned why until last winter, fifteen years later. The tragedy changed both our lives. She responded by becoming a deputy sheriff, working her way up to detective.

But the discovery of the guilty driver's identity a few months back had shaken her deeply, and she took a leave of absence from the department. To rethink things, she said. She'd spent the last few months working with horses in California. She'd returned to her family's guest lodge and dude ranch a couple of weeks ago, and we'd gone riding on Wednesday.

I wasn't entirely sure that she'd finished rethinking.

But while I trusted Ike Hoover to handle the matter well, Kim's presence would have reassured me, in more ways than one.

"We'll come back up in the raft," Adam said to his own BFF. "Lend a hand if they need us, then grab the kayaks."

"Sure." Tanner looked queasy, as if he weren't sure he wanted to come that close to Gerry Martin's body a second time.

Adam took my hand. "We'll walk you back to the shop."

A few feet downstream, I spotted a white paper cup in a clump of snowberry. "Slobs," I muttered and snatched it up.

At the trailhead, the onlookers had dispersed. Both Derek D'Orazi in the ambulance and Deputy Oakland in the sheriff's rig had left, and the gate stood locked again.

Doesn't seem fair that tragedy can strike as easily on a sunny day as under grim or dreary skies. Still, I suppose I'd rather my last vision on this earth be a glimpse of its beauty.

Who had pushed Gerry Martin? Was it in the heat of an argument, or on purpose? What had been his final thoughts? Had he regretted his outbursts of the night before, his angry snipes and bitter retorts? Had the delights of a blue-sky morning on the River Road calmed him and restored his faith in his fellow man—or at least, his fellow musicians?

I could hope.

"All these years, the way you've been talking about this place," Tanner said, breaking the silence, "I thought you were a raving lunatic. I get it now."

We paused halfway down Hill Street to drink in the views of the bay and beyond, Eagle Lake and the Salish Hills. We passed the handsome log building that anchors the north end of the village. Dragonfly Dry Goods quilt and yarn shop occupies ground level, the owner's home above. On the opposite corner stands the historic chalet-style Jewel Inn—no lodging, just great eating. To the right, the recently-restored WPA steps lead uphill to an older residential area.

And to the left, down Front Street, lies the heart of the village. I'd grown up here, gone away, and come back. The village of Jewel Bay fills my heart, and occasionally breaks it.

No one ever expects a small town in Montana quite like this. Most days, I'm happy to go on and on about its restaurants, its art, its music, and all the amazing scenery and recreational opportunities. The rivers and lakes in our front yard, the wilderness at our back, and thirty miles up the road, Glacier National Park.

Today, my Chamber of Commerce patter failed me.

I gripped Adam's hand a little tighter.

We passed Rebecca Whitman's gallery. I supposed I ought to stop to tell her, since she was in charge of the festival, that one of her guest artists was dead.

Let someone else bear the bad news. Being this close to another death made me want to hide.

In front of the Merc, Adam kissed me tenderly and said they'd see me this evening, at my cabin. I watched the two of them go down the street, their strides long and loose, perfectly matched, Tanner a little thinner. They even held their heads the same way. From my vantage point, I couldn't see them speak; I knew they didn't have to.

My feet felt heavy as I crossed the threshold. The Merc, my happy place, seemed a tad less happy than when I'd dashed out the door. Less colorful and inviting. Behind the chocolate counter, Tracy's eyebrows rose inquisitively. I mustered a wan half smile and retreated to my office.

I was startled to realize I still held the paper cup I'd found on the trail. Your standard white cup. I tossed it in the silver mesh waste basket and sank into my black desk chair.

Why did the death of a man I barely knew trouble me so? I'd enjoyed his music, though I lacked Heidi's emotional connection with it. Last winter Martin had put on a private concert down at Caldwell's Eagle Lake Lodge. He'd been pleasant, focused on his performance and the big-money donors he'd been brought to town to court. I'd barely merited an introduction, but I hadn't minded—that's how the money game is played.

Arms and ankles crossed, I swiveled my desk chair back and forth.

Martin's death troubled me because of his behavior last night. Because I'd witnessed too many conflicts to think it an unfortunate coincidence.

And because I don't believe in coincidence. Most times, it's nothing more than events with connections we can't see.

I brought the computer to life and opened my e-mail. Opened the photos I'd sent myself from Derek D'Orazi's phone.

Martin's death troubled me because of what I'd seen—and hadn't seen—on the trail. But Ike Hoover had seen those things, too. His actions, his furrowed brow, the camera angles he'd directed his deputy to get—all told me he had questions and he'd demand answers.

And it troubled me because I'd been in this position before. I knew people would say the town was cursed. They'd sneak odd glances at my mother and Ned Redaway and me, because we'd hosted the party in our courtyard, the last place Martin had been seen in public. Because of what had happened there last year.

Because my boyfriend and his buddy had been the first to arrive.

Because this town depends on tourism, and anything that triggers talk and rumor and fear threatens our livelihoods. And sometimes, our lives.

I stared at Christine's painting on the office wall, the stenciled letters, bright spring green on a yellow backdrop speckled with purple, red, and orange. If she were here, what would she tell me?

She'd toss that long red hair over her bony shoulder, and cackle. *You're screwed, Murphy,* she'd say. *You're in this thing, whether you like it or not.*

Because I'm nosy and snoopy and committed to this town. And because the death of a guest—even a few hours later, even after his rage against me and my friends—is bad karma, bad feng shui, and bad manners.

And my bad luck.

Five

"Erin, are you hiding up there, or working?"

I spun the chair toward my mother's voice. She stood at the bottom of the half flight of stairs, one hand on her hip.

"I want to talk with you," she said.

And I'd thought I had my hands full of trouble before.

Fresca—short for Francesca—surged up the stairs and stood in the doorway. I hooked one foot around a leg of the rolling piano stool, the only spare seating we have room for, and slid it toward her. She didn't take it.

Her lovely oval face, barely lined at sixty-five, bore that *I want you to do something* look every daughter knows. She wore slim white pants and a deep coral tunic that complemented her olive skin. The skin I didn't inherit, instead getting my father's fair black Irish complexion, though the dark eyes that bore into me now were much like my own.

"We've talked about you hiring Lou Mary Vogel. It's time. Before someone else snatches her up."

This was at the least the third time my mother had mentioned the woman. I'd hesitated because Lou Mary wasn't a foodie. And I wasn't sure the Merc had room for another bossy woman, even if we do call it leadership skills these days.

"She knows retail," my mother went on. "She's a serious connector. She'll make the Merc the center of the town and free you up for more of your businesssy stuff."

I frowned. "The Merc *is* the center of town. Has been since 1910."

"In case you haven't noticed, darling, times change. Besides, Lou Mary needs the job. And you need someone who can help you when I can't."

Change was afoot, both in my mother's life and in the Merc. How it would all affect me, I didn't quite know yet.

"What's going on, anyway?" she continued. "You ran out of the Merc like a house on fire, then came back and shut yourself up here without a word."

Your mother knows before you do that you're about to burst into tears. At least, my mom does. Despite doing business with her for the last year, I think of her as "Mom" more often than "Fresca." Hard to undo a thirty-three-year-old habit.

I arched my back and sucked in air. It did not go down smoothly. Mom crossed the room, sat on the piano stool, and rolled toward me, all in one fluid motion. She reached for my hand—the one that wasn't damp with tears and snot.

"Darling, what's wrong? Your brother and sister? Adam?"

"They're fine. But—but there's been another death. And it might not be an accident." I sniffed loudly and filled her in.

Her long, slender fingers fiddled with the neckline of her tunic. "Are you sure? Who would do such a thing?"

"No clue. He had a pickle up his b—backside last night, but it was more like he would kill than be killed. When Dave Barber took that solo—"

"Erin?" Tracy called from the shop. "You busy? I need a hand."

"Be right there," I replied, then turned back to my mother. "I know you'll tell me not to get involved—"

"Darling, I learned ages ago that the worst thing a mother can say is 'Don't do X.' It's a recipe for resentment all around." She lowered her chin, giving me a long look. "Just be careful."

We have our moments, Fresca and I, in business and in life. I have my secrets, and no doubt she has hers. But when friends ask how I can stand to work with my mother, I think of times like this, and the trust she gives me.

She rose. "Wash your face. Your mascara's running."

But she'll always be my mother.

I hadn't seen the Merc this busy in days. Weeks. Months—not since Christmas.

My mother was right—we needed a good hire, and soon. On our way downstairs, she'd reminded me of the reason she'd come in. "Lou Mary," she'd said. "Think about it."

"No thinking needed," I'd replied, though why push Lou Mary for the opening, I had to wonder.

We stopped outside the restroom door and she laid her fingers on my cheek. "Don't forget, tomorrow morning at the Orchard. It's going to be very special."

The announcement. "You'll get to meet Tanner," I'd said. "You'll love him."

In Adam's stories, Tanner had been the jokester, the kidder. They'd been equal partners in boyhood hijinks, especially those aimed at Adam's older brothers, whom he called Cain and Abel. They'd stayed close, despite Adam's decision to head west, texting and e-mailing goofy pictures and tales of their adventures.

And despite the craziness of missing his flight and coming in late, we'd had a great time last night. But seeing Martin fall would rattle anyone. I vowed to make sure he had a vacation to remember.

Face washed and mascara refreshed, I shook off my musings. The scene in front of me called for retail triage.

Fresca had charge of an older couple choosing pastas and sauces from the cooler and the adjacent shelf of jarred Italian specialties. I relieved Tracy at the front counter—the cash-wrap, in retail parlance—and sent her to help a family clustered at the chocolate counter, where sales promised to soar. Her boyfriend had urged her to open her own shop, but I'd enticed her to stay. The Merc needed her. Fingers crossed that she sold well enough to be happy, but not well enough to leave.

Not my most generous thought. I pushed it away and focused on the young women in front of me. "Oh, Luci's Spring Rain body wash. You'll love it. Did you see that she makes a lotion, too? It goes on light, but it lasts, and it's not too smelly."

"I missed that. Be right back." The girl with the ponytail dashed away, and I started ringing up her friend's purchases. After the soap girls came a woman stocking up on Montana Gold baking supplies and Cowboy Roast coffee. I suggested a jar of rhubarb jam for her Sunday morning scones.

"Sold," she said, and I grinned. One of my favorite words.

Twenty minutes later, the tide ebbed. Tracy handed me a bottle of Pellegrino and took a long swig of her Diet Coke.

"The chocolates are flying out of here," she said, the black-and-gold cowboy boots in her ears doing a two-step with her long chestnut hair. The earrings matched the boots on her feet, another consignment shop score.

"Cheers." I tipped my bottle toward her. "But in high summer, we won't be able to handle this without another sales clerk."

"Promise me you won't hire Candy Divine," Tracy said. "Even if she cries."

I made an X over my heart. "I won't hire Candy Divine."

"Not to be mean, but she's so sweet, she makes my teeth hurt."

I knew exactly what Tracy meant. Not to mention that Candy—Candace DeVernero to her parents—has a voice higher than the Merc's sixteen-foot ceilings. Plus she dresses like Minnie Mouse set loose in a lingerie shop.

But the hordes weren't clamoring for the job. Luci, aka the Splash Artist, had helped out during the spring, and she'd worked with my brother-in-law to fire up our new web business. Now it was time for her to focus on making soap. Her line of household cleaners using essential oils held promise.

Fresca pitches in, too, between kitchen stints. But she had other things on her mind, maintaining the Murphy Orchard, a busy place in spring, and spending time with her sweetie, Bill Schmidt.

Since last winter, I'd approached half a dozen retail veterans, but they'd already lined up all the hours they wanted to work at other village shops and galleries. I'd gotten so many turndowns that I'd started to wonder if it was personal, though everyone insisted it wasn't.

Even my cousin Molly, who, like me, had loved traipsing around the store after Granddad as a kid, had said no.

So I had high hopes for my mother's candidate.

"Where is your mom?" Tracy asked.

"Oh." I didn't bother suppressing a smile. "She had an appointment. I can't tell you."

"What, what?"

"I said, I can't tell you. But I promise it's good news."

She cocked her head. "Are she and Bill—"

The door chimed and I glanced up. My smile faded when I saw who it was.

Men with guns are bad for business.

Deputy Oakland blinked rapidly. He scanned the shop, then settled his attention on me. "Sorry to interrupt, Ms. Murphy. I need a few minutes. In private. And I'd like to see your back yard. Outside space. Whatever you call it."

"The courtyard. Coffee? Sparkling water?"

He declined, and I led the way out back. I plugged in the fountain—the soft sound of flowing water soothes both the savage breast and the savage beast.

Not to mention all the rest of us.

I set my Pellegrino on one of the café tables my friend and personal landlady, Liz Pinsky, had helped me choose last summer. Was it proper etiquette to sit before the law enforcement officer sat?

You'd think I'd know by now.

Dang, I miss you, Kim.

I sat. "The fence between our place and Red's is locked. Their liquor license requires it. But we can walk over and see the stage."

The deputy hitched up his gun belt and sat, then took out a small notebook. "Undersheriff Hoover is retrieving the body. With help from Mr. Zimmerman and Mr.—" He flipped back a page.

"Lundquist," I said. "Tanner Lundquist. Visiting from Minneapolis. He got here last night, just in time for the concert."

"Tell me about the concert," Oakland said. He wiped the corners of his mouth with thumb and forefinger, in the manner of a man who missed having a mustache. "The festival doesn't start until tomorrow, does it?"

I explained about the special event, featuring local musicians, a guest artist, and a promising workshop student. "The idea is to serve up a taste of the festival, spurring ticket sales for next week's evening concerts. Last night's proceeds go to the scholarship fund. And special events help reach people who don't want to mess with the crowds." *Crowds* being a relative term. The Playhouse seats four hundred and fifty, and the park across the one-lane bridge holds about that many. But in a town of less than three thousand year-round, doubling or tripling in the height of summer, that's a good turnout.

He scribbled a note. "Who was in charge?"

"Rebecca Whitman, Dave Barber, and the board. It's all volunteer."

"Tell me about the decedent. Mr. Martin."

Decedent was almost as chilling as *the body*. Criminy, I hate that shift, from *Martin* or *world-famous musician* to *the body*. But it beat *the dead guy on the rocks above the river.*

I took a long sip from the green bottle. "I met him briefly last winter when he came up for a fund-raiser. He's played here quite a few times."

Oakland would be talking to everyone involved. I'd let them tell him what had happened. After all, what I interpreted as ego-driven tensions could easily have been dropped cues or mistaken signals, musicians not used to playing together rubbing each other the wrong way.

"Tell me more about this festival."

"It's been around a few years, though this is my first one. Guest artists—big names—perform a concert or two in the evenings. During the day, they visit the workshops, teach special classes, and hang out with the students and other artists, sharing the love of music."

"And it's all jazz? Isn't that trombones and stuff?"

"Oh, yeah. There are workshops for brass and woodwinds. But also guitar and small groups. Martin is a guitarist. He plays with—*played*

41

with—a lot of famous musicians. Wrote a bunch of soundtracks—I couldn't tell you which ones without my friend Google."

The deputy frowned. "Sounds like he got around. What was he doing here?"

"Like I said, playing and teaching. For the guest artists, it's a chance to reach a new audience. And squeeze in a vacation."

"Tell me about last night."

For a moment, I thought he already knew about Martin's bad mood, but then I realized it was simply a question. "Everything sounded great, but I'm not a musician. You'll need to talk to the people he played with, get their perspective."

Oakland pursed his lips.

"I can say he wasn't happy after the concert." I reached for my water, no longer cold, but didn't take a drink. "He made a nasty crack to Rebecca Whitman, and said he'd 'spread the word about this town.' But I have no idea what he meant. All I did was put up a poster and provide half the space."

Oakland made a note, grunted, and got to his feet. Unlike Ike Hoover, he wore the full uniform—brown pants, tan shirt, sturdy black shoes with rubber soles a guy could run in. Not that he appeared to do much running. He wasn't fat, but clearly Oakland didn't make the use of the department exercise equipment that his boss did.

We walked out to the alley and circled around to Red's courtyard. The magic had vanished in the daylight. A group of young men had taken over a picnic table, now littered with beer glasses and baskets of burgers and fries. The aroma set my stomach gurgling.

Oakland pulled a small camera out of his pocket and snapped a few quick shots of the stage and surroundings. For the file, I imagined—or rather, the oversized corkboard that shares one wall of the sheriff's Jewel Bay satellite office with an equally oversized white board. For background.

Because surely nothing that had happened here had anything to do with Martin's murder.

Or did it?

The deputy tucked his camera away and held out a big hand. "Thanks for your time. I'll head inside, see if I can catch Mr. Beckstead or Mr. Redaway."

For half a second, my mind went blank—I never think of J.D. or his grandfather by their last names.

"Deputy, Martin and the killer may have been struggling—we don't know—but in the end, it sure looked to Tanner like the killer pushed Martin over the edge on purpose."

Oakland's face gave away nothing.

"I come from the grocery business," I continued, trying another tack, "where a slip-and-fall is not uncommon. The signs are pretty obvious—a wet spot on the floor, a stray grape. I didn't see anything like that on the trail, and I don't think you did, either. Are you investigating this as an accident, a fight that resulted in tragedy, or as an intentional act? A murder?"

He gave me a long, appraising gaze, his fingers working that spot where his mustache used to be. I did not doubt that he shared Ike Hoover's reluctance to trust the observations and theories of the average citizen.

"Ms. Murphy, I hear you're pretty smart. You know I can't answer that."

I did know. But this isn't your average town. And maybe I flatter myself, but I'm not your average citizen.

Six

Inside Red's, I ordered a hot pepper jack burger and fries to go, then sat at the bar to wait.

At the other end, out of my hearing, the deputy spoke to J.D.

The bartender wiped an imaginary spot on the dark, timeworn surface and shook his head. Behind him, a neon PBR sign glowed. He glanced at the deputy, muttered something, and shook his head again.

In the mirror behind the bar, I saw Oakland slip his notebook into his shirt pocket. His heavy steps and the sway of the gun belt as he left spoke of disappointment, of nothing useful learned.

J.D. continued wiping the counter, a patch at a time, until he stood across from me. Still the new man, though he'd been behind the bar since the first of the year, he had his grandfather's affability as well as his red hair and stocky build. "Hard to believe Martin's dead."

"Deputy tell you what happened?" I asked.

"No. He wanted to know if I saw or heard anything unusual Friday night. Sounds like Martin got too close to the edge. Slipped and fell."

Not so, but I'd promised Undersheriff Ike that I'd keep my mouth shut. "Did you? See or hear anything?"

"Nope." J.D. slid down the bar, checking on his clientele. A handful of patrons sat inside—the lawyer who downs one short Scotch at noon every day, the fishing guide working on a plate of nachos and a dark beer, a couple of men in a friendly spat over whether baseball or football is America's favorite sport.

If Kim were on the job, I might have told her about the tensions I'd sensed between Martin and Barber, and the partial conversation I'd heard between Gabby and her mentor. Though she was a cop through and through, I knew she trusted my observations.

It doesn't take a cop's experience to know that a petty conflict or a trivial slight can fester under the surface until it becomes a deadly heat-seeking missile.

I called out to J.D., and when he stood in front of me, eyes bright with expectation, I took the round-about route. "Ned ready for a big week? You guys are hosting the late-night jam sessions, aren't you?"

"Yeah, we are. Gramps is good." J.D. wiped the spot he'd just scrubbed. "Big events wear him down more than he wants to admit, but they psych him up, too. And they're great for business."

I gestured toward the rows of bottles behind him. "Music sells booze."

"The louder the music, the more people drink."

"Does Dave Barber play here much, or is his stuff too mellow?"

J.D. snorted. "He and Gramps don't get along. Don't know why, but when I came to town, Gramps told me not to let him near me with a scissors." He ran his hand over his close-cropped red hair, a shade lighter than his stubble of a beard.

Interesting. My family had always believed that being active in town is a good thing, and I'd assumed that anyone who pitches in must be a good guy.

Then I remembered what they say about what happens when you assume.

"Lunch time." The kitchen runner handed me a brown box I was hungry enough to eat without opening.

"Thanks," I told her, then spoke to J.D. "Gotta run. Gotta stay on Tracy's good side."

He rolled his eyes and went on wiping.

On the sidewalk, I succumbed to temptation and opened the box wide enough to sneak a big, fat fry. Bit off the tip, knowing how potatoes can hold the heat.

Perfect.

Back in the Merc, I sat at the counter on one of the chrome stools my mother had salvaged from an old soda fountain and topped in cherry red vinyl. The place was quiet, as it often is at lunchtime, and Tracy dashed home to grab a bite and check on her dog. An elderly Harlequin Great Dane, Bozo had gotten too arthritic for the doggy door.

I was down to my last fry when the door opened and in swept Lou Mary Vogel.

"Oh, Erin! I'm so happy to see you. Thank you for considering hiring an old bag like me." She paused near the cash-wrap, her lime green quilted handbag the same shade as her loafers, complementing her floral print blouse. The rough-cut carnelian stones in her necklace matched both her lipstick and the poufy light red hair that, while carefully tinted, could have been her natural shade.

I love retail ladies.

At my gesture, she boosted herself onto the stool next to me, grabbing the counter for support as the stool swiveled. She and my mother were roughly the same age, but the years showed more clearly on Lou Mary. She had the pale skin, splashed with freckles on the cheekbones and throat, that many redheads despair of, and the wrinkles told me she'd battled the effects of sun in vain. But she was one of those women whose eyes—the green of leaves about to turn—and personality made her attractive.

I wiped grease and salt off my fingers and held out my hand. Her touch was light and I noticed her swollen knuckles. She would not be toting cases of jam up the wooden steps from the basement, or helping me haul in coolers of cheese from Jewel Bay Creamery.

That's okay. Youth carries obligations, and one is the obligation to carry things.

She accepted my offer of mineral water and I twisted off the cap for her.

"Retail's been my career. My last job before we moved here was in a scrumptious boutique in Palm Springs. It had its perks." Lou Mary wriggled her fingertips at her necklace. "Of course, this is very different, and that's what makes it *fun*. Every store is unique. You get to know the products and customers, and help them find each other."

"We?" No wedding ring.

"I'm single now." She gave me a rueful smile. "Happens to the best of us."

"Ah. I'm sorry. Where do you live?"

"I'm renting a townhouse near the golf course. For the time being." Her smile wobbled.

Her manner of speaking fascinated me. I'd known in half a second that she wasn't a Montana native, but I couldn't place the accent. When I offered a drink from our cooler, she'd said "no soda pop," which sounded Northeastern to my ears, but then she raved about the new enchilada sauce Fresca made, using a recipe from Ray Ramirez's grandmother, and she gave *enchilada* a Southwestern flair. And when she mentioned lasting one winter in Chicago, she reminded me of my old boss at SavClub, who'd never left the Windy City until a promotion to headquarters in Seattle.

A customer came in and Lou Mary watched as I answered the woman's questions and bagged up her pasta and pesto purchases.

"Your mother was right. You manage the customers beautifully."

I blushed, as if I was being interviewed. As I suppose I was.

"Tell me about your name. It's unusual."

"It was supposed to be Mary Lou—one name for each of my parents. My father handled the paperwork while my mother was half-unconscious—they gave serious drugs for childbirth back then. He claimed the nurse got it backwards. My mother said he did it on purpose." Lou Mary cackled.

"We both have funny naming stories. I'm the youngest of three, and when I came along, my father decided that my mother had gotten her say twice, so it was his turn. Which is why a half-Italian girl is named Erin Margaret Murphy. That, and because I was born on St. Patrick's Day."

More laughter, then her eyes became serious. "Your father must have been a prince, to win Francesca's heart. A beautiful name for a beautiful lady."

I grabbed my water and took a swig, to wash away the prickling at the back of my throat. After all this time, I shouldn't miss him so much, but I did.

Lou Mary reached out a hand as if to pat my knee. "I always say my parents got my name backwards, but I did all the rest myself."

I liked her self-deprecating wisecracks. She was a bit of a throwback—I could almost picture her drinking a martini and blowing smoke rings. But my mother had made a good point about connectors. And while my business instincts are reliable, I don't have the oil-off-the-back temperament for working the floor all day.

I glanced at her hands again. The job didn't require straight fingers. Heck, I had perfectly capable hands and I'd splashed jam all over the floor, barely missing Ann Drake's white pants.

Lou Mary was retail-ready.

"Can you start tomorrow? It will be our first Sunday of the season, and while it would be great to have Tracy here, she's overdue for a day off. Noon to five."

Her eyes sparkled behind the tortoiseshell glasses. "Why not today? Give me an hour for lunch."

Tracy walked in as I said, "It's a deal."

Lou Mary slid off the stool. "The three of us will make a great team."

The door closed behind her and Tracy's wide eyes locked on me.

"It'll be strange to see a new face here," I said, "but I think she's just the ticket."

"Hope so," Tracy replied. "Because we are gonna have a rockin' summer."

"I heard that musician plunged off the River Road," our very next customer said. "Must have been high or drunk."

I tipped my head in a question.

"It's so obviously dangerous," she continued. "I can't imagine why people thought converting that old road into a pedestrian path was a good idea."

Those "people" included my father, my uncles, and my granddad. Originally the homesteaders' road into town, it had long ago been replaced by a highway south of the river, and fell into disuse. In my kidhood, community volunteers led by the Murphy men had worked out an easement with the power company and reclaimed the unpaved trail for a foot and bike path.

"I've lived here more than forty years, and no one's ever fallen," another customer said.

"Not true," the first woman said. "My cousin's friend fell and broke her collar bone. Ten years ago? Twelve? 'Course, it was night and they were loaded."

"Lucky that was all she broke," I said.

"Be a shame if the bad publicity hurt the festival," the other shopper said. "After all the hard work."

The naysayer counted out quarters for three huckleberry truffles. "Musicians," she said, as if it was a dirty word.

"Besides being fun," I said, "the workshop and concerts haul in the money. You know the Krauses from the winery—they came here as students, then bought property. Same for the new cardiologist at the hospital in Pondera. So the festival even sells real estate."

Pahn-duh-RAY, the big town, all of thirty thousand people, thirty miles away.

Unconvinced, the woman bit into a truffle and left, wiping purple goo off her lips.

The door had barely shut when it flew open. Heidi Hunter, my mother's best friend and the owner of Kitchenalia, the ever-expanding housewares shop that brings thousands of visitors—and untold dollars—to the village, marched in. A strand of her long highlighted hair whipped her in the face, and she flicked it away.

"Erin, I can't believe it's true. I can't believe he's dead."

"I know. I'm still in shock."

She took a deep, ragged breath. "This will be so hard on the students. Erin, I *loved* his music."

"Oh, Heidi, I know you did." I wrapped one arm around her. "And he was so young."

"People don't just take a walk in broad daylight, fall down a cliff, and die. You know this could be a problem for the festival."

"I'm not sure why," I said, stepping back. "Accidents happen every day. People get sick, have heart attacks. We all feel terrible, but we don't stop supporting the arts."

Even to Heidi, I didn't want to say the word *murder*. A fight that went wrong would be bad enough, and could result in criminal prosecution. But it was understandable, in a way—a tragic accident. Murder, on the other hand ...

Heidi's voice grew stern. "Erin, it's all over town that Adam and his friend helped rescue the body. And that Ike Hoover hauled them both up to the sheriff's office for interviews."

My jaw clamped shut.

"If—and I'm just saying *if*— his death wasn't an accident," she said, "Jewel Bay could take a big hit. You know we live or die—no pun intended—on how many people spend how much money between now and Labor Day. And it's not just the tourists. The jazz festival brings in hundreds of thousands of dollars in advertising and donations. Word will spread, and we need to be prepared for bad press and the fallout."

Especially once it became known—as it would—that Martin had been pushed to his death.

"You're the head of the Village Merchant's Association," Heidi said, as if I needed reminding. "You have to do something."

Ike Hoover was a good man and a good cop, but his job was to put someone behind bars. It wasn't his job to care about tourism or the financial impact of an investigation on the community. That was our job. My job.

"You have to do something," she repeated.

"Okay, I will. I promise," I said, though I suspected Heidi was thinking press releases and a social media campaign about the virtues of the village. She wasn't thinking I should slink around asking questions.

But every job carries hidden responsibilities. And investigating murder seemed to be one of mine.

Seven

Tanner had not seen who'd been with Gerry Martin on the trailhead. A good handful of folks—locals and outsiders—had a beef with the man.

And it appeared that, unwittingly, I was one of them. Although my only beef was irritation at being pulled into the mystery without knowing why.

I did know one thing: The secret to a person's death always lies in their life. I didn't know much about Martin or his music, but plenty of folks around here did.

Years ago, when Jewel Bay hit a rough patch, a core group of residents set out to give the town an economic boost. They focused on tourism, playing up recreation and the natural charm of the village, the original townsite by the bay. At about the same time, artists discovered the area and created their own community. The trends merged, and Jewel Bay became a place that nurtures potters and painters, sculptors and jewelers, along with hikers, golfers, and boaters. The Playhouse, long a mainstay, boomed. More recently, great restaurants had fired up a new nickname: the Food Lovers' Village. The Jazz

Festival added music to the mix. Many of the original shops and galleries downtown were now in their second or third iteration, new owners adding new flavor.

I strode up Front Street and pushed open the heavy door of Perspective. Not everyone likes the way Rebecca had reframed the old gallery—no more cowboys or Indians—but I found the white walls and uncluttered space soothing. Nothing but a chair or two—themselves works of art—sat in the middle of the room. Nothing to get in the way as the viewer stepped back for perspective.

I'd moved from a Roger Rink oil—a five-by-five semi-abstract of fall foliage—to a Terry Karson collage, a twist on found objects that required contemplation, when Rebecca approached.

"Erin. I heard."

"Oh, Rebecca. What a tragedy, and right when the festival is about to start."

Her strong jaw quivered and she blinked, her turquoise eyes damp and shiny. "None of that's my problem anymore."

I tilted my head, puzzled. "But you're director. Or whatever your title is. I'm surprised to find you here. The last-minute details must be crazy."

"Erin, you disappoint me. I thought the village telegraph ran straight to the Merc."

So did I. Before I could ask what was up, the door opened and an unfamiliar couple walked in.

"Welcome to Perspective," Rebecca called. "Our artists offer a contemporary take on the West. Let us know if you have any questions."

Over Rebecca's shoulder, I glimpsed her shop assistant at an elegant mahogany desk in the next room, opening the mail. No rotating retail clerks here—the gallery relied on a staff of professional artists who each worked a few days a week, staying visible and current. And not coincidentally, freeing their employer for copious amounts of volunteer work.

Which was now prompting a rash of questions. I asked the first. "Can we talk, in private?"

Rebecca led me through the far gallery, hung with black-and-white photographs reminiscent of Ansel Adams's luminous landscapes. I followed her up the wide stairs, my hand trailing over the peeled-pine banister, then through a room lined with drawings. They reminded me of Chihuly sketches I'd seen in Seattle, visions of fantastical blown glass.

She unlocked a door and we entered her private office. Lush and tranquil. Not the hub of activity I'd expected.

Rebecca stood behind her desk and picked up a filigreed silver pen.

"I know you're a great organizer, with a team of well-trained volunteers, but you're pretty relaxed for being in charge of a festival starting in less than twenty-four hours."

She let out a long sigh. "Because I'm not in charge. As of two days ago."

The image of Ann Drake's face, concern showing through the artful makeup, flashed in my mind. Of course she would have heard of her friend's ouster.

"Grant Drake did everything he could," Rebecca continued, as if reading my mind. "But Dave Barber convinced them—well, it doesn't matter."

I lagged behind her on the twisty road we were taking. Why would the board fire its director on the eve of the big event? Surely any problem short of major malfeasance could wait. What had Dave Barber said to the board, and why had they gone along?

And did any of it have anything to do with Gerry Martin's death?

"Sorry to hear that," I said.

"I didn't think spreading the news would be good for the festival. I should have seen it coming."

I pulled out one of a pair of director's chairs, upholstered in brown-and-white cowhide, and sat. "Seen what?"

She snapped her gaze toward me. "Dave Barber wants to run this festival his way. It's fine to make changes, but people like what they like. You change too much, you lose your core audience. The powers that be want to keep their powers, and grab more. They don't see—"

She broke off, her harsh tone hanging in the air. She slammed the pen down and leaned on the desk, hands flat, lips tight, eyes hard.

As Heidi had said, once the news of Martin's death spread, we'd know what the impact would be. For the village, I hoped for a quick resolution, before merchants lost sales, and hotels and restaurants lost reservations. For the festival, on the other hand, the longer the news that Martin had been pushed stayed under wraps, the better. Without the festival, Jewel Bay would lose its place as a musical hub. Teachers, students, and performers would suffer, and so would the rest of us. The village would lose its sound track.

And as president of the Merchants' Association, I would hear plenty of sour notes.

But in the meantime, a bigger worry stared us in the face.

"Rebecca, talk to me about Gerry Martin."

She folded her arms and faced the big west window. The sun had disappeared, and the sky had begun to gray. Even in profile, I could see her struggle to keep her composure.

"Was it personal? Were you—involved?"

She gave a sigh of resignation. "We met years ago, in Austin. I'd already started summering in Jewel Bay. The festival needed a big name, and I suggested him. The relationship always meant more to me than it did to him—typical, I think."

Sad, I thought.

"My friends warned me he was a jerk, but I didn't see it. After I bought the gallery, he kept coming up for the festival and the midwinter fundraiser, and I saw him in Austin a few times a year." Eyes damp, she sniffed deeply. "He'd always traveled, so I didn't think me living in Montana would make much difference, but ... "

Friday night, I'd assumed he was referring to business plans, but maybe not.

"Everybody has a rough patch now and then. But Gerry—he didn't know how to handle it. He blamed everybody else. Fired his manager, blew off his friends. I don't know whether he changed, or I finally saw his true self."

If he had no one left, who would claim his body? Organize a memorial? Leave flowers on his grave?

"And you thought you were next."

Rebecca clamped her lips together and nodded. "Tickets for his concert on Tuesday night barely hit sixty percent."

"It's Saturday morning. The festival hasn't started yet."

"Every other show is sold out." She turned toward me, arms folded. "Barber insists it's my fault. That Gerry was washed up, and I brought him back anyway. He claimed *he* had a line on someone who would fill every seat and then some. Someone who didn't want to play with Gerry."

"The board got rid of you for that?"

"Erin, none of that matters. He's *dead*."

As I knew well. "I'm so sorry. You must be devastated. But I've been puzzling over what Martin said last night after the concert, about plans and false pretenses, and everyone wanting something. What did he mean?"

She stared, as if I was speaking Mandarin. Then she rolled her eyes and waved a hand. "Oh. That. That was nothing. More of Gerry twisting facts around so he could justify blaming other people when he didn't get what he wanted."

I didn't believe her. If Barber had been upset with her over next week's ticket sales, Martin might have been upset, too. I knew nothing about the artists' arrangements with the festival, didn't know whether they were paid a percentage or a flat fee, but open seats did no one any good, especially in a small venue. Sellouts had to be a selling point for an artist booking future gigs.

"I imagine the board will make a statement about his death, but since you were close— "

"Rebecca?" One hand on the door frame, the shop assistant leaned in. "Customer with questions."

"Be right there," Rebecca called. To me, she said, "I feel terrible. If he hadn't come here, if it hadn't been for me, Gerry would still be alive. Please wait, Erin—I won't be long."

After a minute or two, I started to feel antsy. It's hard to wait when you have a million things to do, especially when you have no idea what you're waiting for. Gerry Martin's face beckoned from a stack of CDs on the shelves behind Rebecca's desk. I'd bought his new CD last night, but hadn't listened yet. I stood and walked around her desk to reach for an older recording. A pile of files and papers slid off and crashed onto the floor.

"Criminy." I knelt and started gathering them up. Two thick catalogs for musical gear, sporting labels from the music shop in Pondera. A third catalog lay open, facedown, at the edge of the splayed-out mess. I stretched and snared it, pulling it toward me, and finally got hold of the binding. Started to close it when I realized a loose paper stuffed inside had gotten crumpled. I laid it flat and ran my hand over it, a printout captioned *Quote* with a bottom line approaching six figures. I peered closer. For musical equipment, dated a week ago, listing Rebecca as the buyer. An order for the festival?

Had the story about power and direction been a cover? Was the real problem not bringing back Martin, but unauthorized spending?

A folder from a village real estate agent also lay open. I picked up a handful of pages, not sure what went where. I slipped a listing agreement and a quit claim deed, stamped DRAFT, back in the folder.

"What are you doing?"

Rebecca's sharp tone startled me, and I scrambled to my feet, folder in one hand, loose pages in the other. "Sorry. I bumped the corner of your desk, but I've almost got it cleaned up."

She snatched the papers from me. "I'll take care of it. You can leave now."

"Ohhh-kay." I pushed myself up. "Sorry. I didn't mean to make a mess."

"No one ever does."

Across the street, the Playhouse lobby thrummed. A line of volunteers filed past a table stacked with class schedules, maps of festival venues, and brochures from Jewel Bay businesses and attractions, stuffing them into folders. At another table, a woman laid out name tags in alphabetical order. In the box office, Dave Barber conferred with the Playhouse manager, a woman with an extraordinary eye for details. Nothing dared go wrong on her watch.

But despite the activity and excitement, I sensed an unspoken anxiety. It peered out from hooded eyes, and lurked in the low voices fretting over bad luck and bad publicity.

I picked up a program, Martin's face shining back at me.

"Hello, Erin," Dave said. "What brings you here?" Had I ever seen him without his hat? My mother might frown at men wearing hats indoors, but that rule seems, pardon me, old hat these days.

"I wanted to offer condolences about Gerry Martin's death, on behalf of the Merc, and the Merchants' Association. If there's any way we can help ... "

"I'm worried about cancellations," said a woman who worked as a desk clerk at the motel on the highway, and I heard muttered agreement.

"Are you getting calls? Has this hit the national news yet?"

"Everything's under control," Barber said. "We're rearranging the concert schedule and redistributing his classes. It's a pain, but we'll manage."

That had to be done, sure, but was Martin's death nothing more than a scheduling glitch?

Heaven save me from international stardom, if that's all it means. If you don't form true friendships along the way. If you visit a town half a dozen times and don't touch people's hearts and spirits.

I'd barely known the man, and I felt wounded on his behalf.

"You know, in business school, we studied companies that were hit by tampering and other tragedies, and we learned the importance of being proactive. Since not all your students have arrived yet, you might consider sending out a text or e-mail explaining what's happened, expressing your grief and sympathies, and assuring them that the show will go on, as Martin would have wanted." I wasn't on the committee; this wasn't really my place. "Just a suggestion."

"And an excellent one," the motel clerk said.

"I can handle that," another volunteer offered.

"And you should get that same message out to fans through the press, and your own social media. On the personal side, I'd like to send his family a basket from the Merc, in memory of all he did for the community."

Barber looked like I'd suggested a sunbathing trip to Mars.

"That's a lovely idea, Erin," Ann Drake said. I hadn't noticed her come up. "He had no family, but we've been in touch with his booking agent. We're setting up a scholarship fund, and we'll name the first Gerry Martin guitar fellow next year."

"That's great." I glanced at Barber, who frowned and rubbed the back of his neck. "Count on the Merc for a contribution."

"Perfect," Ann said.

"How is Gabby dealing with the news of her mentor's passing?" The words *die* and *death* don't bother me, maybe because I encountered death so personally, so deeply, so young, but Ann Drake seemed like a woman who would prefer to keep her distance from the inevitable.

"She's shocked, as we all are, but she'll get through it."

"Good. I'll let you get back to work. If there's anything we can do, let me know."

"Thank you, Erin. We'll remember your kindness."

Outside, the clouds had darkened from plain gray to pewter streaked with gunmetal. (With an artist sister, I've learned to see beyond the colors in the standard twenty-four-count box of Crayolas.) The sign advertising the festival whipped in the wind, metal grommets clanging loudly against the Playhouse's awning.

I shivered. Rain is common in late May and early June—we need it, to fend off forest fires in July and August—but the change in the air hung like an omen. In the flowerbeds outside the Playhouse, a late tulip had snapped off and lay on the sidewalk.

"Poor thing." I picked it up, twirling the blossom as I walked, its petals tutu pink with splashes of white and deep red. "A little water, and you can live happily for days on my desk."

The lonely tulip made the reality of Gerry Martin's death worse. No family, few friends to grieve for him. Fans like Heidi would be touched, but they'd move on. Rebecca Whitman and Gabby Drake seemed to have suffered the biggest losses. I knew from experience the guilt that lingers when your last contact with someone before his death was unpleasant.

I would do what I could to bring him justice, and to help them recover.

And to prevent long-term damage to Jewel Bay. Tucked at the edge of the wildlands, at the base of mountains formed by shifting tectonic plates, between two rivers and the largest freshwater lake west of the Mississippi, this town and its residents were no strangers to fire, flood, or earthquake. Even the occasional pestilence, in the form of fruit flies and drought-driven grasshoppers.

If it turned out that someone intimately involved with the festival was responsible for Martin's death . . .

I shivered. Was that truly possible? It had to be. Who besides the organizers and other musicians had any connection to Martin? Unless he'd pissed off a barista but good, or provoked a bartender to a murderous rage.

"Maine, Auntie! I got—"

I spun around on the sidewalk at my nephew's call, my brain sizing up the situation and kicking me into motion before I fully registered what was happening.

"Landon, STOP!"

Rubber ground on the pavement as a driver slammed on his brakes, the back end of his car jerking to a dead halt in the middle of Front Street.

I sprang forward and scooped up the boy, his battered brown cowboy boots kicking my thighs.

The driver climbed out of his car. "Where did he come from?" he asked, voice shaking. My heart pounded and I didn't know whether to yell at the six-year-old, the driver, or God.

Not God, because Landon was okay.

"He's collecting license plates," I said, the heat from the fear and adrenaline rushing through my body as I clutched the boy.

"I got Maine, Auntie," he whimpered into my chest. At my feet lay his stubby little pencil and the crumpled list of states and provinces he kept in his pocket.

And beside them, on the pavement, lay the crushed pink tulip.

Eight

I delivered my teary nephew to his mother and handed her the pencil and list. Then snatched them back and made a big X next to Maine. It was the Holy Grail of license plates in these parts, second only to Hawaii.

Chiara—a name my mother chose, it's said with a hard *C* and rhymes with *tiara*—carted her only child to the gallery's back room. I sank onto the stool behind the front counter. People assume the family retail bug bit us both, but while I love business, Chiara loves art. Retail is a means to an end for her—a means to sell her paintings, jewelry, and quirky kids' hats. She and a handful of artists started Snowberry as a co-op gallery a couple of years ago, and it had quickly become a mainstay on the art trail.

A customer approached carrying half a dozen beeswax candles. This wasn't my shop, and I had to get back to work, but my sister was still busy with Landon, so I rang up the sale for her. Watching her walk through the gallery a minute or two later was a bit like looking in a mirror. I'm two inches taller and she's two years older, but we've got the same heart-shaped face, brown eyes, and dark bob that falls just below the chin, though after the close encounter on the street, mine was messier.

Truth be told, my hair is always messier than my sister's.

"He's napping in the desk chair," she said. "We'll have another talk about street safety tonight. And about sneaking out of the shop without telling me."

"Thank God the driver stopped in time." I reached out to a coat rack, handmade from a fallen birch, and lifted off a green and blue leather bag. "These are new."

"Oh, our new artist. April Ng." Chiara handed me a cross-body satchel in black leather. "Isn't her work stunning? She repurposes old leather jackets and pants, and buys scraps from a coat factory. We should find you a replacement for that filthy blue thing."

"My blue bag has history."

"It shows."

I resisted the temptation to stick out my tongue. "Hey, I hired Lou Mary Vogel. Mom's idea."

"Good. She'll be great."

"Yeah." I bit my lower lip. "But Mom got way pushy about it, which isn't like her. Why zone in on Lou Mary?"

The door opened and three women entered, shopping bags in hand. Time for us both to get to work. My sis threw her arms around me and kissed my cheek. "I'm so thankful you were there."

"Me, too."

But before heading back to the Merc, I wanted to check in with another friend.

The door to Kitchenalia stood open, and jazzy guitar strains floated out. Music by Gerry Martin, unless I missed my guess.

"Those lily pad lids are some of our most popular items," I heard Heidi tell a fiftyish woman studying a display. "They form the perfect seal for a bowl or a pot. They're silicone, so they withstand hot and cold, wash beautifully, and last forever."

"You can even put the small one on top of your water glass to keep the cat from dunking her paw in it," I said.

"Sold." The customer dropped two small and two medium lids in her basket, and moved on to the bakeware display.

"She's stocking her daughter's first real apartment. Are you investigating, Erin? Digging into what happened to Gerry?"

I glanced around, kept my voice low. "Yes. Because he deserves justice. His death means more than lost tourism dollars."

Heidi's lips quivered and her jaw trembled as she swallowed hard. She closed her mouth and swallowed hard. "His music helped me get through a hard time. My interest faded, but not the memories."

I reached for her hand. "Thank you, Heidi. For reminding me that we're talking about a real human here, who touched other people's lives."

The customer called for help from a display of cake pans, and I slipped out the front door.

Back in the Merc, Lou Mary had arrived for her first shift, and bent over the iPad as Tracy showed her how to e-mail customers their receipts. A weight slipped from my shoulders.

Almost before we knew it, the day was over, and I ran Lou Mary through the closing procedures. Tracy hauled the produce cart inside. The lock on the front door balked. Lou Mary blamed her arthritic hands, but I assured her it gave me fits, too.

"Old buildings have their quirks," I said.

"So do old ladies," she replied, pointing a gnarled finger at herself.

She fretted a bit as she watched me count the till, but it came out on the penny, rare even without a new employee. *This might work*, I thought as I watched Tracy and Lou Mary leave. I packed up a jar of enchilada sauce and a few outdated but yummy truffles. Upstairs, I locked away the till.

That done, I reached under the desk for my bag. As I did, the white paper cup in the wastebasket caught my attention.

Could it be important? I'd found it a few feet from where Gerry Martin had gone over the edge. Had it belonged to him, or to a witness? Or to the killer?

More likely, it had lain there for days. *No, it hadn't*, I realized. A hard rain had fallen Thursday night. This cup was stark white. Crisp and clean as it looked, it must have been dropped this morning.

I dashed downstairs and grabbed a plastic bag from our commercial kitchen. Back in the office, I labeled it with the time, date, and place where I'd found the cup and added my initials, as I'd seen Kim do so many times. Holding the outside of the bag, I used it like a glove and plucked the cup out of the trash, then zipped the seal shut.

"Now to keep it safe. Preserve the chain of custody." In case the cup turned out to be significant. But there was no spare room in the one locking file drawer. "Ah—that's it." I opened the ancient wall safe again and tucked the bag inside.

"Thanks for dinner, Erin." Tanner stretched out one long leg, picked up his wineglass, and leaned back against the couch. "That was terrific."

He'd pushed away a half-full plate. Adam had said his buddy would eat anything, but apparently not my chicken enchiladas. So much for my plan to fatten him up. At least the outdoor activities Adam had on tap would put a little color in his face.

"I told you she was a great cook," Adam said.

"Yeah, but you think dumping soy sauce on ramen noodles makes them gourmet."

Adam opened his mouth to protest, then saw me grinning. "I've changed. My tastes have matured."

Who laughed harder, Tanner or me, I couldn't say. We were sitting on my living room floor, dining at the coffee table. My cabin is compact. Two can sit at the kitchen island. The tiny deck offers giant views of the lake and mountains, and its café table is perfect for morning coffee, but too small for dinner for three. Besides, the weather was a bit unsettled for dining *al fresco*.

That had left the living room, ideal for one woman and a pair of cats. Stir in two tall men and it gets a bit cramped, but tonight the coziness made me warm and happy.

"Oh, no, you don't." I grabbed Pumpkin around the middle and relocated her to the slate hearth, well away from my plate. "That's mine."

"So this other guy owns a restaurant and it's his recipe, but you can it," Tanner said. "Jar it, or whatever."

"Right. We both sell it, and I'm working on developing outlets in other towns." I finished the last bite, and Adam got to his feet. He loaded the plates, with their tempting tidbits of red sauce, into the dishwasher, away from the full-figured orange tabby's reach. "Can you believe—a cat who likes spicy food."

Tanner topped off my wine, leaving his glass empty. "I can see the ad now. One bite, and you and your cat will be hooked."

I picked up my glass and twirled the divine red liquid. "On small quantities, shipping costs kill us. It's not like SavClub, where we shipped pallet loads, mainly in our own trucks."

"Or like your T-shirts. Flat and light." Adam set a plate of truffles on the table. Mr. Sandburg raised his head, then returned to his nap. My cats couldn't have been more different, from their sleeping habits to their taste in human food. They had in common excellent hunting skills, and the fact that each had come to me after the death of their original owner, both good friends.

"I love my hoodie, Tanner, by the way. Thank you." I stretched out my arms, admiring the black-and-white stripes. "And it's made from plastic bottles?"

"Some of it. Mainly post-industrial and post-consumer fibers." He arched his back as if it ached. After today's events, no surprise.

"Post-consumer—that would be the old T-shirts you take back, right? But what does post-industrial mean?" I looked up at Adam, flipping through my CDs on the shelves next to the fireplace. "Adam, sit."

"I'm trying to find different music. Your CD collection sucks."

"Use my iPod." I couldn't blame him for feeling restless. He'd dealt with countless tragedies in Search and Rescue, but he always said that if it ever stopped bothering him, he'd know it was time to quit. And finding a body on the rocks when you're out having fun had to be doubly unnerving.

One more reason for me to help solve the crime. As long as I stayed safe.

"Post-industrial means remnants from other industrial uses. We buy short bolts. Odds and ends. A fifty-yard remnant that's useless to Champion or Under Armour will last us for ages."

"Oh, like this cute handbag I saw today, at my sister's gallery. The artist buys leather scraps and remakes old jackets into bags."

"Exactly like that." Tanner explained the process of sourcing and manufacturing while an early Coldplay CD began. He'd dropped out of college to start the business, determined to build a company that made good, lasting products average people could afford, while keeping what would otherwise have become waste out of the landfill.

Doing good while doing well, as the sustainable business gurus say.

Or as Adam had told me, to create something of his own. Important to a guy who'd regularly had to leave everything behind when he got shuffled off to a different foster home.

No sign of Adam. Then I heard him on the floor behind the couch, tossing a cork for Sandburg. "Are we boring you with business blather?" I called.

No answer. Tanner watched me, expressionless.

"Pick a new topic, then. Anything you want."

Adam popped up, peering over the back of the couch. "I like hearing you two talk business."

Then why was he hiding out with the cats?

"Hey, Z, you give any more thought to that commercial solar coffee roaster?" Tanner asked.

"Solar? Here? No chance. Anyway, I have enough going on." Adam flopped over the back of the couch. Sandburg jumped on his leg, crawling up to settle on his chest.

"You don't need a hundred percent sunny days. You just need somebody who understands accounting better than you do, and I think you found her." Tanner got to his feet, smacking his buddy on the shoulder on the way to the bathroom.

"Do you want to talk about it?" I said softly after I heard the door close.

Adam's gaze darted toward me, wide-eyed and worried. He shook his head quickly, then stared over my shoulder at the gas fireplace, the flames burning low. "It was nothing I hadn't seen. You, either. Tanner's never stumbled across a dead body before, far as I know. But he did okay. He stayed back while we carried the body down and got it loaded up. Then we brought the kayaks in. Went up to the station and gave Ike Hoover our statements." Lips tight, he gave a quick *that's all—no big deal* shrug.

I didn't think that was all, and I darn well knew it was a big deal.

"Ike ask you about tracks and signs, what you saw when you climbed up?"

Adam nodded. "Yeah, but that dirt's too fine and sandy to hold much moisture. You saw how faint the tracks were up top—same thing on the cliff. It was pretty clear where Martin went over and where he landed, but in between all we saw were a few scrapes in the dirt."

"Ike's going to investigate like it's murder until he's sure it isn't."

Adam sat up, Sandburg in his arms. "Erin, I need to tell you—"

I heard the toilet flush. The door opened and footsteps neared.

"Hey, Lundy, they played this in that concert we went to, didn't they?" Adam called out.

What else had he wanted to say, without Tanner hearing? He shot me a look that could have meant a dozen different things, from *let's not talk about murder in front of my buddy* to *stay out of it.* I knew he trusted me, and I knew he was proud of my success in past investigations, but that didn't mean he wasn't worried.

Some things go without saying.

Nine

"We should call you Enchilada, not Pumpkin." I hoisted the cat, all thirteen pounds of her, out of the sink and set her on the kitchen floor. My restless sweetie had done a great job on cleanup duty. But he'd left the baking dish soaking, and Pumpkin had practically stood upside down to get at the bits of sauce stuck to the edges.

Scrubbie in hand, I set to work removing temptation. It didn't take long—she'd been thorough.

I laid the baking dish on the drain rack and reached for a smudgy wineglass. Most times, washing dishes relaxes me. But tonight, I'd caught a bit of Adam's agitation. I'd wanted him to stick around and let me soothe it—Tanner would be here all week—but he'd made no move to stay, and I hadn't wanted to ask. Instead, I'd been content with a long, sweet kiss after Tanner headed for the car.

I reached for another glass. My internal PowerPoint flipped through a series of images: Gerry Martin's body lying on the rocks, the roiling river, the short stretch of trail with an unprotected edge, Gerry Martin on stage last night.

The slide show kept playing: Martin bristling at Barber, then barking at Gabby. All they'd wanted was a piece of his spotlight. Oh, and earlier, Martin scowling at Sam for a missed cue.

Who had pushed Martin?

And why?

I wiped my hands on the kitchen towel and spotted Pumpkin, crouched hopefully on the kitchen floor. "That's the point Holmes was making to Watson, right? About the dog in the night? If two people tangled and one slipped and fell, the ground would have been beat up. The dirt edge would have been broken and shrubbery torn. There should have been signs, at the edge of the trail and the top of the cliff, of Martin slipping and trying to catch himself. Of the other person trying to grab him."

Was I placing too much importance on signs that should have been plain as day, but weren't there?

On the page and on screen, Holmes never betrayed a lick of doubt. Oh, for such certainty.

What did I actually know about Gerry Martin? Not much—jazz guitar had never been my thing. I put on his new CD, then settled in the chocolate brown leather chair with a fresh glass of red and two truffle rejects. Pumpkin eyed me from the rug a few feet away. Sandburg was nowhere in sight.

The liner notes gave the air-brushed version of Martin's life. Born in Pittsburgh to a father who plumbed by day and drummed by night and a mother who taught piano. Child prodigy on the keyboard, until he—like so many kids—discovered the guitar at thirteen. Unlike most, he stuck with it, joining a popular jazz band at sixteen and working regularly in the city's bars and clubs. He hadn't bothered with college, getting his musical education on the road and in bands large and small. He was praised for his tone, his rhythm and harmony, and his versatility. Even I'd heard of some of the artists he'd recorded and toured with.

I reached for a truffle. The mark said double chocolate, but with rejects, you never know. Martin had seventeen Grammy nominations, five awards. "Mmm. Raspberry."

Rebecca had said his career had taken a downturn recently. Ebbs and flows had to be common, but she'd made it sound more serious.

I dug out my laptop and searched his Grammy history. Impressive as the numbers were, the last award had been eight years ago, the last nomination six.

No obits online yet, though a couple of small pieces reported that Martin had "apparently plunged to his death while hiking in a remote Montana valley, where the innovate performer and composer had been scheduled to teach at a music festival before dates in Seattle and Vancouver, and an Asian tour."

Remote, shmote. Interesting that Ike had not revealed that there was a witness, or that he suspected that old demon, foul play.

I flipped to the website for Dimitriou's Jazz Alley in Seattle. Next to Martin's name on the schedule was the ominous word *cancelled*.

When I lived in Seattle, a boyfriend—using the term loosely—had taken me to Jazz Alley to hear Diane Schuur, the hometown singer and pianist. She'd been fabulous; the guy had been a fail. My dating life in the city had been a cross between *Survivor* and *The Apprentice,* with me repeatedly voted off the team as one guy after another climbed corporate ladders leading elsewhere.

Martin, on the other hand, had climbed the ladder of success like a monkey streaking up a palm tree. Surely he'd made a few enemies along the way. Was one of them here for our festival? One of the other artists?

Of course, you can't find out who hates a guy enough to kill him by checking his website. I dug the program I'd grabbed this afternoon out of my bag.

No clues there, either. I ate another truffle—cherry, as marked, but with an imperfect bottom.

I stood, unkinking a leg, pondering. Glanced into the bedroom. Sandburg lay on the chaise, staring out into the night.

I sat beside him and ran my hand over his sleek fur. From a distance, he looks black, but he's a sable Burmese—dark chocolate with black pointing on his ears, face, feet, and tail. I'm no expert on cats. We had a cat at the Orchard when I was a kid, but after a hawk killed him and my sister bawled for days, my dad brought home Sparky the border collie and we became dog people. Sandburg was my first feline roommate, and until Pumpkin came, he ruled the place. They tussled with each other the first few weeks, hissing and snarling, one cat deliberately taking the other's favored spot or eating out of the other's bowl. I'd wondered about my sanity, thinking two regal pretenders could occupy six hundred square feet and leave room for me. But they'd since settled into an uneasy truce, sharing the throne.

The metaphor ran its course. If he was the King and she the Queen, who was I?

Their humble servant.

Back in the kitchen, I poured another half glass and took a sip. Rebecca had said she and Martin had known each other in Austin, and she claimed credit for bringing him here. Too late to call her, but if I sent a text, she could answer when she wanted.

Which turned out to be about three minutes later. No, she wasn't aware of any other artists on this year's schedule angry with Martin, but she wouldn't know, would she? Since he hadn't been talking to her much, and when he was, he obviously hadn't been truthful. Sorry she wasn't much help.

She got that right.

I grabbed the program and flipped to the page of featured performers, or in the trendy term, emerging artists. First on the list, courtesy of alphabetical order, was Gabrielle Drake. A smaller version of the photo on our poster smiled out at me. Truly a beautiful young woman. The program described her as "the voice of a new generation," the words Gerry Martin had used to introduce her, saying she'd been raised in New York City and Connecticut, and now studied at Indiana University, "the finest school of music in the country." I didn't know about that, but I did know a little about sales puffery. Every performer listed was "the finest," "iconic," "stellar," and otherwise super double groovy.

Maybe Gabby Drake deserved all the praise. She'd outshone Gerry Martin, I knew that for sure.

And I knew for sure that he hadn't liked it one bit.

She had no website, but I did find her Facebook page, her Twitter stream, and her Instagram feed. She'd be busy this summer, with performances scheduled all over the country. I had no idea that music festivals had become so popular—obviously the thing for the "emerging artist." Ours was a little different, combining big-name concerts with daytime workshops, and welcoming serious adult musicians as well as the younger set.

I clicked on a series of YouTube videos and sank deeper into my chair. Gabby had entered a nationwide contest for singer-songwriters. Each week, contestants were given a topic and a key, then required to write a song with those elements and submit a video. Fan voting ruled the early rounds. A clickable version of *The Voice*.

Part way through Gabby's first piece, Pumpkin jumped on the arm of my chair and trained her yellow-green eyes on the screen. I reached for my wine to prevent a clash between tail and glass.

Gabby had an ethereal, haunting sound, her lyrics betraying her youth, all romantic angst and searching for identity. Her guitar playing, I couldn't judge. A few early clips had obviously been recorded on a phone in her dorm room.

With three weeks to go, Gabby clung to the top five. I voted for her latest song, then opened the festival's website. Martin's face shone from the front page. A small text box said the festival "mourned the passing of a great artist," and dedicated this year's events to his memory.

Rebecca was still listed as Executive Director. I knew most of the board members, including Dave Barber and Marv Alden, but none well. Grant Drake, I'd just met.

Meaning I'd have to work for insider knowledge.

Though she wasn't on the board, I started my search with Ann Drake, soprano. No joy. She must have performed under her maiden name. She'd mentioned the Met.

"What do you think, Punk? Gabby's a junior, so let's call her twenty-one. Ann's about my mother's age. Can we narrow the search that way?"

Bingo, by jingo, as Ned would say. Ann Fletcher had been a cast member for thirteen years. As she'd said, minor roles, some as understudy, and several tours. She, too, had attended Indiana University's school of music.

A twenty-five-year-old wedding announcement for Ann Fletcher and Grant Drake lauded her musical career, noting that the groom "worked in finance." It also said the groom was attended by his sons. No children were mentioned for Ann. As I suspected, Gabby had been a later-in-life addition to the family.

So what? None of that had anything to do with Gabby's relationship with Gerry Martin, or with his death.

The Drakes were protective. Righteous anger on a child's behalf is understandable, even expected. But would a parent kill to avenge a slight against a child, if the slighter stood to harm that child's professional aspirations?

Extreme, yes, but hardly unheard of.

If Martin had threatened to withdraw his support for her career, then her parents might have done almost anything.

So might she, for that matter.

I squinted, trying to picture who'd hung around after the performance, who might have heard more of Martin's tirade. The other musicians had been busy on stage, unplugging amps and cords and packing up instruments.

I frowned. When Martin stormed out of the courtyard, Jennifer Kraus had run after him. She might have seen or heard something. I hadn't remembered that when I gave Deputy Oakland my statement, but he would have talked with her by now.

What was I looking for? What was I expecting to find?

I was too keyed up to sleep. I refreshed my wine, decided I'd had enough truffles, and sprinkled a few treats in the cats' bowls. They came running from opposite ends of the cabin. Their bowls were mere inches apart, yet they managed to avoid each other completely, as if each had cast a protective spell around their territory.

Heck, maybe they had.

"The photographs." My feline companions ignored me as I scrolled through the pictures I'd sent myself this morning from Derek D'Orazi's phone. I sat at the kitchen island and studied them. Nothing jumped out at me: just dirt, smudged here and there. Who could say how a body had tumbled, whether it should have gone this way or that instead of that way or this?

I shivered. Death is a messy business.

Ten

his is where you grew up?" Tanner's voice rose in awe as I steered my sage green Subaru up the dirt lane leading to the Orchard. My family's usual Sunday evening gathering had been converted into brunch so we could all attend the festival's opening concert tonight. "No wonder you don't want to leave."

"I left twice. First for college in Missoula, and then out to Seattle for ten years." We rounded the last curve and I pulled up behind my mother's ancient Volvo, parked underneath the carport. Why my parents had never enclosed it into a full-fledged garage, I had no idea. They'd bought the house from my grandparents, who built it when my dad was a toddler, his younger brothers in the offing, and people can be funny about changing family property.

Adam unfolded himself from the backseat and stood next to Tanner as he absorbed the view. I took Adam's hand. He gave me a smile that could melt glaciers.

How had I ever walked away from that smile? Or more accurately, failed to notice it. Last night, over enchiladas and red wine, Tanner had gotten me to admit that I barely remembered Adam from college—not that Adam had any illusions otherwise.

Back then, I'd been an overly studious business major, reeling from my father's death, seeking comfort in my classes. Adam had been a tall, skinny woods geek, one of dozens who came west as much to play outdoors as to get an education. Not that there aren't plenty of trees and lakes in Minnesota and the other places these boys—and a few girls—had left, but Montana had called to them.

A handful stayed. "There's the home you start from," Adam had said last night, his fork full of chicken and tortillas, "and the home you make."

And the home you come back to, I thought as I gazed down the hill toward the lake, glistening in the mid-morning sun, *and know the place for the first time*. To mangle T. S. Eliot's words.

"Adam!" Landon's shout broke my reverie, and nearly broke my eardrum. He tore through the orchard, the blossoms gone, the apple, cherry, and plum trees nearing full leaf.

"Hey, buddy." Adam crouched to six-year-old height and a handshake–fist bump ritual followed.

"Jason Phillips." My brother-in-law trailed his son and held out his hand to the newcomer. "That little wild man is mine, I'm afraid."

"Tanner Lundquist. What a great place."

"We were up in the tree house. You can see for*ever* from there. Come on!" Landon took off, then stopped and looked back. "Come *on*, you guys."

Adam tossed me a grin, and he and Tanner loped after the boy.

"I heard." Jason's voice cracked. "Thank you. Not a scratch on him."

"And he got Maine," I said. Jason's wry half smile mirrored my own, and he took the bag of cranberry-rhubarb muffins from me. I grabbed a chilled bottle of Prosecco from the backseat, and we headed for the house. My mother might tell her daughters we don't need to bring anything to family gatherings, but neither of us believe her.

A few minutes later, Tanner and I strolled through the upper meadow, a riot of green thanks to last week's rain. "The property stretches to the top of this ridge." I yanked down the sleeves of the striped hoodie Tanner had given me, and tugged the hem of my short black skirt. The nip in the air had prompted my mother to decree that we'd be enjoying Sunday brunch inside, instead of on the stone terrace with its lake and mountain views, so I was giving Tanner a quick pre-feast tour. "That's Trumpeter Mountain beyond."

"Fresh snow," Tanner said. "Somebody live in that shack? It's about to fall down." He rubbed an elbow and winced, as he had last night. Too much paddling?

"My brother Nick used it as home base for years. He's a wildlife biologist, specializing in wolf behavior. Last winter, he inherited a cottage and an old church a few miles away and that's where he stays when he's home, which isn't often." Nick had offered the cottage to me, but the prospect of living so close to where I'd found Christine—twice his fiancée but never his bride—dead made me too sad. I pointed northeast. "You met my sister and her family. They bought the original Murphy homestead, through those woods."

"Auntie! Tanner!" Landon summoned us to the main house.

As we made our way back, I couldn't help wondering what Tanner was thinking. Hands in his pants pockets, he seemed distracted, or tired. "A few family friends will be here, too. I hope the chaos doesn't send you screaming back to the Midwest."

"Are you kidding?" His face came alive, Nordic blue eyes sparkling.

Landon stood outside the kitchen door, hopping from one foot to the other. A hummingbird feeder hung from the roof line, and a Rufous dive-bombed him before taking a quick drink.

That old feeling murmured in my gut, the one I couldn't quite articulate. A mix of *Why did you ever leave?* and *You had to leave, to come home.*

The air buzzed with my mother's surprise. I glanced at my sister, the excitement building, but she'd bent down to wipe Landon's face.

I led Tanner inside. "Did you meet Heidi and Reg last night? They're here, along with the rest of the family."

My mother put a champagne flute in Tanner's hand and led him into the fray. My Murphy uncles and aunts had been summoned to hear the news. We get along fine, and both Mick and Dan live nearby, but they have their own families and Sunday traditions, and don't usually join us.

I filled a flute, took a tiny sip of Prosecco, and readied for the sneeze the first bubbles always bring. That done, I sat next to my cousin Molly on the couch. My mother believed a mid-century house deserved to be furnished with updated 1950s classics, like this three-seater with wide bentwood maple arms, its black fabric splashed with red hibiscus blossoms and jungle green foliage. Pepé, my mother's Scottie, jumped into my lap.

"Tell me about your new job," I asked my cousin. "When do you hear if you passed the real estate exam?"

"Soon. Soon. Part of my job is updating our MLS listings." Molly's got pale, freckled skin, lively green eyes, and curly reddish hair. Our grandfather Murphy had said she and her brother, and my uncle Dan's kids, "had the map of Ireland on their faces." We half-Italian kids he'd lovingly called "the dark ones."

That map crinkled now as she explained. "That stands for Multiple Listing Service, the computer system that shows every property available in the entire county. It's crazy."

"But you love it."

Her eyes sparkled like the wine. "I love it."

"Good. If you turned me down for a job you hated, you'd be in serious trouble."

The tinkling of a spoon against a glass interrupted the conversation, and we all faced my mother, who stood in front of the marble-topped cabinet that served as the bar. In a black boat-neck T and a long skirt reminiscent of a poppy field gone mad, she glowed. Bill appeared beside her, his salt-and-pepper beard and hair neatly trimmed.

I leaned forward on the couch, clutching my empty flute. The nerves along my shoulders and spine tingled, and I couldn't keep from grinning.

"Thank you all for joining us on this special morning," Bill said. He reached for my mother's hand, and anticipation rippled through the crowded living room. "We hope you'll all join us in a few weeks for another special occasion. I've asked Fresca to marry me, and she's agreed."

It takes a lot to quiet the Murphy clan. That did it. Briefly. Then Uncle Mick raised a half-full glass. "To the woman who made this Irishman drink fancy Italian wine on a Sunday morning—"

"He's on his second glass," his wife interjected.

"—and the man who's made her happy again."

"Hear, hear." "Cheers!" "Salut!"

Happiness rang through the room, though no one sounded genuinely surprised. The only surprise to me was that my mother had waited so long. She'd dated, and over the years I'd met several beaus who'd clearly been head over heels for her. But she'd held back, and I'd never known why.

I raised a toast with the rest of the family. Beside me, Adam gave me another of those toe-tingling smiles. More Prosecco flowed, with and without fruity additions—the peach puree of a Bellini, or the orange juice that makes a Mimosa. I wondered about other flavors. A dollop of strawberry-rhubarb jam might be terrific, if unconventional.

Wedding plans were revealed—the first day of summer, in the orchard.

And then it was time to fill our plates. With all of us and my uncles' families, we overflowed the dining room and living room. Molly and her younger brother, Henry, sat on the floor. It was a sweet house, surprisingly modern, but the remodeled kitchen was due for another update.

The couch squeaked as Adam and Tanner sat on either side of me, and Tanner rose instinctively. "Sit," I said. "It's sturdier than it looks."

They sat. So did Pepé, her nose in the air. I pried a bite of bacon out of an omelet muffin—a mini crustless quiche—and raised it like a communion host before letting her gobble it.

"Is that how you make friends, Erin? Bribery?" Uncle Mick said. He could have been my father's twin.

"Whatever works."

"What do you call this?" At the buffet Tanner pointed to a slice of sweet flat bread—or what passes for flat bread in classic Italian cooking—studded with orange peel and raisins, and topped with sliced almonds and powdered sugar.

"*Schiacciata.*" Skee-yah-CHAH-tah.

"What do you call this?" He pointed to a fat sausage grilled with peppers and spinach.

"*Salsicce con pepperoni y spinaci.*"

"And this?"

"You idiot," Adam broke in, "don't you recognize a sliced pear when you see one?"

"From the Conti family orchard in California. One of my mother's brothers raises tree fruit, and the other grows grapes and runs a winery there."

But despite the verbal enthusiasm, I couldn't help noticing that Tanner didn't eat a lot.

Conversation ran the gamut: Tanner's business and his thoughts about Montana. Henry's summer internship. More about Molly's new job. She and my mother exchanged knowing looks, and I wondered if Fresca had helped Molly land the post at Jewel Bay Realty.

I ate another egg thing, apologizing to Pepé for eating the bacon myself.

One voice was missing from the cacophony. I glanced around, wondering where Chiara had gone. "Outside," Jason mouthed.

I excused myself, dropping my dishes in the kitchen on my way out. The morning chill had burned off, leaving a clear sky, the orchard grasses damp around my bare ankles. The tree house has always been my hideout, but when Chiara needs to get away, she takes refuge in her own special spot.

The wild shrubs had not yet fully exploded into summer glory—another day or two of rain and a blast of sunshine and they'd be thick with new growth. I made my way up the narrow path and found my sister on a giant rock beside the stream, arms wrapped around her knees, long skirt covering her feet. The spring green fabric was nearly the same color as the thick moss at the trail's edge.

Jason likes to say that in our family, Murphy's Law means no silence can last longer than two seconds. But even I can keep my mouth shut sometimes.

"I was fine with it, when she told us last week," she said finally, sounding exhausted. "I love Bill, and he adores her. It's just that—oh, God. Dad's been gone for years, and nothing could ever bring him back, and sometimes I can't remember him quite right, you know? It feels so unfair."

"That she's remarrying?" My feet sunk into the spongy moss. "It's been years, Chiara. She deserves this."

"No, that's not it. It's so unfair that Dad never got to see what his kids became. He'll never know Landon, or your kids, or Nick's."

"If either of us ever has any."

"You will." She raised her head, her eyes brimming. "I sound like an awful bitch, don't I?"

"Not awful. It's a crazy time, with summer coming on. And you have the biggest heart and freest spirit of anyone I know." At the edge of the woods, a chickadee chirped.

"You didn't say I wasn't a bitch."

No, I didn't.

"I asked her once why she hadn't remarried," she said, "right after Jason and I moved back here, when Landon was really little. We'd had too much Prosecco. She said she felt like Dad wanted her to move on, but until his death was solved, she couldn't."

And now that had shifted, freeing her to make a new commitment.

"You gave her that gift," she said, and I heard an unfamiliar tone. Jealousy? Resentment? Both so unlike her.

I kicked at a small, moss-covered rock, bright against the toe of my red shoe. "Yeah, who'd a thunk your kid sister could solve a crime the cops couldn't."

"That's not what I meant." Chiara's dark eyes flashed. "I thought— I thought you of all people would understand." She slipped off her perch, stumbling on the soft ground. She grabbed her skirt with both hands and rushed up the trail toward the orchard.

Criminy. What was I supposed to understand?

I perched on the rock my sister had abandoned. Mom's news that she and Bill were engaged had made sense of a few things. A casual comment about travel, her urging that I expand the Merc's partnership with Ray and the Grille.

And her determination that I hire toot sweet. Though not why she'd insisted on Lou Mary.

You think you understand your family, and then *whoosh*! In two sweeps of the minute hand, you realize you don't understand a thing.

∞

"Erin, come with me."

"I've got to get to the Merc, Mom. Tracy's off, and Lou Mary doesn't have keys."

"You can spare a minute." She strode down the hallway, the black skirt with its red-orange poppies swinging.

In the bedroom, Mom stood at her dressing table. A silk kimono, deep green with purple trim, lay draped over the bench. My mother is the only woman I know who actually uses a dressing table—this one a waterfall design in butterscotch walnut. (Details I learned helping her scavenge the set from my great grandparents' homestead house before my sister moved in. Every few months, Chiara contends that the pieces ought to come back to her house, where they belong. Mom just rolls her eyes.)

I could see her reflection in the beveled mirror. Her graceful hands held a small square black box. Though I had never seen it before, its meaning was unmistakable.

"I've been saving this for you, darling. I think it's time."

My hands remained at my sides, frozen. She reached for one and placed the box in it.

No matter what your inner turmoil, you can't not open a box. Especially a box like this.

A flood of emotion washed through me as I stared at its contents. I was astonished, stunned, awestruck, joy-struck, love-struck, and terrified all at once.

"It's—it's your engagement ring. From Dad. It's so gorgeous."

"White gold. The center diamond is a princess cut. I always felt like a princess when I wore it."

I slipped the ring out and held it up. If there's any light at all in a room, a diamond will gather it up and give it back to you, doubled, tripled, and more.

"But, what about Nick?" I met her gaze. "Don't you want—shouldn't he—I mean, he'll find someone else."

"Your grandfather gave him your grandmother's solitaire, years ago. You remember—he gave it to Christine."

Who'd offered it back when she broke their engagement, but he'd refused. As if he'd known they'd need it someday.

"But—"

She took the ring from my trembling fingers. "No *buts* about it, darling. He can decide for himself what he wants to do with that ring. This one is yours." She slipped it on my right ring finger.

I stretched out my hand. Small channel-set diamonds tapered toward the center stone. The ring fit as if it had been made for me. I caught my reflection in the mirror.

My mother stood behind me, her hands on my shoulders, her eyes moist. A moment later, she stepped back and cleared her throat. "No strings attached. You can wear it, you can sell it, you can have the diamonds reset. You can put it on a chain around your neck."

Like she'd done with the matching wedding ring.

"No strings attached," she repeated.

But that didn't keep me from feeling them tugging at my heart.

Eleven

Adam had left his car—a perpetually dirty black Xterra—at the top of the long driveway that led past my cabin, also known as "the caretaker's place," and down the hill to "the big house" on the lake, my landlords' summer home.

"Promise me you won't do anything dangerous this afternoon," I said. "Not one word tonight about whitewater, rock climbing, or mountain bikes. And no more dead bodies."

"From what I hear," Tanner said, "running a retail shop is at least as dangerous as running the rapids." He stepped nimbly out of my reach, Adam behind him, laughing. I rolled my eyes and climbed into the Subaru.

Less than ten minutes later, I was unlocking the Merc and apologizing to Lou Mary for making her wait.

"Normally, we set up the till first, then restock the produce cart and get the day's samples ready before we open, but Sunday should be slow enough that running late won't be a problem." Thank goodness Wendy's crew had cleaned up the courtyard after yesterday's bridal shower.

Lou Mary followed me around the shop like an eager puppy, the wooden heels of her apricot loafers slapping the plank floor. I wondered if she had a pair in every color.

I'd given Tracy the day off, which meant training Lou Mary and tending to customers, and leaving business details for another day. Fine with me—sometimes I get so caught up in invoices and orders and product development plans that I forget how much I love working the shop floor.

Technically, my mother owns the Merc. My grandfather gave it to my father, and when he died, the building went to her, although she calls herself the custodian, holding it for the three of us. Nick and Chiara are more than happy to let me tend to the old pile, and I knew her remarriage wouldn't change the arrangement. Some adult children get anxious about money and inheritance when a parent remarries, but I couldn't see any of us fussing over that. She and Bill were both financially comfortable, fair-minded, and relatively young and healthy. If they wanted to run off to Maui and blow their wad, fine with me.

Not that I expected them to do that. Maui, maybe, but they were too smart to do anything really dumb.

Unlike me. I'd just dumped a bag of Montana Gold crackers onto the kitchen counter instead of into the bowl.

I cleaned up my mess and hoped Lou Mary hadn't seen the mishap.

No such luck. The woman was a retail queen, eyes in the back of her head. Happily, she knew when to bite her tongue.

This was our first Sunday open since Christmas, and my expectations were modest. About half the customers were workshop students and their families, checking out the town after checking in at the Playhouse. As they shopped, they tossed out comments about this class or that artist. Gerry Martin's name came up a few times, but not as often as I'd expected.

And not one word about murder, thank goodness. Though the rumor mill's temporary silence gave me little comfort.

Lou Mary didn't know all products and their stories, but she had an amazing ability to set customers at ease, to chat in a relaxing way that didn't set them up as marks.

Tracy and I could learn a few things from her.

Teaching her and the customers about the jams and jellies, meat and cheese, and other goods kept my mind off the murder, my stormy sister, and the ring in the box tucked deep in the bottom of my blue bag. If Tanner hadn't been with us, I might have shown it to Adam. Or maybe not. The last thing I wanted was for him to think I was trying to wheedle a proposal out of him.

Ha. He would think that was my mother's plan. And he might be right.

"Penny for your thoughts." Lou Mary rested an elbow on the front counter. I'd finished ringing up a customer, and we were alone in the shop.

"Big family do this morning. I can finally share the news I've been sitting on all week. My mother is getting married."

Lou Mary's eyes brightened and she clapped her hands, the jade and mother-of-pearl bangles on her wrist jangling. "Bill and Francesca! It's about time. When?"

"First day of summer. I'm not sure if they mean that to be symbolic, or if it's easier to remember the anniversary that way."

"Well, I'm not surprised, but I am delighted." She gave me a knowing look. "Aren't you?"

"Of course I am. Bill is wonderful, and he adores my mother. And she loves him right back."

"But ..." Her voice trailed off suggestively, and I had a sudden urge to show her the ring.

I dashed upstairs and returned with the box.

"She gave me this. The ring my father gave her in 1970-whatever. I think she's trying to tell me something."

"Put it on."

I slid it on to my right hand, as my mother had, fingers trembling.

"It's gorgeous," Lou Mary pronounced. "It suits you. Wear it," she said as I started to slide it off.

"It doesn't feel like mine yet."

"Jewelry never feels like yours until you wear it." She reached up to finger the jade beads around her neck. "That takes time. And don't feel strange about it having been your mother's. Good jewelry always tells a story. From what I hear, this ring carries good vibes."

The door opened. I slid the ring off my finger and tucked the box into the back of the cash drawer. The gift symbolized a big change in my mother's life, and I supposed I wondered how that would change who she was. Who *I* was.

Or whether I was ready for the answer.

The afternoon sped by profitably, thanks mostly to sales of picnic baskets for the concert. About four o'clock, we hit a lull. It's typical, even in high summer. The golf widows have finished shopping for the day, and the casual browsers have tired themselves out. They've all gone home to rest before dinner and the evening's entertainments.

"Mind if I sneak out for a few minutes?" I asked Lou Mary, busy studying the Montana Gold grain products. "I want to run down to the park and see if they decided the weather will hold, or if they're moving tonight's concert indoors."

"You go. I'll be fine."

I grabbed a pemmican bar and headed out the front door. The temperature had dropped four or five degrees since noon, and a cluster of gray clouds, bruised around the edges, filled the sky.

Halfway down the block, I caught up with a man I knew largely by sight.

"Doesn't look good, does it?" Marv Alden ran a hand over his shiny head. He peeled off his rimless glasses and polished them with a white handkerchief as we walked down Front Street toward the bridge.

Across the lake, sunbeams had broken out from behind the edge of the clouds, and lit up the tops of the mountains. "It's clearing. We may get lucky."

Alden's footsteps slowed as he put his glasses on and adjusted them, then tucked the hankie back in the front pocket of his pleated khakis. "Luck would be a nice change."

I swallowed the last bite of pemmican, buffalo meat mixed with berries. "Martin's death must be upsetting for the festival board. And a logistical challenge." The bridge's plank walkway wasn't quite wide enough for two, and I glanced at him over my shoulder.

"It's both. Wife and I moved up here for good a year ago, when I retired. The board sounded like an easy gig. Keep me busy, help us meet more people." He rolled his eyes, his bushy salt-and-pepper brows waggling like wooly worms. "You know what they say—no good deed goes unpunished."

We'd crossed the bridge to the small parking area. The Greek Guy, the ice cream wagon, and a couple of other food trucks were gearing up for pre-concert business, their generators drowning out the sounds of the river, the aromas pricking my nostrils.

And, nose out, a sheriff's vehicle. A patrol deputy I didn't know stood beside it, shades on, arms folded. Even without a murder, extra deputies would be on duty, plus the reserves, to respond to emergencies. To keep the rowdies in line, simply by their presence.

"Like I told Dave Barber, if there's anything you need from the Merchants' Association, let me know."

"I'll do that," he said.

We started up the grassy slope leading to the covered stage, past a white tent lined with posters for this year's concert. A table stacked high with programs waited for Ann Drake and her volunteer ticket takers. I thought I saw her near the band shell.

A friend of Adam's directed two men stacking a bank of speakers. I tried to remember his name—Rocky? No, Rocco, from the music shop in Pondera. On the lawn, men and women scurried back and forth, some toting gear, others shouting instructions and responses.

"Busy place," I said. "Buzzing like the bees in the cherry trees."

"That's what I like to see," Alden replied. "Enjoy the show." He hustled across the lawn to the sound booth, under a canopy by the giant golden willow.

"I thought for sure we'd be hauling a—hauling our backsides down to the Playhouse," Jennifer Kraus said. I hadn't seen her approach. "It's a ton of work, moving from one venue to another, and another. We'll be playing three places in four days."

"That's what happens when you cram a big festival into a little town."

"Everybody wants their piece of the pie."

That wasn't quite what I meant. To me, it was about being involved—for the good of it, not to get your share.

Sam appeared at my other elbow. "Shaping up to be a great night. Nacho?" He held out a red-and-white paper boat filled with gooey chips and cheese.

"No, thanks. Nachos always make me want beer, and it's too early," I said. Besides, I needed to save room for my mother's picnic feast.

He extended his offering to his wife, who crossed her arms and scowled.

"So crazy, everything that's happened since Friday night," I said. "Good news is the crowd had a great time, despite the problems on stage. Sweet of you to try to smooth things over with Martin."

Jennifer gaped at me blankly, then recognition hit. "Right. Lotta good that did." She marched off toward the food trucks. Sam raised his eyebrows at me and wandered after her.

I strolled back up to the stage, hoping to see Rebecca's big gear investment. At the foot of the steps to the stage rear, voices stopped me.

"The only reason I care that's he's dead is that it's bad publicity. We didn't need that has-been yet another year. If she hadn't kept insisting we bring Martin back, we could have attracted serious names. Guys who sell tickets, and would put us on the map. I had Lee Ritenour and Bill Frisell talking to us."

I frowned, trying to identify the speaker. Male. And who was the *she*? I snuck up another step.

"On the other hand, his studio would have been a major draw to the community. Not that it matters now." A second man's voice.

I peeked around the corner into the wings. No sign of Ann Drake, which didn't surprise me. Everyone involved with the festival knew her daughter had a lot riding on that association with Gerry Martin. No one would diss him to her now. Hard enough that Gabby was going to need a new patron.

His back to me, Marv Alden blocked my view of the other man. Then he shifted his weight and I caught a glimpse of Dave Barber.

I heard footsteps and turned quickly, as if I were leaving. A crew member toting two guitar cases came into view and I flattened myself against the wall, then hopped down the steps into the open.

Though the music wouldn't start for another hour or two, the evening's performers had begun to gather for a sound check. I neared the parking area and paused to study the sky. No clouds. I pulled out my phone to check the forecast.

A moment later, Gabby Drake emerged from behind the Greek Guy's truck, nostrils flaring, her hands cutting through the air. Behind her, wearing a pleading expression, came her mother.

The crowd chattered. The generator hummed. From the stage came the sound of a sax, mournful and bright.

So all I heard from Gabby was "don't deny" and "push."

Ordinary words, I told myself. *They could mean anything.*

But they gave me the shivers anyway.

Twelve

My hands gripped my upper arms. My heels echoed on the wooden planks of the bridge. Below, the waters of the Jewel River raced by.

Dave Barber's animosity toward Gerry Martin had been simmering long before Friday night's performance. Why had it reached a boil on stage?

Had he planned to take an unrehearsed solo, to test Martin's reactions and goad him into—what? Had he meant to embarrass a guest artist he didn't want to welcome?

Rebecca had called the incident Martin showing his inner jerk. The same could be said, I suspected, of Dave Barber.

I reached the cottages where Martin had been staying. Once upon a time, another pioneer family had owned this property beside the river. Generation by generation, they'd moved away. The farmhouse burned one night when I was in high school—smoke huddled in the air for weeks. Then a newcomer with California money bought the property and we held our breaths, expecting a trophy home. Instead, he built a dozen jewel-box cottages, each a sweet getaway ringed with flowerbeds and small trees. They looked as if they'd always been here.

A narrow, paved lane wound through the complex. A trumpet rang out through an open window. Cars parked beside the cottages bore plates from all around the country. I shuddered at the memory of yesterday's license plate incident, but if he came down here with an adult—preferably by the hand—Landon could check off a few more states.

I seriously needed to get back to the shop—I'd left Lou Mary alone too long—but I couldn't stop myself from detouring into the complex. It's odd how a building can project a mood, but I knew I'd reached Gerry Martin's cottage before I saw the yellow tape stretched across the door.

The deck held a pair of wooden chairs, brightly striped cushions on the seats, a small round table between them. Up the steps I went. I shaded my eyes with my hands and peered in the window.

A black rolling suitcase stood next to the door. Beside it sat a sturdy guitar case. I squinted to scope out the rest of the living room and a tiny kitchenette tucked in the corner. No signs of occupancy. No signs of trouble.

I walked back the way I'd come, puzzled. If the sheriff had already packed up Martin's belongings, why keep the cottage off-limits? Had someone else packed them?

"Thanks—enjoy your stay." The manager, a woman I knew mainly from the Merchants' Association, stood outside the office. A couple sauntered down the walk. I smiled and stepped aside to let them pass.

"You're full up," I said. "That's great."

"Without the festival, we wouldn't be at full occupancy till mid June. I could have rented Martin's cottage three times today, if the sheriff would let me."

"What's the holdup?"

"Don't know. Probably tomorrow, he said." She crossed her arms. "Martin had barely unpacked when he packed up again."

I waited.

"Ike and the deputies crawled all over the place yesterday. Tried to interview the guests, but most of them were out. Quizzed me up one side and down the other, but all I could tell them was he'd been booked for the week, then Saturday morning he said he'd be leaving early."

So Martin had packed the bags. "Did he say why?"

"Not a word. But he paid me for Saturday night, in case I couldn't rent it out on short notice."

First generous thing I'd heard about Martin.

"At least he didn't die here," I said. "That's bad for business."

"You're telling me," she said, whistling as she headed inside. Halfway to Front Street, I recognized the tune. I'd be singing John Denver's "Leaving on a Jet Plane" all week.

That's a music festival for you.

As predicted, the skies had cleared by evening. I was sitting on the park lawn on an old quilt my Gran had made, Tanner on my left, Adam sprawled out on my right. Chiara leaned over from her blanket and handed me a glass of rosy-pink cava, the Spanish sparkling wine.

"Champagne twice in one day," Tanner said. "You guys know how to live."

I clinked my plastic flute against his beer bottle. Around us, others spread out their blankets and picnics, popping corks and bottle caps. I recognized many of the folks who'd crowded the courtyard Friday night. The area closest to the stage had been reserved for students and faculty. Tracy and her beau, Rick, sat one blanket away from us. I waved to Kim, walking in with her parents, folding camp chairs in her arms. Each tall, slim, and blond, they could have been an ad for their dude ranch.

Walt and Taya Thornton, who run the antique shop in the block north of the Merc, approached. One of our picnic baskets swung from Walt's hand.

"Fresca, Bill," Taya cried. "We heard. Congratulations!"

A round of kisses and hand-shaking followed. Seeing my mother and Bill so happy made me all tingly inside.

My sister handed out plates and forks, and we started passing dishes. No mustard or mayo in my mother's potato salad: diced potatoes, barely-cooked green beans sliced the long way, olive oil and wine vinegar, capers, and fresh herbs. Tanner handed me the tray of deviled eggs sprinkled with smoked paprika.

"Better take one now," I said. "You won't get another chance."

He obeyed.

Next came tortellini salad with Adam's favorite spicy salami. Then the leftover sausages, cut in bite-sized pieces, because it's not a picnic without some kind of burger or dog, and there was a six-year-old in the crowd.

"Save room for dessert," Chiara told Tanner. "We've got iced coffee and rhubarb bars."

After all, we were the Murphys.

I took a bite. The park was filling up. Good. Music lovers were not being put off by the bad news. So far, anyway.

We'd passed several uniformed deputies on our way in. Now, a few feet behind the ticket booth, in front of the long hedge separating the concert area from the park below, I spotted Ike Hoover and Deputy Oakland. The deputy had dressed like his boss—always good strategy—in khakis and a polo, a fleece jacket not quite hiding his gun. Not that he necessarily meant it to—they were here to see, yes, but also to be seen.

I turned back to the crowd. I didn't want to think about murder and motive tonight.

Gabby Drake sat to our left with her parents. They'd brought a picnic, and Grant filled wineglasses. At the entrance, Jennifer stopped briefly at the ticket booth, then zeroed in on an open spot. Sam straggled behind her, carrying chairs and a small cooler. She never looked at him.

Uh-oh. Trouble in winemaking paradise?

"Do they always eat like this?" Tanner said to Adam.

"Why do you think I hang around?" my sweetie replied and winked at me.

Dave Barber took the stage, and the babble died down. I reached over to the cooler and refilled my flute from the magic pink bottle.

"Welcome—welcome, once again to the Jewel Bay Jazz Festival. Our shows this year will be bigger and better than ever." He paused and we filled the gap with applause. "We have some phenomenal, and I mean *phenomenal*, rising stars here this week. And our guest artists— well, the lineup is second to none."

More applause. Standing near the hedge, Rebecca Whitman bounced from foot to foot, a white sweater tied around her shoulders.

"First, I need to acknowledge a loss in our festival family. Gerry Martin was a master guitarist. An innovative performer. Every one of us, from the oldest hand to the newest volunteer, valued his presence, and we all mourn his passing."

Adam pushed himself up from one elbow to sitting, and crossed his long legs.

"Tonight's concert is dedicated to Gerry's memory, and half the proceeds from the ticket sales will be earmarked for a scholarship for an up-and-coming jazz guitarist."

I tucked my glass between my knees and joined the crowd in applauding. Out of the corner of my eye, I saw Rebecca. Arms tightly crossed, she glowered at the stage.

"Tonight, our opening night, we offer a taste of the week to come, a sampler to whet your appetite. Put your hands together for the finest Gypsy jazz ensemble in North America." Barber's voice rose and he extended his arm. "From Seattle, pleeease welcome Pearllll Djang-gohhh."

Applause erupted as the musicians took the stage. Adam skooched closer—not easy to do on a quilt on the grass—his arm behind me. I leaned into his shoulder as the bright, swinging rhythms filled the park.

"Mommy, I need the bathroom." My nephew's words rose over a quiet moment in the music, and I heard a chuckle behind me. Chiara shushed him, and they hurried out, Landon tugging at his pants with his free hand.

A Brazilian trio took the stage next, blending American jazz and the Latin sound. Then, intermission. We all stood, stretching arms and legs, except Tanner, who folded his hands behind his head on the quilt.

"Nap time. You wore me out on that hike."

"Where did you guys go?"

"Wolf Creek. Let's take a walk." Adam took my hand. As we passed the stage, the crew rolled the grand piano into place and I remembered Jennifer's gripe about moving gear. She'd always been upbeat, until the past few days. What had changed?

Hand in hand, we strolled through the park and out the entrance. We crossed the bridge back into the village. Adam's purposeful steps told me he had a destination in mind. Or a conversation.

I thought about the announcement my mother and Bill had made this morning. I thought about the ring I hadn't been ready to wear.

Was he thinking what I was thinking? My chest felt all fluttery. I glanced up.

My beloved looked like we were heading for the firing squad.

He led me to the greenbelt that lines the bay. A lawn slopes to a path above the seawall, a gravel beach below. Fed by the Jewel River, the bay flows out into Eagle Lake. The water levels hadn't fully risen yet, and the public docks stuck out above the muck.

Adam aimed for a bench with a view.

"Did I tell you I heard Pearl Django once when I lived in Seattle?" I said. "Great fun."

"Erin, we need to talk."

It's funny. Every woman I know says she wants more conversation in her relationship, but when a man says "we need to talk," it never sounds good.

"Adam, we went over this last winter. You said you understood my need to dive in, to protect what matters to me. You said you loved that about me. You said—"

"This isn't about you investigating, Erin. This has nothing to do with Gerry Martin or the festival or the village."

I raised my face to his, stunned. "Then what's it about? What's wrong?"

For the next ten minutes, he told me what was wrong. He told me why Tanner had finally made good on his threat to visit, on short notice, and the appointment that had made him miss his flight. He told me how the leukemia that struck Tanner first as a teenager, then again a few years ago, had returned.

He talked. I listened, my gut twisting, my hand to my mouth.

"I wondered if he was sick," I said after Adam finished, "when he didn't eat. But I figured he'd picked up a bug on the plane. I never thought—he's been in remission for years. When did you find out? Why didn't you tell me sooner?"

"Saturday, after we left the sheriff's office. After I'd dragged him out on the river, then up a cliff. He was out of breath, and I gave him a hard time about being out of shape."

That's why they'd gone to Wolf Creek today. Stunning views, but an easy walk from a trailhead you could drive to.

"I almost told you last night. This morning, I didn't want to upset you at a family gathering."

My chin quivered and I reached for his hand. "What's next?"

"He starts chemo in ten days. He wants me there while he goes through treatment."

I twined my fingers through his, and we watched the western sky turn a muddled gray. No glowing pink-and-orange sunsets tonight.

"We've been buds since the first grade. We didn't have great childhoods—you know all that—but we've always had each other's back. I said no last time. But now …"

"Go," I said. "Don't worry about the camp. Let your boss figure it out."

"One more thing." He took in a long, slow breath and let it out. What he was seeing with those gorgeous deep, dark eyes, I couldn't imagine. "The business he's so proud of, that he built from scratch. By himself."

The business Tanner had told me about last night, with a drive I admired, a passion I understood.

"He's giving half of it to me now. And if he—" Adam's voice broke in midair. "If something happens, he wants me to have it all."

Thirteen

Adam matched his stride to mine and gripped my hand. I did not let go when we left the bench and greenbelt, when we wound our way back to the bridge, when we strode through the park.

I was not letting go.

The clouds grew darker, denser as we neared the concert lawn. The air felt heavier, too.

Almost as heavy as my heart.

"*S'wonderful, s'marvelous.*" We'd missed the start of the second half, and the vocalist was in full swing. I tried to channel her beat, smiling broadly, swinging my hips. Acting "as if"—one of my mother's sure-fire remedies for turning a frown upside down.

At the family spot, Tanner glanced first at Adam, then me. He knew. They'd planned this. I dropped to the quilt, and kissed his cheek, for once unable to speak. He returned my thin smile. Over his shoulder, I saw Landon sprawled across his father's lap, asleep.

Sometimes I longed to be six again.

∞

"What a difference a day makes." The singer's closing lines echoed in my mind as I parked the Subaru next to my cabin. When the thunder rolled and lightning flashed through the sky behind the concert shell, the crowd had disbanded quickly. We'd snatched up our quilts, grabbed our coolers and picnic baskets, and scurried to our cars. The first drops had fallen as we'd reached the parking lot behind the Merc.

"I can take him home, then come down," Adam had said, and I'd wanted to say yes. Then the sky had opened up, and Tanner had shouted "Z,. get your ass in gear."

"You take care of him," I'd said. "Don't let him get a chill." Then I stretched up for a kiss that lingered on my lips.

Now I gathered my things and dashed to the covered porch. Inside, I toed off my shoes and dropped my blue bag on the bench. Somewhere in my misadventures, the bag's metal clasp had torn loose, ripping the leather beyond repair. As I dug out my phone, I noticed a hole in the lining. Chiara might be right—no harm flirting with a new bag.

Little cat feet crept up beside me. "Hey, Sandy. You two play nice while I was gone?" I bent down and rubbed the velvety patch under the cat's chin. He closed his eyes and purred. Males are so predictable.

Well, in some species.

The tortellini and deviled eggs had long worn off, and I'd missed the rhubarb bars, handed out while Adam and I had gone walking by the bay. I poured a glass of Cabernet, then filled one of Reg Robbins's red bowls with vanilla ice cream and chocolate-Cabernet sauce, a Merc bestseller. Before curling up in my comfy brown leather chair, I popped in the CD Chiara had bought me of tonight's featured artist, the jazz singer from Denver with the smoky voice.

"It had to be you, wonderful you."

At least the CD player and the cats were mine. The leather chair, the tables and lamps—they all belonged to the cabin. To Bob and Liz

Pinsky, my snowbird landlords and friends. I'd lucked into a great setup—a lovingly restored log cabin with a great little kitchen and a picture-perfect bed-and-bath addition, five miles from town. And rent-free. The Pinskys called me the caretaker, but they hired a man to plow in the winter and a crew to mow, weed, and trim in the summer. Bob took care of plugged gutters and dripping faucets while they were here, and he made clear I should hire out any maintenance or repairs the place needed when they were gone. All I had to do was leave a few lights on and make sure the property looked occupied.

Sweet deal. I licked a stray bit of chocolate off the back of the spoon.

I was thirty-three, and what kind of life had I made for myself? I ran a shop I didn't own in a building I didn't own. Slept in a bed I didn't own.

And I'd had about enough of the unintended rootlessness.

From her perch on the brown leather couch—another piece I didn't own—Pumpkin ogled my bowl. "Don't even think about it."

I'd thought Adam and I had a future together. I still thought so. But now ... Heat pricked at my eyes, and I blinked hard. Spooned up a double bite.

Not for one minute did I think Adam should not go to Minneapolis. "I'm all he's got," Adam had said.

"He's got me, too," I'd replied, meaning every word.

The lights flickered. The music stopped, mid-beat. In the momentary silence, I heard the wind whipping through the woods. A limb from the giant spruce behind the cabin hit the logs with a deep *thwack*. Tiny cones and branches skittered across the metal roof.

The lights came back on, and the music resumed with a drum roll.

But Tanner's plan for his company changed everything. Adam could be a silent partner from twelve hundred miles away, but he wasn't the silent partner type. When I talked business, he always listened, and was a great brain-stormer. The solar coffee roaster intrigued him, with its combination of green technology, innovation, and coffee. A lot like Tanner's business, minus the T-shirts.

How tempted was he to go back and join his buddy, especially now that he was half owner? Especially now that Tanner was sick?

I scanned the bowl for stray chocolate and saw none. Safe for cats. "Have at it, girl. Polish the bowl."

She hopped up on the table. Not good care-taking or cat-parenting to let her eat on furniture I didn't own.

"Don't you look at me like that," I told Sandburg, his green eyes glowing. "Besides, you don't like ice cream."

Monday mornings always come too early, but in this mood, I wouldn't be able to sleep. I tossed my skirt and hoodie on to the bedroom chaise and pulled on the stretched-out black yoga pants and oversized gray T-shirt that pass for my jammies. Grabbed my laptop and headed back to the living room.

Spreadsheets comfort me. I find solace in resizing columns and labeling rows, in the blank spaces waiting to bring order to an untidy world. Plus filling them in makes me feel like I'm in control, like I'm taking action.

Even if I'm fooling myself.

"Easy, girl," I said as Pumpkin knocked the spoon out of the bowl in her zeal for one more drop, but I knew as it clattered on the slate table top and tumbled to the floor that I was talking to myself.

Deep breath in, deep breath out. I held my fingers above the keyboard. *You know how to do this. Start at the very beginning.*

First column: Motive. Next, Means. Third, Opportunity. And fourth, Questions.

First row: Gerry Martin. I had lots of questions about him. The first was his relationship with Rebecca Whitman. I clicked on the top row and inserted a column between opportunity and questions, labeling it Relationship to Victim. Then I added Rebecca's name on the left, though she wasn't my first suspect. I could reprioritize later.

"Oops. Nearly forgot my favorite." I added a new column, Whabouts, short for Whereabouts. Not a word used much in daily life, but the key to a successful investigation.

Time to focus on suspects. Below Rebecca's name came Dave Barber's. Had he struck back, angry over Martin's attempt to shove him off the stage—or lashed out for some other reason? In his backstage conversation with Marv Alden, Dave made clear that he'd wanted Martin out of the way—and that a woman's insistence on keeping Martin on the playlist had been a major obstacle. He had to mean Rebecca.

What about other suspects? I set the laptop on the table and started pacing—not easy in a space sixteen feet by twelve. I paused in front of the fireplace to scoop up Sandburg and made the half turn. You have to be careful with dark-furred animals—both Sandy and Pepé the dog had suffered the errors of outrageous footing far too often.

His paw snagged my silver hoop earring as he draped one front foot over my shoulder, and I wriggled the hoop free. Gabby shared Tracy's love of unusual earrings; my tastes are simpler.

"What about the Drakes?" I asked Sandy. Had Gabby lost her cool over the slight?

I reached the wall between living room and bedroom and pivoted. I hated to think about a man's death in such calculating terms.

But both the reality and the prospect of death demand hard, scary questions. What if Tanner died? What if Adam stayed in Minneapolis, to run the business? I couldn't ask Adam to sell the company his best friend had built from the ground up. Tanner had taken it from a dorm room dream to an innovative operation employing dozens of people in its mills and sewing rooms, not to mention its sales force and other staff. Sell it off to some faceless conglomerate that saw "green manufacturing" and "sustainable, American-made" as nothing more than marketing slogans?

Whoa, Nellie, as my granddad used to say. *You got the cart halfway down the track while the horse's nose is stuck in the feedbag.*

I studied Sandy's small, neat face. He opened one eye, the other barely a slit. "You're right, I'm overreacting. Getting it over with, so I can behave rationally when the time comes."

He gave me a *yeah, sure* look and nestled into my shoulder.

The CD ended, the machine clicking and whizzing the next disc into place. I had no idea what was in the player. The lyrics began.

One hand cradling Sandy against my shoulder, I pushed "stop," then "forward." I did not need Willie Nelson's advice on being lonely. I wasn't blue or lonely, just sad. And a bit uncertain.

I punched more buttons and the Gerry Martin disc began to play. I let it continue. The man had been *good*. He deserved an audience.

He deserved justice, even if no one in town liked him very much. Tanner's illness had reminded me that life is fragile, and unfair. Maybe Martin had hit a rough patch, mad at the world for not going his way, as Rebecca had said. Letting his jerk flag fly. Maybe he wouldn't have gotten over it. Or maybe he'd have come out the other side the Mother Teresa of the jazz world.

It didn't matter. We didn't get to judge him. But he'd died in my town, and I wanted to do everything I could to get him justice.

I sat, tucking the cat next to me with care. Added Gabrielle Drake to the lineup. But I couldn't overlook Ann and Grant.

Gabby's overprotective parents had put a lot of stock in Martin's patronage. Had they feared he would use a youthful misstep as an excuse to block her promising career?

Two more rows filled in.

"You can't leave him out just because you like him." Reluctantly, I added Sam Kraus to the list, then clicked on the Motive column.

The look Sam had given Jennifer this afternoon, when I thanked her for soothing Martin's ruffled feathers, came back to me. I added *jealousy—affair?*

I huffed out a ragged breath, then typed in *resentment—musical success? Musical tensions?* Hard to imagine salt-of-the-earth Sam summoing murderous rage. But investigating shows you faces of people—people you thought you knew—that you've never seen before.

And sometimes, you wish you could go backwards. Unsee what you had never expected that now felt glaringly obvious.

I peered at the rows and columns. They mocked me.

I could almost hear Kim telling me to stop before I put myself in danger. If it came to that, I would stop. Ike Hoover might pin his badge to a polo or a fleece quarter-zip, but he carried a gun and the keys to the jailhouse. There are things people won't tell a cop, no matter how much they like him or how piercing his eyes.

Talking to me is different. I'm their friend and neighbor. The cute girl who runs the shop down the street, who sells their favorite strawberry jam, carries free-range chickens that actually had run free, and is almost always willing to help with any village event.

I stifled a yawn. Closed Excel and powered the laptop down. Those empty boxes would have to wait.

Thinking of Ike made me think about my father. My mother's remarriage would redefine our family. Bill had been part of "us" for nearly a year now. But marriage changes things.

I put my wineglass out of cat reach and padded over to the bench by the front door. Dug in the bottom of my blue bag for the black box. Opened it. Peered at it. Carried it into the bedroom and slipped the ring on my right hand.

With the rest of the clan so near, and his revelation about Tanner's illness, I had not had the chance to tell Adam about my sister's weird reaction to my mother's engagement.

When he left, what else wouldn't I get to tell him?

A few weeks away, a month or two—that would be fine. We'd text and talk, and in those moments when nothing but the other person's face would do—well, they make apps for that.

But what if …?

I sat on the edge of the bed. Stretched out my arm and held up my fingers. The center diamond caught the light from the lamp on the nightstand and sparkled. The channel stones glistened, and the white gold, worn thin from so many years on my mother's hand, gleamed.

I slipped the ring off and slid it on to my left hand. Outside, the wind picked up. A branch hit the side of the cabin, and the lamp flickered.

I drew my knees to my chest, laid down my head, and cried myself to sleep.

Fourteen

I'm telling you guys. You won't have any friends left if you keep killing them." I picked up the dead mouse on the bottom step, carried it by the tip of its tail to the edge of the clearing, and flung the evidence of my cats' crimes deep into the woods. Wiped my fingers on my skirt and glanced down.

"Ohhh."

I crouched and cradled the nest in both hands. Built by beak and claw, as expertly as any human basket weaver's work. But nothing could have kept the weathered twigs and branches safe in last night's storm. I scanned the duff along the edge of the woods, afraid of what I'd find.

And there it was, nearly hidden by the moldering leaves and needles. Lightly speckled, the palest, softest blue, the tiny egg lay crushed on one side.

"Get back, Pumpkin." I didn't think my fat tabby cared about the empty nest or broken robin's egg—she was simply curious what I might be up to. But I couldn't bear to leave the egg behind, so I slid my curved fingers underneath it and laid it gently in the nest, then stood.

"Come on, you two." Pumpkin trotted after me, Sandy running ahead and leaping up the steps to our deck. It's not that they're actually trained or obedient—they are cats—but they know I pour them each a few tasty tuna treats before I leave for work.

I tucked the nest into the corner of the kitchen window sill, sniffing back a tear. It would be safe there—as if that mattered now—and I could see it when I washed up.

A few minutes later, I stood in the driveway, surveying my domain. The calm waters and clear skies belied last night's winds.

That was equally true in town, I realized a few minutes later. The few branches that lay along the narrow highway gave no hint that major gusts had stormed through. And you couldn't tell that a man had been killed, a festival threatened, plans ruined.

Plans. Gerry Martin's plans to build a recording studio intrigued me. I'd heard about it first from Gabby, then in the conversation I'd overheard between Barber and Alden. A town like ours needs a diverse economy—anything that provides construction work, followed by a few steady jobs, is good. If it brings in outsiders and their cash, double good.

And it meant moving his home base here. Where Rebecca, the maybe-ex-lover, lived.

I passed by my usual turn into the village and the entrance to the state park. The natural place to dig for more info, or to start recruiting someone else to open a studio, was the music crowd. They were busy this week.

So I'd start with the builders' crowd.

Oversized pickups filled most of the parking spaces in front of Perk Up, the breakfast-lunch-coffee joint on the highway, next to the gas station and convenience store. I slipped the Subaru in between a red rig advertising Jewel Bay Construction, aka Chuck the Builder, and a log home builder's mud-splashed blue truck.

"Coffee, black." The woman behind the counter wore a denim shirt with CYNDI embroidered on the breast pocket. I took half a step back for a better eye on the pastry case. "And a sugar twist."

"Hey, Erin." Chuck the Builder stood and swung a wrought iron chair out for me. "What brings you in here?"

"Classing up the joint," the log home builder said, his baby blues twinkling.

"Change of pace." I set my plate and cup on the table, and sat. "Good to see you guys."

The morning paper from Pondera lay on the table. The feature photo on the front page had been taken from the river, looking up. The headline read MUSICIAN TUMBLES TO HIS DEATH ALONG POPULAR TRAIL.

"You just missed Ike Hoover," Chuck said. "Not that any of us knew anything, or that Ike would say anything. But I have to wonder, the way he's poking around, if that body ended up on the rocks by accident."

Cyndi refilled his cup. "That poor man."

I presumed she meant Martin, not Ike, but in the middle of a death investigation, it could be either one.

"Why all the fuss about music?" asked a man I didn't know. "Most of it's noise to me."

I took a bite of the twist, all sugar and air.

"And they wonder why you spend three nights a week at the bowling alley," the log guy replied. "Takes all kinds."

The bowler chuckled. "Ain't that the truth."

"His name was Gerry Martin. He was planning to build a recording studio somewhere around town." I took a teeny sip. Too hot, thin, bitter. I'm not the coffee snob Adam is, but this stuff tasted burned.

Chuck had angled his chair away from the table, making room to stretch his legs. Now he leaned back, scooting down an inch or two in his chair, but said nothing.

Patience, Erin. I dipped my twist in the coffee, hoping the fried dough would soak up enough caffeine to give me a decent dose without me having to drink the stuff.

"Don't suppose it matters now, but yeah. I worked up the plans for him and his sound engineer down in Texas. Woulda been a good piece of work." Chuck held his coffee mug in front of his chest, his tongue prodding his cheek as if he was working a tooth. Or thinking.

"You suppose anyone else would be interested? Town could use a good clean business like that."

"Easier said than done," the bowler said. "You were talking half a mill, weren't you? Apart from the land."

"Or better," Chuck said. "Though land wasn't a problem."

That surprised me. "So Martin already owns property here? I didn't know that." I turned to the bowler. "You gotta admit, noise or not, the festival's a boon for the local economy."

He grinned. Chuck set his cup on the table and rose. "Those two-by-fours aren't gonna nail themselves. Good to see you, Erin. *Danke* for the java, Cyndi."

When the leader of the pack departs, the rest get restless. Besides, we all had our own two-by-fours to nail, metaphorically speaking.

In my car, I pulled up the county property tax records, a gold mine for the serious sleuth. Too small to read on my phone.

A few minutes later, I rounded the corner in front of the Jewel Inn. A runner sped down the hill from the River Road and headed up the way I'd come—a young woman in a white T-shirt and tight black running shorts, on a good clip.

Took me longer than it should have to recognize her.

Why was Gabrielle Drake out for a run? The workshops should be starting any minute now.

I parked in my usual spot in the Back Street lot. Other teachers—both the regular faculty and the guest artists—would have been thrilled to have her in a class on vocals, jazz guitar, or ensemble work. But emotions don't always cooperate.

When my father was killed, I'd been at the Playhouse for a rehearsal. I'd been ticked off at him, for some long-forgotten reason. And in my seventeen-year-old pea brain, the thoughts and self-recriminations had gotten twisted and tangled, and I'd felt so guilty for being angry the very last time I'd seen him that I might as well have killed him myself.

Losing a mentor wasn't the same. But it had to suck.

I climbed out of the Subaru, not bothering to lock it, and crossed the alley. In the next block, Rebecca's nearly identical Subaru stood behind her gallery. The semi-official car of Northwest Montana.

After nearly a year, our courtyard still made me tingle with delight. Liz Pinsky would say that's how feng shui works. Maybe so, but it could as easily have been the industrial-strength cleaning and a few well-positioned planters.

Or the fountain—metal mountains and fish in front of a corrugated metal backdrop. Chuck had introduced us to the man who created it. Chuck's niche is remodeling, the more complicated the better. And more profitable. He'd worked in Red's last fall, after my mother bought the property—not a high-end or high-dollar project, but the building was nearly as old as the Merc and needed an experienced hand. He'd also done the build-out for Le Panier and Chez Max next door, a newer building than ours but more of a hodgepodge.

If I remembered right, Chuck had created that swanky apartment above the gallery for Rebecca, too.

She must have introduced him to Martin. The log home builder had called the studio a half-mill project. Five hundred thousand is a lot of money. If the project had gone south, that might explain both Chuck's reluctance to talk and the accusations Martin had flung at Rebecca.

I needed real coffee. I marched through the Merc and into Le Panier.

"Double shot," I told Wendy. "Your very best."

She raised one eyebrow and focused on her espresso machine. That's Wendy for you.

"Croissant, Erin? Or *pain au chocolate?*" Michelle, the other barista, asked.

I am a creature of good habits, but after the sugar twist, my system needed more substance. "The veggie quiche. For here."

In the seventies, Jewel Bay outgrew itself and much of the town's commercial enterprise moved from "the village," aka downtown, up to the highway, where more land was available and visibility higher. The hardware store became a full-scale building supply. The gas station moved and added auto parts.

The new supermarket all but put Murphy's Merc out of business. My granddad had been offered the opportunity to buy in, but his three boys had chosen other careers and he preferred to stay small and stay put. He'd remained the unofficial mayor of unincorporated Jewel Bay, but with a splintered kingdom. Occasionally, tensions flare—the town's many festivals tend to be held in the village, and a few owners of highway businesses get irked at being asked to sponsor events that don't send foot traffic past their doors. But most understand that bringing people in to town helps us all. Tourists need gas and groceries, and the more jam I sell, the more money the jam-maker and I have to spend elsewhere.

But while the highway cadre patronizes the Perk Up, there's always a morning crowd at the Jewel Inn, and another klatch that favors

Le Panier. I sat at a tile-topped table with Heidi and Ginny Washington, our veteran bookseller.

"We were chatting about Gerry Martin," Ginny said. "I always stock a rack with local music and CDs by festival artists. Sold out of his yesterday."

"I'm not surprised." Heidi's bracelet slid down her arm as she raised the white china espresso cup to her red lips. "He wasn't as popular as he used to be. I don't know if he'd gone out of style, or lost his touch. But death sells."

That it did.

"I heard last night that there have been some cancellations," she continued. "Now that his death is national news."

"Students? Fans?"

"Both," she said. "And questions from sponsors. But the board is reaching out, like you suggested, and that ought to help reassure people. Reporters can't be far behind."

With Ike and his deputies asking questions all over town, that would be inevitable.

"What are you wearing?" Ginny reached for my hand. "Your mother's engagement ring?"

I nodded, my throat tight, and changed the subject. "Turns out, Martin was so ticked off after Friday night's concert in the courtyard that he decided to leave early. What I don't know is whether he told anyone, or whether he meant to ghost them and disappear."

Michelle set my breakfast on the table. "He came in about nine, nine thirty Saturday morning. Ordered a double cappuccino and left."

Half an hour before Tanner witnessed his fall. The cup in my safe? I didn't know if it was evidence or not, but I ought to get it to Ike and let him make the decision. Next chance I got.

Michelle stood behind the counter, within earshot.

"Do you remember who else was in around that time?"

She tipped her head, thinking. Pinched her lips together. "Sorry, no."

Considering the foot traffic a downtown bakery and espresso shop gets, she probably wouldn't have remembered Martin coming in at all if his death later that morning hadn't burned it into her brain. I couldn't blame her. That's retail.

"Thanks, anyway." I concentrated on my quiche as Heidi and Ginny chatted. Odd that Martin had gone for a stroll up on the River Road before leaving. He hadn't struck me as a guy who'd want to see the sights one last time. Maybe he wanted to stretch his legs before the long flight home.

Or maybe he'd been meeting someone.

Had he planned a hike? What kind of shoes had he been wearing? I swallowed the last bite of quiche, scooted back my chair, and picked up my coffee. Wendy wouldn't mind if I brought the mug back later— I needed to capture these thoughts on the Spreadsheet of Suspicion before they vanished.

"Oh, Erin, I meant to tell you." Ginny laid a hand on my arm, keeping me in my seat. "Both Dylan and Zayda got into film school. Now the challenge is to keep them from running off and getting married the week after high school graduation."

"You're joking, right?"

One side of her mouth shifted, her cheek rising. "I wish I were. If you get a chance, talk some sense? They might listen to someone closer to their own age. Besides, they owe you."

"Not that much." Although you could argue that Zayda George owed me her life, but that argument went both ways.

Back in my pint-sized office, I booted up the system running the weekly sales and inventory figures, and opened my spreadsheet. Entered my questions about Martin's morning walk, and made note of the man's connections to various locals. Skipped a space below my list of suspects and started adding potential witnesses. Tanner. Chuck. Me.

Tracy would burst in any minute, eyes wide with word that I'd dropped into the Perk Up, one of *her* morning haunts. Then Lou Mary would rattle the door and we'd launch into a full day of retail sales and training. I'd be lucky to get the weekly paperwork done before tonight's concert at the Playhouse. I didn't plan to go to all the events, but Pearl Django was playing and as co-sponsors, the Merc and Snowberry had each scored two tickets.

I brought up the property tax site and clicked furiously.

But my searches for Gerry, Gerald, or Gerard Martin came up empty. I sat back. A lot of people own property under business names, but I had no idea what to look for.

Molly had been telling me yesterday how she was learning the ins and outs of all the computer systems and property records real estate agents use.

And if you can't ask your family for help, you can't be much of a spy.

Fifteen

It was early afternoon before I could get away.

They say fifty percent of business is problem solving. In retail, make that sixty. When you've got new vendors, a new employee, and an old employee changing roles, all as you're gearing up for sales season, you're talking seventy-five percent, minimum.

No sooner had Lou Mary tucked her bag away—a dusty lilac, to match today's loafers—than vendor deliveries began. Thank goodness I'd run the weekly figures and could input the new deliveries without confusing myself too much. Just because the inventory system is automated doesn't mean there isn't plenty of work involved. Huckleberry and chokecherry syrup had somehow gotten the same product number. Each new soap scent needed a separate code—one reason I'd cautioned Luci to keep her line simple. And because her supplier had sent the wrong size bottles and she'd filled them before learning—from me—that she could insist they correct the mistake at their expense, we had to input that change and update the price list on the display.

I griped a bit but didn't really mind. Focusing on the details kept my mind off murder, off my mother's engagement and my sister's bewildering response, and off my boyfriend's best friend's life-and-death battle.

"Well, this is the place to be, isn't it?" A sixty-ish man in a nubby blue short-sleeve shirt strolled in behind his wife. Hands on his hips, he surveyed the scene. My jam and pickle makers were busy restocking their wares while I stood behind the counter with my iPad, updating the inventory. It's less work for us if vendors restock their own products. But their presence also invites conversation with customers. And that leads to sales.

On the other side of the shop, Tracy fussed over chocolates. Near the front, Lou Mary tucked colorful cloth napkins from Dragonfly Dry Goods into empty spots in the wine rack, camouflaging our wine shortage.

"If we don't have it, you don't need it," I said. But we needed wine. Where was my Monte Verde delivery?

Lou Mary bustled over to give the newcomers the nickel version of the Merc's history, mission, and product line. I called Sam.

"Sorry, Erin. I've got the van loaded, but—well, there's been a glitch in the matrix. We're not going to get into town today. Is Thursday soon enough?"

It probably was, but I like my ducks in a row. "Why don't I run down after lunch? Say, three cases?"

"Great. I owe you." He clicked off, as if in a hurry. That's the modern world, all of us juggling too much with too few resources and too little time.

I dashed upstairs to finish the weekly deposit. I zipped the bank envelope shut and tossed it into my bag.

Back downstairs, I spotted Gabby Drake at the chocolate counter.

"Love your earrings," she told Tracy, whose fingers flew to her miniature Eiffel towers. Ann stood a few feet away, inspecting our hand-blown martini glasses, a new item. She flicked her eyes toward the earrings, obviously unimpressed.

"Good morning, Ann. I think it's still morning. Hey, Gabby. You have a good run?"

Gabby jerked her head toward me, her black pony tail swaying. "How did you—yeah, thanks. Sometimes I need to get out and move."

"You're skipping the workshops this year?"

"I ... " Her super-short shorts showed the effect of regular runs, and her platform sandals made her nearly as tall as her mother, who wore leopard print flats with black leggings and a gold tunic. "I'd planned to, but after—what happened ... Maybe later in the week."

"Teachers are clamoring to have her join their classes. No point letting his misfortune slow you down, dear."

Murder or accident, surely death was more than misfortune. The girl—she looked very young at the moment—glanced away, lips pushed out, eyes darkening. Ann continued to inspect the pottery and glassware, unruffled.

I wondered how much of this musical dream belonged to the daughter, and how much to the mother.

"These will be absolutely perfect," Ann said. "I'd like place settings for twelve. And serving pieces, of course. I'm still thinking about the glassware."

I didn't bother to hide my pleasure. "That's great. Reg will be thrilled. I'm sorry I didn't get to introduce you Friday night. Do you want to take what's in stock with you, or have all of it shipped at once back to—" I broke off. No need to reveal my snooping.

"Oh, no need to ship," Ann said. Her left hand floated through the air. "They're for the house here."

A morning full of surprises. "I didn't realize you have a house here."

123

"We don't," Gabby said. She'd wandered over to the display of wooden crates, accented by an antique washboard and a metal tub, that held Luci's soaps and lotions.

"We're in the market," Ann said, her tone smooth and sharp at the same time. "There's been a bit of a holdup, but I think the deal will go through now. Meanwhile, we're renting a small condo on the harbor."

Gabby dumped a pile of goat's milk soaps on the front counter, followed by half a dozen bottles of shampoo, conditioner, and lotion. "If you're buying dishes for a house we don't own yet, I can buy the soap." Then she grabbed two large bottles of Luci's newest product, a nontoxic all-purpose household cleaner.

Her mother shifted her focus back to the glassware. Turned out the voice of a generation could be a little bratty.

"Isn't the festival the most fabulous thing? Music, food, and parties." Lou Mary spoke too brightly, as if determined to get us back on neutral ground.

"Marred by unanswered questions," Ann said, inspecting a wineglass. "I wish that sheriff of yours would say once and for all that Martin's death was simply a tragic accident, that he slipped and fell, so we can move on."

Surely Ike had questioned Ann. But he'd been clever enough that she didn't know another person had been involved. Did that mean she was on his list, too?

Gabby set a jar of lavender bath salts on the counter with a loud thunk.

"Too soon," I said.

"It's tragic, but people will flock to the festival." Lou Mary seemed to realize she'd put her loafer in her mouth and tried to pull it out. "Once they know what a beautiful place Jewel Bay is, and what wonderful talent it draws."

"Ann, that reminds me," I said. "That recording studio Martin wanted to build here. With one foot in rock and one in jazz, he'd have been a great draw. With your contacts in the music world, any thoughts who might be willing to take that on, now that he's gone?"

Ann took a long moment to reply. "That's thoughtful, Erin, but Gerry Martin was truly one of a kind. I can't imagine anyone else having the wherewithal to truly succeed with the endeavor."

By "wherewithal," I didn't think she meant money alone. But Ann Drake would never say "balls" unless she was talking tennis.

"Mom, you *hated* Gerry." Gabby spat out the words. "You only put up with him because you thought he was my ticket to the success you never had." She stomped out, her heavy steps filling the silence.

Ann ignored her daughter's behavior. "Erin, please call the potter and place the order. I'll make arrangements to pay later, if that's acceptable. As for these things—" She gestured at the bars and bottles covering the counter.

I flashed out both hands, in a *don't worry* gesture. She thanked us and followed her daughter out the front door.

Lou Mary and I reshelved the soaps and shampoos, then I sent her on a lunch break and asked Tracy to handle the store. Much as I hated to leave again, I had a mission.

Five minutes later, I walked in to Jewel Bay Realty, crammed into a skinny space between a boutique and Rebecca's gallery. At the front desk, Molly stared at the computer screen. Behind her, the agents' desks sat empty.

"You eat yet?" I raised a fragrant bag from Le Panier and set two bottles of San Pellegrino mineral water on the desk.

"Oh my God, Erin, you are a savior." Molly sniffed the white-wrapped sandwich I handed her, eyes half closing in rapture. She might not share my half-Italian genes, but she shared my devotion to Wendy's grilled panini.

After we'd taken a few bites, I asked if she could figure out whether Gerry Martin had been trying to buy real estate in the area.

"If the purchase is pending, or just closed, it wouldn't show on the property tax records yet." She wiped her mouth. "I'm pretty sure we didn't represent him, but let me see if he was a buyer on any of our recent sales."

I watched her fingers fly over the keyboard and took a long draw on my Pellegrino. She turned back to me, shaking her head. "Erin, I probably shouldn't ask, but why do you want to know?"

"Following a hunch." I'd tell her my idea about the music studio later. The plans had already been drawn up, according to Chuck. If we knew what property Martin had meant to buy, Molly could help one of the agents recruit a new buyer to take on the project. Her first big deal. Meanwhile, I fibbed. "Next question—and this is my curiosity. Ann Drake ordered a ton of pottery for their new house, but I didn't get to ask her where it is. Do you know?"

Her eyes widened. "What? They found a place? They've been running their agent ragged, showing them properties. They've got to have lakefront, but they also need mountain views. They want an orchard—"

"HA. Everyone wants an orchard, until they actually have one and have to figure out what to do with it."

"Tax break," she said. "Your waterfront trophy home gets treated as farmland if you have enough acreage planted in saleable fruit. I can't believe, after all the hours and hours we've spent searching for listings and hauling them around, they would buy through someone else. No wonder the agents say buyers are liars." She clapped a hand over her mouth.

"Guess I misunderstood. Maybe she got so excited when she saw Reg's pottery that she jumped the gun."

Molly clicked a few more keys and closed the screen. "No offer officially on file. But Ann Drake doesn't seem like a woman who gets carried away over dishes."

No, she didn't. "Well, don't tell anybody I said that. In case I'm wrong. Because I'm sure I'm wrong."

Molly fixed her green eyes on me. "Erin, I won't tell anybody because you asked me not to. But you are almost never wrong."

"There's always a first time." I stood. "Thanks, cuz."

On my way up Hill Street to the bank, I paused to drink in the view. *We are so lucky to live here.*

And then I remembered Adam, and Tanner, and Minneapolis, and felt like a cloud had passed in front of the sun, though when I shaded my eyes and looked up, not one cotton wisp obscured the big yellow ball.

Fifteen minutes later, I'd finished the banking, and was speeding down the highway toward Monte Verde Winery.

Crystal clear may be a cliché used to sell window cleaners, but it's also exactly the right phrase for the waters of Eagle Lake and the skies overhead. The Mission Mountains on the east side of the valley were carved by the glacial hand of God, with help from the earthquake fault lines we all ignore. (In high school, we learned that a handful of quakes hit the area every day, each so small they barely disturb a pine cone, let alone an actual structure. They wouldn't even have rattled the robin's nest I found this morning.)

The mountains to the west always remind me of the silk screen print Kim and I made together in freshman art. Each receding layer of mountains stood a smidge higher than the one in front, each a paler shade of that amazing blue-green-black that forested hillsides become in late afternoon. We still knew how to work together then, and we'd gotten an A. My framed print, number one of two, hung in the front hall of my mother's house.

Maybe it was time to reclaim it. Find a place of my own to hang it.

I drove with one hand and reached for the CD player. Empty, and I'd tossed the spare discs out of reach to make room for the guys yesterday. My iPod was at home. I punched on the radio. But the BBC World News clashed with my mood. Light rock, classic rock, alt rock, country—different channels, same mood.

I punched the off button.

At twenty-eight miles long and eleven miles wide, Eagle Lake is the largest freshwater lake west of the Mississippi, and on this late-spring afternoon, it was a vast expanse of glory. In some places, the narrow highway hugs the shore; in others, it veers away, past orchards and through woods, by small lawns starting to green and long drives sloping to the water. Cherry houses—roadside garages used for fruit storage and sales—dot the roadside. The homes, both visible and hidden, are a mix of new and old, kempt and shabby, in all sizes and styles. Real estate season was upon us, and FOR SALE signs had begun to sprout like glacier lilies, one of my favorite wildflowers. I suspected most of the signs would have a longer life than the lilies.

People often ask me what's different between living here and living in Seattle. Top of the list is driving, followed by shopping. Driving in Seattle is a nightmare if you have to take a freeway, more manageable if you're staying in town. And parking is a task that would try the patience of Glinda the Good Witch.

Driving under the Big Sky is a joy. In decent weather, anyway. You do have to watch for deer, and occasionally you get stuck behind a semi or a road whale—a bus-size RV towing an expensive SUV. But mostly, it's four wheels and happiness.

Halfway down the lake, Monte Verde Winery's cherry house—remodeled in Spanish Mission style, with pale yellow stucco and red tiles—came into view, and I slowed at the driveway, signal on. To my surprise, a sheriff's rig pulled onto the highway, Deputy Oakland at the wheel. A quick flicker of the eyes said he'd recognized me.

The rutted dirt road wound past an older white clapboard house, the screen door hanging loose. Beyond it, at the edge of a sparse patch of pine forest, stood three or four ancient frame houses. Cracker boxes, my granddad would have called them. The paint was peeling, the siding bare in places, though one house had recently been repainted. An old red Subaru wagon, its back quarter panel bashed in, stood beside it.

I followed the road downhill, fruit trees on one side, grapevines on the other. The bottom of my car scraped the high, hard crown of dirt at a hairpin turn, and I cringed. Even the recent rain hadn't softened it. A few feet farther on, I held my breath, as if that would make the car lighter, and eased over a patch of exposed rock. It worked—no more scary sounds. Sam seriously needed to regrade the entire half mile of road.

Speaking of Sam, there he was, tossing broken and blown down branches on to a six-foot-high slash pile at the edge of the orchard, his faded Cal State T-shirt soaked with sweat.

I stopped and lowered the passenger side window. "All that blow down last night?"

"Hey, Erin." He walked toward me, wiping his forehead with the back of his arm. "About half. Long as I was out here, I figured I'd pick up what I missed over the winter and spring."

"Hop in. You can load up my wine."

He opened the door and slid in, bringing with him the scents of sweat, mud, and pine mixed with cherry wood.

"I passed the deputy on my way in. What's up?" Before Sam could answer, I hit a deep rut I hadn't seen. The steering wheel jolted out of my hand.

He groaned and stared through my dust-and-bug spattered windshield.

"The road needs work. The trees and vines need work. Everything about this place needs work. My life needs work. My marriage." At my gasp of surprise, Sam flicked a glance my way. "And according to the good deputy, I'm the number-one suspect in a case of murder.

"Know any lawyers who trade for wine and cherries?"

Sixteen

Sam sat on the back end of my Subaru, wine boxes loaded, gripping a can of Mountain Dew.

"They can't seriously believe *you* killed Gerry Martin. Why—because he chewed you out over a few sour notes?" I picked up a stray pinecone off the gravel parking area in front of the winery and squeezed it, the sharp points on the scales biting into my palm. I hesitated to suggest something more.

"They won't say. But I can read the handwriting on the wall." He gestured behind him at the winery's elaborate false front. "Even if I can't maintain the walls."

Wine-making, bottling, and storage took place in the old metal Quonset hut. They'd added a tasting room and fashioned it all, like the cherry house, in Spanish mission style. I squinted. The cracks in the stucco I'd thought faux-finishing were real.

"But surely Jennifer made them see sense. You're not that kind of guy. And you were never more than twenty feet apart all evening."

He took a long swig. "That's part of the problem. They won't actually say I need an alibi, but they keep asking where I was, when I left the village, when I got home. Who pays attention to time in that kind of detail?"

We have clocks in our cars and on our phones, and some of us wear watches. And Red's keeps several clocks, but bar clocks are notoriously wrong, often on purpose.

Was it Sherlock Holmes who'd said beware of the man with an ironclad alibi, because only a guilty man needs one?

Or maybe that was Columbo.

I put my foot on the bumper, forearms on my knee, and leaned forward. "Sam, don't drive yourself crazy over this. They have to track the movements of everyone who had a beef with the victim, no matter how petty." The Whabouts, in my personal shorthand. "When that's out of the way, they can focus on the suspects. Once Jennifer assures them that you were barely out of her sight."

"She can't say that." He rose, squeezing the empty pop can till it made a metallic clang, and I took my foot off the bumper. "She drove into town early, to talk to somebody, I don't know who. I came in later with the gear."

"Okay, but you left Red's at the same time, right? You packed up your gear and followed each other home."

He pressed his lips together and breathed out through his nose, a big breath rough with pain and anguish. He gave me a sidelong glance, and at his side, both hands were fists. The mangled pop can lay at his feet.

"Tell me," I said. "I can't help you if you don't tell me."

"After the last set, Jennifer left the stage. I thought she went inside to the bathroom, so I started packing. I kept an eye out, but I didn't see her." He reached for the pop can and started twisting it in his hands. The sound of aluminum grating on aluminum was like fingernails on a chalkboard, but I kept my mouth shut.

"Finally, I had all our gear stowed in the van, out in the alley. I didn't see her in the courtyard, or inside Red's."

I hadn't notice him searching, focused as I'd been on Adam and Tanner. But the memory of Jennifer dashing out after Gerry Martin, her blond hair flying, the skirt of her turquoise dress whipping around her strong, tanned legs, flashed in my mind. Busy wrangling speakers and soundboards, Sam must have missed that.

A sour taste wriggled down the back of my throat, and I was afraid I knew where this was leading. *Criminy*. "Go on."

The pop can tore in half, and he stared at the pieces, as if he didn't know what to do with them. "I didn't see her car, so I assumed she'd headed home. I came straight home, Erin, I swear. I never went near Gerry Martin. I never touched him. Even though I thought …" His voice trailed off.

"Even though you thought she was having an affair with him." She and Sam had seemed so solid, this place a dream come true.

We see what we want to see.

"Was she parked next to you?" I asked.

"The lot was half empty when I finished unloading, so I got a good spot close to Red's. Next to your car. She came in a few minutes later. I never saw where she parked."

I closed the hatchback and leaned against it, arms folded. "Sam, when did you first think she might be—involved with Gerry?" *Tell me it wasn't until after he died, so the sheriff has no reason to suspect you.*

His Adam's apple bobbed. He plucked a leaf off a Lapin planted at the corner of the building and tore it into tiny green shreds. "Friday night. When I got home and she wasn't here. When I realized I had absolutely no idea where my wife was. She—she's been hiding something from me for a while now."

"That doesn't mean she was having an *affair*. With a man who's here a few weeks a year." And who'd been involved, until recently, with another local woman.

"But what else could it be?"

That was the question. Maybe I'd been right in thinking she just wanted to ease the tensions Friday night. Obviously, she hadn't succeeded. Sam suspected her of cheating, and the sheriff suspected him of murder. Manslaughter, murder—I didn't know all the degrees. All I knew was that one happened unintentionally and one on purpose, and that both led to prison.

"Anyone see you between the time you left Red's and when Jennifer came home? And when was that?"

He scuffed the sparse gravel with the toe of his worn work boot. "Not that I know. She got home about ten minutes after I did. Erin, I swear I didn't kill Gerry Martin."

If Jennifer had been involved with Martin, she'd had enough time for a quick smooch, but not much else. If "else" was even going on.

As Sam had said, what else could it be? Love and sex may be the first things we think of when we think of tensions between men and women. But there's a million other stories—stories of money, jealousy, anger, revenge. Stories of friendship gone wrong, of mistakes, of misunderstandings.

"When she got home," I said, "did you fight? Wait. We're focusing on the wrong time. He was alive the next morning." I nearly clapped my hand over my mouth. According to the news accounts, Ike had said only that Martin died on the rocks and had been spotted by a pair of kayakers. He hadn't revealed Tanner's identity, or that a second person had been involved. He'd mentioned the time of death, and asked anyone who'd been on the trail at about that time to contact the sheriff's department.

"They didn't tell me that."

"That's their MO. They don't tell you everything. They make you worry and sweat, and hope you'll say something they can use against you. What you need to show is where you were Saturday morning, between—" I thought back. Michelle the barista had served Gerry his cappuccino around nine or nine thirty, and it had been close to ten when Tanner saw him tumble to his death. "Between eight thirty and ten, give or take."

"I was here, working on the cooling system. The alarm went off at five that morning—the compressor's been acting up. Took me half the day to get it fixed." He ran a hand through his hair. "Making wine sounded so romantic. Never figured I'd have to be an electrician, and a plumber, and a roofer, too."

"That's good. I mean, it's bad for the wine, I get that, and I'm glad you got it fixed. But Jennifer can vouch for you, right? Even if all she did was hand you a wrench and listen to you gripe." Wrenches always make me gripe. "Where is she, anyway?"

Sam's face fell lower than an earthworm's belly, as my granddad used to say. "She went for a run. She runs every morning."

Without an alibi, there was no way to prove he hadn't reached the same conclusion as the sheriff's men and gone after Martin. Sam was bigger, stronger, younger.

"Oh, pooh. Just remembered—I forgot to send her the e-mail about the bottling equipment you guys wanted. I'll make myself a note, right now." I opened my car door and started to reach inside, but the expression on Sam's face stopped me.

"She asked you about that? I thought we'd agreed—look at this place. It's our dream." He gestured. Once you saw the signs of neglect, they were everywhere. "She says we need more volume, more production. I keep asking what's wrong with staying small, making a little money. Not a lot, but enough."

"Sounds like your dreams took different directions." I ached for them. But we had to solve the problem at hand, to give them a chance to work things out. "So who do you think killed Gerry Martin?"

"I can't imagine anyone in Jewel Bay hating him enough to kill him."

Hate, I had learned, isn't the only reason people kill. It's waaay down on the list. "I've gotta get to back to town. You hang in there, Sam."

"At least I have my music," he said, his expression forlorn, "and my friends."

I gave him a hug. He was the kind of man I liked, a dreamer and a hard worker. I prayed he and Jennifer could mend the breach.

I aimed the Subaru up the rutted road, thinking about what triggers murder. Martin had been upset with Sam for mistakes on stage. Whatever Sam had felt, he'd kept to himself. Barber, on the other hand, had deliberately stepped on Martin's solo. If I'd understood Rebecca's comments and the stage whispers right, Barber had wanted Martin out of the way long before the festival began. Had he been trying to make Martin look bad, costing him fan support, or to goad the man into quitting the festival?

In that, he'd gotten his wish. Martin's bags had been packed, ready to go.

But wouldn't he have worried about talk during the festival? And if he'd wanted Martin to leave, why kill him?

Barber had never been part of my family's circle, and I didn't know much about him. But J.D. had said he and Old Ned didn't get along. And Old Ned is always willing to share his opinions, at least with me.

A movement on the shoulder caught my attention and I braked hard. A red fox sped across the road and disappeared into the brush behind a Jewel Bay Realty sign.

Keep your eyes open, girl. As the business gurus preach, you can't conduct a reliable analysis with a specific conclusion in mind. Doubly so for a murder investigation.

Which meant I had to consider Sam's motives to kill objectively.

He swore he'd been stuck in the winery's mechanical room till noon. That sounded plausible, and it would put him in the clear. But he had no witnesses. What would have stopped him from jumping into his van and running up to the village, tracking Martin down, following him, and pushing him over the cliff?

Nothing, I had to admit. Not even my conviction that he was a fundamentally decent man. In small towns, we always think we know everything about everyone else, but it turns out we're wrong. People harbor secrets, no matter where they live.

I passed another FOR SALE sign, from another real estate office. A lot of these properties had changed since I'd been a kid in Jewel Bay. Older houses had been converted into rentals, or torn down and replaced with trophy homes. Orchards had been uprooted, the acreage subdivided. I wondered again where Martin had intended to build his studio, and what property the Drakes had their eyes on.

I passed by the road to Murphy's Orchard, and a few miles farther on, my own road.

My hands tightened on the wheel. My mother's remarriage had me thinking about the family homestead and its future. Tanner's illness and his request of Adam had me thinking about my own future.

Though the thought made me cringe, murder was a mighty convenient distraction.

Seventeen

You hired *her*? Without even talking to *me*?" Candy Divine made no effort to hide her dismay.

I'd meant to stop at the Merc for two minutes to fetch the paper cup stashed in the safe, then run it up to Ike Hoover. Instead, I'd been way-laid by a sobbing pink mess in front of the customers and Lou Mary. *Where was Tracy?* And in front of Fresca, who'd paused her chopping and whirring to eye us. The Kalamata olive tapenade she was making smelled heavenly, and I wished I could sit at the counter with a healthy sample rather than deal with Candy, but there was no escape.

I grabbed two bottles of Pellegrino from the cooler and led Her Pinkness to the courtyard.

"When you said—when Luci—when Tracy—"

"Sit." I set one green bottle on the round tile-topped table in front of an empty chair. Candy obeyed. I took a long draft of mineral water and sat across from her.

She hiccupped and reached for her water. I hoped she wouldn't choke—and that I could talk myself out of another sticky situation.

"When you and Tracy decided she could focus on her chocolates"—Candy paused for a breath and a big sniff—"I knew you'd need somebody else in the shop. And I thought ... " Another sniff, and a sob. Today's hair bow was a darker pink than usual, almost the same deep fuchsia as the streak in her black hair. The bow flopped dangerously as her head bobbed.

I couldn't say I hadn't known she needed a job. She'd said nothing outright, but homemade candy is not a career path, not when there's already a chocolatier in town. And she'd dropped broad hints of interest to Tracy, who'd begged me not to give in.

"You found Luci a job last winter." Candy's tone hovered between a plea and an accusation. "I wanted—I need—and now you've hired Lou Mary."

Lou Mary didn't have a speaking voice that made a door squeak sound melodic. And while she had a penchant for color-coordinating, she didn't wear pink from tip to toe, and she never dressed like Minnie Mouse on a bender.

I gave my lucky stars a quick swipe and dove in. "Lou Mary came along at the right time. And Luci knew web design, which my brother-in-law needed to get our web sales going. Tell me your job skills, besides making candy, and let's brainstorm."

My corporate experience had been buying groceries. HR was totally out of my league. But if you want to prosper in a small town, you have to be a connector.

That's when it struck me. "You sew, right? You make a lot of your own costu—clothing." Her outfits appeared well-made, if on the frothy side.

My guess hit the mark. Her face lit up, then fell. "But what could I do?"

"Kathy at Dragonfly Dry Goods always needs women to make napkins, placemats, tablecloths. Aprons. Quilts and decorative items for display." Candy would try Kathy's patience, too, but at least she wouldn't be working in the shop. "Or, you know Sally at Puddle Jumpers. She designs super-cute children's clothing, and she always needs seamstresses. Especially with summer coming." At least, I hoped she needed help.

Supersweet Candy and Sally Sourpuss. A lamb to slaughter, or a mismatch made in heaven?

Candy sniffed. "That would be fun."

I offered to take her across the street to see Sally, but she wanted to run home and change first.

"If I'm going to offer my dressmaking skills, I need to show off my very best." She pushed back her chair, hitched up her wide satin belt, and reached down to pull on a loose shoe, a black pump trimmed with a fuchsia satin shoe rose. Shoe not quite on, she stumbled across the stone courtyard to the back gate, the rosette at the small of her back in need of freshening.

I drained my Pellegrino. One bullet dodged.

Back inside, I spotted Tracy and asked her to join me in my office. "Be calm, and be kind," I muttered to myself as I got the evidence bag out of the safe.

She climbed the steps heavily and stood in the doorway, shoulders slumped.

"Trace, I know you're excited to focus more on chocolate and less on the sales floor. And you know me, chocolate is Vitamin C. But honestly, what were you thinking, leaving Lou Mary here alone on her third day on the job?" My words sounded harsher than I'd meant.

Her jaw tightened and she took a long time to speak. "I always go to lunch at noon. And Fresca was here."

Meaning it was my fault. I hadn't been here. I glanced at the wall clock—quarter after one.

"I'm sorry. But it's not enough that my mother was working in the kitchen. No one can cook and watch the shop floor—that's why we changed your schedule."

She pressed her lips together, then raised her eyes to mine. "I don't see why it's any big deal. You keep saying Lou Mary's such an old retail hand."

"It's a big deal because even an old retail hand—and she would hate hearing us call her old—needs time to get to know the place. Lou Mary could sell ice to an Eskimo, but at this point, she barely knows a bag of lentils from a bar of soap."

That drew a teeny, tiny hint of a smile.

"Next time I'm running late, I'll check in. And if you need to leave while I'm gone, you call me. Deal?" She nodded, but I wondered what else was going on. This passive-aggressive stuff wasn't the Tracy I knew. "The Merc needs you, Trace. I need you."

Jaw tight, she nodded several times, then left, her long denim skirt sweeping the wooden steps.

I did not have the brainpower to manage a conflict between my employees, or their personal problems. My spreadsheets and the calendar on my phone might keep the investigation and my shop organized, but keeping my head straight was another story.

And though this was the worst possible time to leave the Merc, I was sitting on possible evidence.

I grabbed my bag and let Tracy and Lou Mary know I was stepping out. The sheriff's Jewel Bay satellite office sits off the highway, behind the volunteer fire department and ambulance service. The downside of not being an incorporated town is lack of services, like our own police force, mayor, and trash pickup. To a lot of folks, that's also the upside. Fortunately, the current sheriff never stinted on services to the unincorporated areas, and I expected Ike to do the same when he became sheriff.

If he became sheriff. An unsolved murder of an international celebrity might be a sticking point.

Two official rigs sat in the rear parking area. The official seal marked the tan metal door of the office, though I could see where amateur graffiti had been covered up with slightly darker paint.

Weird, weird, weird to walk in and see Deputy Oakland at the desk in the outer office instead of Kim.

"'Lo, Deputy. You're becoming quite the regular down here in the Bay."

"I don't mind the overtime," he said, "but I'm sure sorry we got a major crime on our hands."

"Thought I heard a familiar voice." Ike Hoover leaned against the door frame of the inner office.

I raised my makeshift evidence bag. "Saturday morning, on the River Road, I found this cup in the shrubbery, about fifty feet from where Gerry Martin went over. I picked it up, thinking it was trash. I still had it in my hand when I got back to the Merc."

He took the bag, eyes narrowing slightly as he read my notes and saw what was inside.

"I threw it in my office trash. Then I stopped in Le Panier this morning, the bakery and coffee shop next to the Merc. The barista—Michelle is her name—said she made Gerry Martin a cappuccino around nine Saturday morning. So this cup could be his. Or his killer's."

Something I couldn't read flickered behind his eyes. "You know this could have been there for days."

"It rained overnight Thursday. Heavily. But the cup isn't muddy or wrinkled."

He gave the bag an appraising scan, then turned his gaze on me. Did I imagine it slightly less stony?

Our relationship had grown smoother since my father's death had been solved. But it would always be a little uneasy, because Ike would always feel guilty about not having closed the case sooner.

And I would always be the half-orphaned girl who reminded him of his failure. Doubly so, since I was the one who nailed the killer.

I barged on. "I know you and your deputies have been pounding the pavement, and the dirt roads, identifying folks with a gripe against Martin. Any idea yet whether it was heat of the moment or premeditated?"

His lips curved, but you wouldn't call it a smile, his lowered chin saying *nice try, but I'm not telling you.*

"Okay." I rested one hand on the back of the plastic chair in front of Oakland's desk. "We know Martin had just bought a cappuccino, and the manager of the cottages told you he'd decided to leave the festival early, despite being scheduled to play Tuesday night, work with students all week, and join in the finale Saturday. Do we know whether he told anyone about his change in plans? Besides the manager?"

Ike continued to study me in silence.

I changed tack. "I saw a lot of live music in Seattle. Most rock guys live in jeans and a T-shirt. Some of the hot tickets suit up. Bob Dylan wears a coat and tie. So does Paul McCartney. Gerry Martin's in between. Friday night, it was black pants and a dressy black shirt. Short black boots. You weren't there, but he does this kind of shuffle thing." I bent my arms and shifted my hips, replaying the scene on stage. "Like he's dancing to his own music. You can't do that in running shoes or hiking boots. You need smooth soles."

Tiny shifts in Ike's face told me he knew where I was taking this.

"If he had those boots on—if they were his traveling shoes—then they might explain why he slipped in a struggle. But I don't think he

143

would have climbed Hill Street and started up the trail in slick-soled city boots if he'd gone for a walk on his own. I think he went up there with someone. I know it's a long shot, but his killer might have tossed that cup away." I pointed at the bag in Ike's hand.

Ike eyed me a long while, then spoke to his deputy. "Log in Erin's evidence. Then check the trash can at the trailhead for similar cups. With any luck, it hasn't been emptied yet."

"I'm on it." Oakland's chair squeaked as he rolled back from the gunmetal gray desk.

"Then take another run at talking with the guests at the cottages. Those people have to be home sometime." Ike studied me, one hand on his office door. "You know, Erin, I'm beginning to think you missed your calling."

Eighteen

My heart pounded as I climbed in the Subaru and followed Deputy Oakland toward the village. I was an adult now, not the teenager I'd been when I first met Ike. But challenging a cop does make the pulse race a bit.

At the corner of Hill and Front, the deputy continued up toward the trailhead. I toyed with traipsing after him, but Ike's directive to do the footwork reminded me to do my own. I didn't need another view of the scene of the crime. I knew Martin had been pushed to his death.

What I didn't know, I thought as I wound through the village, was who had lured—or followed—Martin up the trail, and why. Answer one question and I'd answer the other. It didn't matter which came first.

I parked, shouldered my blue bag, and marched down Back Street to where it met Front, then on past the library slash community center to the cottages. Midday, most guests would be out and about, but you never know when you'll get lucky. And I was hoping to find one with reliable info before Oakland got here.

No car stood outside the first cottage, its windows dark. I knocked on the door. No answer. I dug for an old notebook in my bag and started a list. (I love tech, but I'm good with no tech, too.) *Mon, 2:02 p.m. Cottage No. 1—no answer.*

Next door, same result, same note.

As one of my SavClub supervisors once said the difference between a sales call and a sale is making your own luck. The same holds for investigating—without a little extra effort, it's just snooping.

Not until the fourth cottage, the one next to Martin's, did I find anyone home. Then came the tricky part, explaining why I was there. I'd already decided to be honest and straightforward. Lying is too much work.

A few minutes later, I was sitting on the deck with the Carters, sipping sweet tea. I'm not fond of sweet drinks, but refusing the offer would have closed the door on confidences. That's how hospitality works, and while Jewel Bay was my town, this cottage was theirs for the week, front porch and all.

"Such a pretty little village. We fell in love with it, didn't we, James?"

"We sure did. Started to tell you, we flew out to Spokane"—he said it with a long a, the way people from other regions sometimes do, but in his Southern black drawl, it came out more like *kyne* than *cane*—"to visit an old Navy pal. Rented a car and drove over here. My Rosie had a hankering to see Glacier National Park before it melts."

"Didn't know half the park would be snowed in, but what we got to see was simply gorgeous," Rosie said. A wild rose bush bloomed in the bed below the deck, and I thought how aptly she'd been named.

"Plows won't finish with the Going-to-the-Sun Road for weeks," I said.

"I'd be tempted to stay," James said. "But we got grandchildren back home to spoil. Our Georgia peaches. Now you asked if we'd seen your friend Jennifer talking with the gi-tar player next door after the concert."

"Gerry Martin," I said.

"That concert was a treat, by the way. We hadn't heard a peep about it till we walked into Red's to wet our whistles, and heard the hubbub. That man sure could play."

We were silent a moment, in unspoken agreement.

Rosie leaned forward, dwarfed by the Adirondack chair. "Afterwards, we took a stroll down by the bay. Your friend was just leaving as we came in. The guitar player—Martin, you said?"

I nodded.

"—was standing on his porch, hands on the rails, watching her go."

"So you didn't hear their conversation." My hopes sank in a puddle of sweet tea. "How did she look?"

"Not theirs, we didn't," James began as his wife said, "Hurt. One glimpse of her face and the way she walked, and I knew. Hurt and confused, that girl was."

All of a sudden, Rosie had given me a lot of information to unpack.

Rosie gazed over the top of her glasses at me, sitting on the steps. Her dark eyes shone. "We raised three girls and a boy, all of 'em grown now. You learn to tell a lot from a little."

Truth to that. "Did you hear Martin talking with someone else?"

James answered. "Yes. The man who'd been playing with him."

"Which man? The drummer or the guitar player?" *Careful, Erin. Don't let friendship affect your hearing.*

"The guitar player, in the cowboy hat. Played that nice long piece in the middle. Good of that Martin fellow to let him show his stuff."

These two, observant as they were, hadn't picked up on the tensions between Martin and Barber on stage. "So what happened?"

"We called out hello, and thanks for the music. I said if y'all come to Atlanta, we wanta hear. He said thank you—he was polite and all, but not real talkative."

Unlike the Carters, thank goodness.

"We went inside and got ready to call it a night. Five, ten minutes later, I heard harsh words. Angry words."

I glanced between them, wondering if this was going where I thought it was going.

"Put my pants back on. In case I needed to step in." James's voice, already deep, had dropped a notch as he remembered. "I told Rosie to keep her phone close, and I stepped on to the front porch." He gestured with one big hand toward the empty porch of the next cabin.

"Martin stood in that doorway. The cowboy had hold of the railing, one foot on the bottom step." James paused for a long drink of his sweet tea. "They broke off when they saw me. I called out, 'Evening, gentlemen.' They both stood real straight, they did."

That, I believed. Even relaxing on his front porch, James had a commanding presence I was sure had served him well in the Navy, and in the family.

"The local man, he took his foot off the step and started to leave. But before he did, he looked at Martin. 'We're not done,' he said."

"Did Martin reply?"

"He did. He said on the contrary, he thought they were, and the cowboy—what's his name?"

"Dave Barber. And he actually is a barber."

"You don't say? He took off. We said our goodnights, and I went inside. I didn't hear any more arguing. This mountain air puts us right to sleep, it does."

"Did you see Martin the next morning?"

"No, young lady, I didn't. We're early risers. We had us a nice breakfast up at the Grille, and took a drive down the valley to the National Bison Range." He gave Rosie a tender look. "The manager told us about it, and my wife thought it sounded like a real nice outing, so off we went."

Not because he did what his wife told him to do, but because he wanted to do what would please her.

I pushed myself up. "Thank you both so much. This is all so horrible—it's helpful to know what you heard and saw."

Rosie stood and took the glass from me. "Everyone's been so kind here. Friends back home warned us about the Wild West, but we moved around a lot when James was in the Navy, and we know most people are good, 'most everywhere."

Her husband rose and held out his big hand. "We sure were sorry to hear what happened. I pray he was right with the world when he passed."

I had my doubts. "You told the sheriff's deputies all this, didn't you?"

"They left a card, but we keep missing each other." The sound of an approaching vehicle in the narrow lane drew his attention, and mine. "Looks like we're about to get our chance."

"Erin," Deputy Oakland said a minute later, as he climbed out of his big rig.

"Deputy," I said. "Enjoy your sweet tea." His eyebrows squished together in puzzlement, and I strode on by.

Visiting with Martin's other neighbors would have to wait—I wasn't bold enough, or foolish enough, to quiz them under Deputy Oakland's wary eye.

I needed to know who Martin had run into after he got his coffee Saturday morning. He had a few hours before the afternoon flight out of Pondera. Had he run into anyone from the festival? Wandered the village?

Who else would have been out and about? Too early for shoppers, and the shopkeepers would have been busy, like I'd been. Tracking down the casual passersby—folks like the Carters—would be impossible.

A stakeout at the trailhead was too long a shot. I'd leave that to Ike's crews.

I made my way up Front Street. What about the woman who walks the two pugs every morning? But she was usually heading home about the time I came in, eightish.

The man on the unicycle? I hadn't seen him in weeks. He's like the stray cat you realize hasn't been around in ages, then spot the next day.

One more question for the spreadsheet.

I angled across the street—taking a lesson from Landon's near-miss and looking both ways twice—to my sister's gallery.

The new bags called to me. I stroked a black-and-green leather triangle with two flaps that opened into a full-sized tote.

"You can wear it as a backpack, or"—Chiara demonstrated—"zip the straps together and sling it over your shoulder. She calls it wearable origami."

"I like." I fingered another, in black and turquoise with a row of colored inserts, like piano keys, along one edge and a leather loop-and-stone closure.

"They're so versatile. This one's your colors." She handed me a tote with outside pockets and blue and green decorative patches that reminded me of sixties op art.

I unzipped the bag and poked around inside. "The iPad would fit, easy." Not to mention the occasional piece of crime scene evidence.

"Her style is contemporary, local but not overly Western. You know, fringed suede or tooled leather with silver clasps that look like rodeo belt buckles."

The boots-and-britches West versus the hiking boots West. "I love my rodeo queen belt buckle."

"But you didn't buy it in a secondhand shop, or fork over hundreds for a replica to impress strangers. You won it."

That I did, on a late spring day much like this one, fifteen years ago. I'd been riding for broke, fueled by grief and anger over my father's death and my best friend's abandonment. In the process, I'd taken the crown Kim had longed for ever since she learned to ride and rope, and alienated her further. Only last winter had I discovered that my lucky season had not been the true cause of the breach in our friendship.

"I'll think about it." The bags were tempting. I stroked a buttery-soft version in a warm caramel. We were alone in the shop. "Sorry I upset you Sunday. I don't get what's bugging you."

Chiara let out a long breath. "Me, neither. Bill's great, and he adores Mom." She picked up a celadon green tea bowl and cradled it in both hands.

"You just don't want to imagine our mother having sex."

She shot me a big-sister glare. "And you do?"

"No, but I'm willing to admit that she does."

She set the bowl down a little too hard, not meeting my eyes.

"Hey, I need to talk with you about one other thing," I said, eager to change the subject. "About Tanner."

"Oh, he's a doll. If I weren't married—"

The front door opened and we gave the newcomers our best retail smiles. Behind them, I saw someone I very much wanted to see crossing the street.

"Gotta run." I kissed my sister's cheek. "Remember, you are a spiritual being having a human experience."

She rolled her eyes. "Tracy's been reading you tea bag tags again."

"You know it."

Across the street, Old Ned stood behind the bar, looking like he'd been there for decades, though he'd walked in just ahead of me.

"Hey, girlie." He reached into the giant cooler and by the time I'd settled on a barstool, a sparkling glass of mineral water with a fresh slice of lemon sat in front of me.

"Quiet in here."

"You wait a few hours. Open mic out back tonight, after the concert." He wiped the spotless counter. "Used to be mid June before the crowds came. The festival's good for business. I hope it stays that way, with news of that fellow's death spreading. Some reporter from Texas called, but I had no comment."

151

That was hard to imagine. I sipped, the mineraly taste countering the leftover sweetness of the iced tea. "You hear a lot of things, Ned. Have you heard talk about changing the direction of the festival?"

He paused, giving me an appraising eye. "By pulling the plug on the big name. By shoving him off a cliff."

"Maybe that wasn't the intent. Maybe there was an argument, and that was the result." I gave the place a once-over, making sure we were alone. "J.D. says you don't care for Dave Barber."

"That your nominee for troublemaker?"

I circled the glass with my hands. "I'm wondering, that's all."

"Well, I don't trust him. Never have."

I waited. Old Ned—everyone calls him that, and he says at seventy-five, he's earned it—is a self-described curmudgeon. But he's not mean-spirited. And he's not a gossip. But he would tell me what he thought I needed to know.

"Three, four years back." He leaned heavily on the bar. "Before you and your sister came home and gave us all a boost. There was a rift, you might say. We all pooled together funds for advertising the village, when we took on the new slogan."

Jewel Bay, the Food Lovers' Village.

"A few business owners put together the campaign. I don't remember if your mother was involved. Anywho, we ran newspaper ads from Billings to Calgary to Spokane. Put up them big billboards. The whole she-bang. And it worked." Ned paused, staring into the past.

"Then all of a sudden, we were short on money. Barber was the treasurer. Said the bills came in over what we'd budgeted and the fund was broke."

I sipped the last of my mineral water.

"Everybody was up in arms. Short version, the Chamber offered to take over the promotional stuff, and they've done a bang-up job.

About the same time, some of the gals decided to reactivate the Village Merchants' Association, to spice things up down here."

"Seems like that's all working well," I said.

"Like a charm." Ned reached for my glass and slid me a refill. "Problem is, Chamber hasn't had any trouble keeping expenses in line. Why did we?"

"So you think Barber pocketed the money."

"I think he found himself holding a lot more cash than a two-bit barbershop brings in. Before you know it, he's got new guitars and speakers and musical whatnot. He's making contributions to the festival and getting himself on the board."

A shiver of suspicion ran down my throat.

"And you think ... "

"I'm not saying I think anything, girlie. Not about that death I know is on your mind, whether it was an accident or not. But Dave Barber is building a monument to himself while he's got the chance."

Harsh words. I'd always considered Ned a pleasant curmudgeon, not a bitter one.

"I know you, Ned. What else is on your mind?"

His face darkened and he grunted. Ned grunts a lot. "I can't say there's a link. But it does put me in mind of an ugly incident oh, maybe thirty years ago."

"What happened?"

"When Eileen, my younger girl, was a senior in high school, she and her best girlfriend were in charge of the Homecoming dance and all that hoo-rah. It was a big deal, and she did a good job. But a bunch of money turned up missing. No one had the guts to accuse her outright, but she went through a rough patch. You know how kids can be."

I did.

He went on. "This was before Excel spreadsheets and all that, but I'd taught her to keep track of income and expenses, so I checked her records. I had a pretty good idea where that money went, but we couldn't prove it, so we let it go. Dave Barber was in that class, and he was dating her best friend."

"And you think he absconded with the Homecoming money your daughter and his girlfriend collected."

"Bingo. Pamela got pregnant, and right after graduation, they got married. Instead of rock and roll, he found himself a teenage husband and father. Went to barber school and started working with his dad. When the old man died of a heart attack, Dave took over the shop. They moved into the folks' house—ramshackle wreck north of town. Had a couple more kids, and the day after the youngest finished high school, Dave left her."

This was all news to me. "She still around? I don't know her."

"Moved to Pondera. Works in the big bank. My girl keeps up with her, says life beat her down a bit, but she's bouncing back."

A couple sauntered in from the courtyard and sat a few stools away. Ned slid down to say hello and take their orders. Barber had argued with Gerry Martin. He'd wanted Martin gone. He did not care for some woman involved in the festival. He may or may not have sticky fingers.

I'd seen Dave at the Playhouse Saturday afternoon, prepping for the workshops. If he'd been there in the morning, he could easily have spied Martin coming out of Le Panier and urged him to take a stroll up the River Road, a stroll Martin had not been prepared for, that ended in his death.

Two episodes of missing money, decades apart and neither ever proven, hardly made a man a killer.

But they might make him think he could dip into the till one more time.

154

Bingo. Murder as a cover-up, though I didn't know yet how Gerry Martin figured in the mess.

But the info I'd picked up today would fill in a lot of rows and columns in the Spreadsheet of Suspicion. And the bits and bytes would add up to the whole story. Soon.

Nineteen

 rin, I heard the news!"

"They caught—?" I turned at the sound of my name amid the chit and chatter of the pre-concert cocktail party in the Playhouse lobby, then stopped myself. I was so wrapped up in murder, so sure that Dave Barber was a killer, that I'd forgotten it was all in my head—so far.

"Bill is a wonderful man," Mimi George from the Jewel Inn said. "Tony and I are so happy for her. For all of you."

My mother always says "change your shoes, change your mood." So I'd put on my lucky red cowboy boots, a short blue and white skirt, and a red tank, and grabbed a white sweater that tied at the waist. I felt like a flag, hung out a week before Memorial Day. I did not feel lucky. But that had nothing to do with my mother and Bill.

"It's great!" I said. "And about time, don't you think?"

Chiara broke in, greeting Mimi with an air kiss and an apology. "Need my little sis." She carried a single champagne flute she stuck in my hand and pulled me to an upholstered bench in the alcove next to the concession stand.

I thanked my lucky stars that I'd slipped my mother's ring—*my* ring—back in its box.

"What did you want to tell me about Tanner? Quick, before they get here."

I told my sister about Tanner's illness recurring, and what he'd asked of Adam.

"You're not saying you don't think he should go. He has to go. They'll hold his job."

"No. Yes." I squeezed my eyelids shut and opened them, waving my free hand in a *stop* motion. "No, of course he should go. And yes, they'll hold his job. I hope. He was going in to talk to his boss today. The problem is—"

Was that all in my head, too?

"The problem is"—I swallowed hard, hating to think about this—"Tanner has no family. If he dies, he's leaving the company to Adam. What if—what if Adam wants to move back? He can't run that business from here. It's hands-on. It needs daily management. It needs—"

"Erin. Erin, stop." Chiara's voice sliced through my fear. "Adam is not going back to Minneapolis. His work is here. His *life* is here." She jabbed a finger toward the tile floor.

"But—"

"But nothing. He is not leaving you."

"He—he couldn't live with himself if he let Tanner down. And I couldn't live with myself if I insisted he stay here for me."

Kyle Caldwell zoomed toward us, Kim behind him. I quickly rearranged my face.

"There sits trouble." Kyle's fedora tumbled off and he grabbed it, laughing. "Trying to be hip for jazz night, but it's not me, is it?" Though he, too, had the tall, slender Caldwell build, Kyle kept his hair too short to show much color, and had long given up the Western look the rest of the clan favored. I didn't know when I'd last seen him without a ball cap.

"Hey, Kyle. Hi, Kim," I said to the cousins. Only a year apart, and both single, they often hung out together. "You two snare the Lodge tickets tonight?"

"My first time in the Playhouse since the Film Festival," Kim said. "Nice—all bright and shiny."

"The gem of Jewel Bay," I said lightly. With the tin ceilings, the colored Tiffany-style light fixtures, and the columns covered in tiny iridescent tiles, "bright and shiny" was spot-on.

"Where's the big guy?" Kyle said.

My neck heated up. Kyle had been teasing me about boyfriends since we were kids, and it had a way of getting to me. "His buddy's here from Minneapolis. They've been out sightseeing, but they'll be along."

"I heard they found the body on the rocks," Kyle said. "You investigating?"

My flush deepened. "Hey, with Kim on leave, somebody has to."

Kim stiffened, but Kyle grinned. "I'm trying to rope her into working at the Lodge, now that she's hung around some other outfits, seen more of the hospitality biz. My dad and hers aren't gonna want to work forever. And I can't run the place from the kitchen."

The rosy spots on Kim's high cheekbones darkened into splotches. We'd seen each other a couple of times since she'd been home, and talked about resuming our regular rides, but she hadn't mentioned taking a role in Lodge management. She'd carefully avoided all mention of the future. Our rift had scabbed over, but while I understood now why she'd acted as she had after my father's death, the wounds went deep, and the inner layers of emotion were tender at the edges. For her, too, judging from the wary slant of her eyes.

"Here they are," I said, as Adam and Tanner crossed the lobby toward us. Thank the stars for the well-timed interruption. Adam introduced Tanner to the Caldwell cousins.

"The ringers who kicked your backsides all winter in pool league?" Tanner said.

"They cheat," Adam replied. "I just can't figure out how."

I pointed a finger at Kim. "Wednesday noon, we're going riding. No excuses this time." After barely a word in fifteen years, we'd reconnected last summer and gone riding on Wednesdays when her schedule allowed. And while I needed to spend every minute at the Merc this week, who knew how long Kim would be around?

And then it was time for small plates of yummy things, and more visiting. I adore seeing the community spirit in action. Every so often, someone thinks Jewel Bay ought to incorporate, until they do the math and realize it will never happen. Others argue that incorporation would strangle volunteerism. If we had a street department, would three hundred people brave a chilly Saturday morning in November to hang garland, tie bows on trees, and create Montana's Christmas Village—then come back in frigid January to take it all down? If we had our own sanitation crew, would neighbors clean up along the highways and the River Road?

That reminded me of the paper cup I'd found. I hoped Ike would take my trash-picking seriously, and send it to the state crime lab.

The lights dimmed, then brightened. Adam gestured to Chiara, then took my hand and we followed her into the theater.

I hadn't gotten to ask about his conversation with his boss.

Our seats were in the twelfth row, in the middle. Adam stopped in the aisle to greet a camp parent, and Chiara motioned Tanner in first. I crossed my fingers that she wouldn't put him through the conversational ringer.

Down front, Dave Barber stood at the corner of the stage, arms folded, waiting to introduce the first band. The place was three-quarters full, but he did not look happy.

He was glaring at Rebecca Whitman, entering the row ahead of us. Her soft green shawl gave her a fairy-like delicacy, the lights picking out copper strands in her hair. She was with the Drakes, and if she sensed Barber watching her, she showed no sign.

How could I investigate the possibility of embezzlement that Ned suggested? Would the Drakes talk? Or Rebecca?

"Tell me you aren't investigating," Chiara whispered as we took our seats.

I flicked my eyes at her but didn't answer.

"*Erin.* You have enough on your plate. A business to run. Mom getting married. *Adam.*"

"He'll be gone for weeks. I'll have time on my hands."

She made an exasperated sound and trained her eyes on the stage.

I glanced back at Rebecca, her profile strong, the fairy-like appearance gone. Had she questioned Barber's handling of the festival finances? Confronted him about his plans? Was that why she'd been tossed out?

Not tonight. Chiara was right.

Adam made his way toward the empty seat. Was I overreacting, fearing I would lose him? He'd certainly never hinted that he might go back to the Midwest. He always said Montana was home now.

A few seats away, Tanner looked pale but less tired than when he arrived. What must it feel like, facing cancer for the third time at thirty-three?

The first time, I supposed, you could call a fluke. The second time seemed more ominous.

The older you get, the more you see the fragility of life. And the third time does not seem so charming.

160

Not tonight, Erin. Tonight is for music and friends.

Adam dropped into the seat next to me. I took his hand and held on tight.

∞

Pearl Django jazzed and rocked and rippled for an hour before clearing the stage for the second half's performers. I needed a break, too, but despite the remodel expanding the women's room, a line had formed by the time I got there. The downside of good seats.

Sally Grimes grabbed my arm. "Erin, I can't thank you enough. My best seamstress retired last winter, and your friend Candace will be the perfect replacement."

Friend. Eek. "Oh, good. Her sense of style seems like a good fit for you. Assuming princess dresses still sell."

"Thank God for Disney," she said, and charged off.

"You did Sally a favor? On purpose?" Adam handed me a glass of wine. "Wonders never cease."

"Where did you guys go today?"

"Pondera, to the Art Museum. Then we poked around the gear shops, seeing if any of them might be interested in carrying his stuff. He's doing good, but I can't be running him up and down mountains all week."

The fear and sadness mingled in his voice nearly broke my heart.

Over by the concession stand, Tanner and Kim were deep in conversation, each holding a beer. Rebecca strolled by, not seeing me.

Ann Drake stood alone, and I introduced her to Adam. After a moment or two of chitchat, another camp supporter came up to talk with him.

"What a great concert," I told Ann. "Fun party, too. You and the board must be so pleased."

"Thank you. It's gratifying to see it all come together."

"But you're on eggshells until the last guest goes home?"

"Precisely."

"The festival has given the local music scene a terrific boost, all year long. It's fired up the weekend musicians, given them a chance to up their game." The clichés tripped off my tongue. "And now more residents are stepping up to help keep things running smoothly, like Dave Barber."

Her jaw tightened. "Dave does know everyone. I'm sure he's barbered most of the men in this room." Her gaze flitted around the place, then landed on me. "He—has a vision for the festival. Bigger, and grander. International."

"Does that mean bringing in new artists?"

She shot me a sharp look. "Audiences want to hear their favorites, on the one hand, and make discoveries, on the other. That balance is different for everyone."

That was the mantra I'd repeated to my mother again and again when I first came home and took over the Merc. If a business doesn't change, it dies. My mother finally got it, once she saw the results.

"But something about Barber doesn't sit well with you."

Her cheek twitched, her eyes on the crowd. "You've been talking to Rebecca."

Not yet. Not about that, anyway. I made a mental note.

"Ann, who's the board treasurer? I've been wondering about finances."

The lights dimmed. Around us, feet shuffled, and voices rose and fell as people moved toward the theater. In the shifting light and angles, Ann's face paled despite her makeup.

"Have a lovely evening," she tossed over her shoulder as she pushed forward into the crowd. Away from me.

I spotted Adam—the advantage of a tall sweetheart—and snaked my way to him. "Finally, no line. Meet you inside."

Not tonight, I had told myself, but when the ideas come running thick and fast, I'm not going to close the gates. In the women's room, I fished out my notepad and scribbled *Who is treasurer? $$$??? Tension—Dave and Rebecca.*

And one more: *What is Ann afraid of?*

The lobby was nearly empty when I emerged.

But not quite.

Ike Hoover stood beside the theater's inner doors, now closed. Arms folded, face unreadable, clearly waiting for me. I pushed away the memory of him waiting for me the night my father died.

"Didn't know you were a jazz fan," I said. "Or is this an official visit?"

"Semi-official." He jerked a thumb toward a long table covered with trays, the tasty treats picked over. "Nothing says I can't enjoy myself while I'm working."

"Don't you live west of Pondera? You didn't make the trip for the snacks."

"Forty-two miles one way, but the EMTs lend me their bunk room now and then."

This building had replaced the town's original movie theater, the Bijou, destroyed by fire in 1970. Wendy's parents had started a summer repertory company here ten years before that, and kept it going until one of their sons and his wife took over a few years ago. In the off-season, community theater, the Children's Playhouse, and high school productions fill the space, along with occasional concerts. Last winter's Food Lovers' Film Festival had been such a success that plans for next February's event were already underway—without me, thank goodness. The moment the last jazz note died, the summer season would begin. Three hundred nights a year, this theater works.

In the concession stand, a young man cleaned out the espresso machine. On the other end of the lobby, a woman sat at the open ticket window, a display of CDs on the counter.

I sat on the long bench my friend Iggy had painted. Ike joined me.

"So you're here to listen, to more than the music. To watch, but more than the performance."

"*Bingo*, as your friend Ned would say."

"Your deputy finally caught up with the Carters, so you know about the argument James overheard between Gerry Martin and Dave Barber." Ike nodded, almost imperceptibly. "I know you have to consider everyone, and you can't rule out Sam Kraus, especially once you found out that his wife had a private conversation with Martin that upset her. But I think Dave Barber deserves a closer look."

"We're looking at everyone. We always do."

"I know you talked to Ned, but I suspect there are a few things he didn't tell you." Things Ned wouldn't volunteer, and Ike wouldn't know to ask. I filled him in. "Ned Redaway is a pretty good judge of character. Dave Barber didn't want Martin to be a permanent part of the festival. That's why he stepped all over Martin's performance. I think that's why he went to the cottages later that night. I can't work out why Barber would kill Martin the next morning, unless he didn't know that Martin had decided to leave early. And I don't know the financial impact of Martin's presence—or his departure.

"I'm telling you, Ike. Whatever Barber's up to might not be murder. It might be theft, it might be a frame. It might not be criminal at all." I could not see past Ike's inscrutable features, but I knew the wheels were churning. "But he's after something, and he's driving hard."

"Thank you, Erin," he said a moment later. "I do appreciate your perspective. Now, I have a favor to ask you."

"Don't ask me to stay out of this."

"I know better," he said wryly. His manner became somber. "I'd like you to talk to Kim about returning to the force. We need her. She'll listen to you."

I wasn't convinced of that. "Are you sure that's what I'll tell her? That it's time to stop playing with horses and get back to work?"

Ike put his hands on his knees and pushed himself up. "Ned Redaway's not the only good judge of character around here."

Twenty

When you plug numbers into a spreadsheet, they add up. If they don't, you check your figures and tweak your formulas. But when you plug in people, no such luck.

I stared at the columns and rows. Sandburg batted at one of my red boots, lying beside my brown leather chair.

"This doesn't make sense," I muttered.

After leaving Ike, I'd snuck back in to the darkened theater and crawled over knees to my seat between Chiara and Adam. He'd been enthralled by the music—first, Pearl Django's tribute to the greats of Gypsy jazz, Django Reinhardt and Stéphane Grappelli, and in the second half, brass, brass, brass. It wasn't the time or place for whispered questions about what shoes Martin had been wearing when he fell, or what Adam's boss had said. Later, I hadn't wanted to spoil the mood—Adam had been so happy. Grinning at Tanner, holding me close.

Exactly what a festival night with people you love ought to be.

And though a van from KNUS, its broadcast dish mounted on the roof, had been parked on Front Street, and more uniformed officers stood around than usual, the only damper I'd noticed had been the rain.

The rain had returned while we were inside, and we'd splashed and dashed to our cars, laughing. This time, Tanner had held out his hand for Adam's keys.

"It's barely a mile," Adam said as he folded himself into my passenger seat and reached for the door handle. "Don't get lost."

And now here I was, in the middle of the night, the cats in their beds, my sweet honey in mine, while I sat in the living room staring at facts from a case that wasn't technically my business, but that I couldn't leave alone.

Plinks and plunks on the metal roof told me the winds were whipping up again. Exactly how I felt inside.

I wanted to believe Dave Barber was the killer. I'd been so sure when James Carter told me about the argument he overheard, until I ran that thought through the analytical side of my brain. Barber was getting what he wanted: Martin was leaving the festival. His early departure created a short-term crisis—juggling the schedule for events long advertised, and explaining the changes to the students and the public.

If Martin was the jerk everyone described, he might have relished that thought.

The clattering on the roof woke Pumpkin. She jumped off the ottoman and crouched by the French doors to the back deck.

I had a hunch the other artists would grouse a bit, for the fun of it, but take the changes in stride. They were pros, and pros know not everyone acts like a pro when they should. Tempers flare, personalities clash, enormous changes happen at the last minute.

C'est la vie.

Pumpkin let out a yowl. "What, girl? Storm scaring you?" She didn't answer, and I went back to my musing.

But why would Barber kill Martin? If he'd known Martin had decided to leave, I could see no reason for them to have exchanged more than a few words of "good riddance" the next morning, let alone take a walk together.

If Martin hadn't told him he was leaving early—I had no idea when he'd made that decision—would tempers have flared back up Saturday morning on the trail?

What did Barber have to gain, now or in the future?

I needed to know more about both men.

Sandburg emerged from the bedroom and crouched next to Pumpkin, a rare sight. The tabby let out another yowl.

"What's up, girl?" The power flickered. "Not again."

It's a common joke that if you don't like the weather in Montana, especially this time of year, wait five minutes.

The wind threw another wave of branches and cones against the cabin. Beneath the wind came a sound I couldn't identify. Metallic, but not quite. Not natural.

Both cats raised their heads, then craned their necks to look at me. I was leader of the pack. I was supposed to do something.

And as the nominal caretaker, that meant taking care of things. I left my warm, comfy chair and rummaged in the coat closet slash laundry room by the front door.

Behind me, a light went on. I started, one hand still fumbling in the junk drawer.

"What are you doing?" Adam stood in the doorway. He rubbed one eye with the heel of his hand, his dark curls sleep tangled. All he wore were plaid boxers he hadn't been wearing when I'd last seen him.

My fingers found what I'd been searching for, and I held up a sturdy black metal flashlight. "Looking for this."

"Why? Come back to bed. It's all warm in there, and I'm awake again. Sort of."

168

And it had been sweet, to let the tensions of the last few days melt away in his arms. But I couldn't dismiss Pumpkin's noise-making as a reaction to a wild animal, not after what I'd heard.

I lifted my slicker off the hook on the back of the door. "I heard something. I don't know if a branch ripped a soffit or damaged the chimney, but I have to check it out."

He dropped his hand. "In this weather? Don't be crazy."

"I'm supposed to be the caretaker." I thrust one bare foot into a snow boot, good in all kinds of wicked weather. Adam made an exasperated noise and disappeared. I bent to dig the other boot out of the pile of winter gear in the corner. By the time I'd found it and tugged it on, Adam was back, in jeans and sneakers, wrapping a coat over his bare chest.

I raised my hood and stepped outside, lights off so we could see better.

A gust swirled onto the covered deck and slapped me in the face. I blinked and stared into the darkness.

"I don't see anything," Adam said. "Or anyone."

On the front step, I paused. The same noise I'd heard earlier rippled through the woods.

"That," I replied, the wind whipping my hair and my words. A car engine? A car door?

We were far enough from the highway that traffic noise was rare. But stormy nights play havoc with sounds and sensations—and emotions.

Another gust sent the heavy boughs of the giant spruce swaying. Another loud crack, this one thunder. Then rain.

"I don't know what it is," Adam said, "but I'm sure it's not coming from the cabin. And it's too far away to be coming from the big house. Wait till morning."

He was right. Besides, the Pinskys wouldn't expect me to go out in this weather on the odd chance that a fallen branch had ripped a shingle off the roof.

Morning would come soon enough.

"*Criminy.*" I tugged on the cabin door but the wind held it shut. Adam reached past me and pried it open, and we tumbled inside. A gust tore at the edge, and if the door hadn't been so heavy, it would have whipped out of his fingers.

Inside, we collapsed, catching our breath. Adam's eyes were wide.

I did what I rarely do: I locked us in.

We shook out our coats and hair, but neither of us was ready to go back to bed. I set the flashlight and a lighter next to the pillar candles on the kitchen island. Liz had chosen them for ambiance, but if I had to use them, I would.

I tossed a fleecy throw at Adam and he sank on to the couch, wrapping the blanket around his shoulders.

"I need a drink." Strong drink, to me, means red wine. Even at two a.m. I scrounged in my wine storage—a crate in the hall closet.

"Do you think—? I mean, it was more than wind. It had to be a car, and close," I said. "No lights, though." Either the driver kept them off—gutsy, on a twisty driveway in the woods in the dark, with no stars or moon—or I was imagining things.

Neither option was very appealing.

I popped the cork on a bottle of J. Lohr Cabernet that Kyle Caldwell had given me for my birthday and poured two glasses. Kyle wanted Kim to take a bigger role in running the guest lodge. Ike wanted her to return to the force, and wanted me to give her a push. She would want me to let all this go.

But there are times when you can't do what other people want. And this was one of them. If someone was out there, if I hadn't been imagining things, then this was getting personal.

Adam's head bobbed in a mix of a nod and a shake. "But who—why? There's no reason for anybody to be prowling around here, not in the middle of a storm."

Pumpkin's big eyes watched every move we made, ears back, tail low.

I set the glasses on the coffee table and settled in next to Adam. He tucked half the blanket around me, and we each took a sip. The wine went down easily, full-bodied but smooth. Monte Verde made a decent cab, still young, and their cherry wine had a similar mouth feel, but neither came close to this. Last summer I'd connected Jennifer to a wine buyer at SavClub, to give them a boost. But they might need more help than that to fulfill their ambitions.

Make that *her* ambitions.

Adam switched off the lamp. He'd shed his wet jeans and his bare leg touched mine. "My guess is a tree fell on the highway, and a driver had to stop and clear the road. You know how the wind throws noises around during the night."

"Yeah, probably." I snuggled closer, his arm around me. My eyes drifted shut, and as if the backs of my eyelids were screens, the spreadsheet and its empty boxes jumped into view. I blinked them away, and raised my face to Adam's, drinking in all the comfort he offered.

The next morning, I stood at the edge of my driveway, staring at the blowdown littering the road. My slash pile would easily rival Sam's out at the winery.

Adam and I had migrated from the couch back to the bed, tangled up in each other. But I hadn't been able to sleep. At first light, I'd dressed and come outside to survey the damage. I wanted to believe Adam's explanation for the odd noises—a downed tree on the highway, the wind playing tricks.

I wrapped my arms around myself against the chill. Against what I might see.

That's when I noticed the tire tracks. I suppressed a shudder and followed them down the driveway toward the big house. They didn't go that far. Instead, they turned left on a dirt access road that served the property to the south. It hadn't been used in years, but it was passable.

Not entirely. About twenty feet in, a fallen white pine blocked the way. I could see where someone had pulled in, then backed out.

If this car had been the one Pumpkin and I heard, why had we seen no headlights? I'd left a light on. Why not stop and ask for directions?

Must have been a man.

Or someone with another plan. This time, I didn't suppress my shudder.

An object glistened in the long grass between the ruts. I picked it up. A muddy guitar pick, a tiny hole at the base. This one had been an earring.

I wiped off the dirt with my thumb. Black, streaked with coppery-brown. Pretty.

Who had lost it? Guitar pick earrings weren't uncommon, but I couldn't remember anyone except Gabby wearing a pair lately. Red, white, and blue, if I remembered right. This one wasn't hers.

This one was a message.

Red-hot fear gripped my brain. I eyed the pick, my hand shaking. I closed my fingers around it and shoved my fists in my coat pockets.

But what was the message?

And who sent it?

Should I call the sheriff? No, I decided. After a big storm, all the emergency services would have their hands full, dealing with fallen trees, downed power lines, damage to cars and structures. In a wild storm last fall, docks had been ripped off their pilings, boats smashed on the rocks. Every few years, a crashing tree killed a passing driver or a homeowner inspecting his property.

Like I was doing.

I headed back to the cabin. The sheriff's department had already summoned the reserves to handle traffic and security at the festival while Ike and the detectives talked and retalked to everyone in town, even the weekenders. And it wasn't like crime or other daily duties stopped in the rest of the county while Jewel Bay had a crisis.

I had no evidence of any wrongdoing, and no idea who the trespasser might have been. The sheriff's office didn't need to hear from me.

I circled the big house on foot, spotting no damage. But a larch and a lodge pole pine had both uprooted, and lay across the backyard. Liz's favorite cherry tree, a rare Rainier, had split in two.

The smell of fresh coffee greeted me when I opened the cabin door, and Adam put a warm mug in my hand.

"So, what's it like out there?"

"Lots of downed branches. Two old trees came down by the big house. I'll call a tree trimmer, and Bob Pinsky. The buildings look okay, like you said."

He wrapped an arm around me and kissed the top of my head.

But the guitar pick in my pocket sang a different tune.

I dropped Adam off at his house, a remodeled bungalow not far from the athletic club where he worked, running outdoor programs and a wilderness camp for kids. In the village, I parked behind the Merc and walked up to Rebecca's gallery. Rubbed my lucky stars and raised my eyes. Her usual morning perch was empty. I peered in the gallery windows. Dead quiet.

Pooh, and double-pooh. I'd planned to quiz her over coffee about Martin and Barber.

Grant and Ann Drake were sitting at the table in the window of Le Panier. I'd already had coffee, but couldn't resist the opportunity to chat.

They were dressed for walking, in long pants and light sweaters.

"Shame we can't lick our plates in public, isn't it?" I said, seeing an orange plate with a few crumbs and a crumpled napkin on the table. Grant smiled broadly. Ann blinked several times, tightening her fingers around a white espresso cup.

I sat at the next table to wait for my latte and *pain au chocolat*. "I trust you and Gabby enjoyed the concert last night."

"We did, though I think she enjoyed the jam session afterwards at Red's even more." Another too-broad salesman's smile. "We snuck out of the condo so she could sleep in."

"Glad she's getting out to play. Did she change her mind about the workshops? I hear some of the other guest artists are terrific teachers, and it would be a shame to miss the opportunity, since you've come all the way out here."

"Under the circumstances," Grant said, as if I could fill in the blanks.

"Must be a challenge, figuring out who will take Martin's Master Classes and his performances. And the money—I bet that gets messy. Who handles that on the board? Marv Alden? I hear he's got a lot of financial experience. Or Dave Barber—I guess he's the chair. Since you don't have a director at the moment."

Ann lifted her cup an inch or two, then set it down again. Grant rose, one hand ready to help with her chair. Cup as unspoken signal.

What I understood, as I watched them walk out to the street, Ann adjusting the sweater draped over her shoulders, was that they were nervous.

About Gabby's career, now that her mentor had shuffled off this mortal coil?

About me, the village nosy parker?

Or—what?

And were any of the Drakes linked to the tracks on my road, and the broken earring in my pocket?

"What spooked them?" Michelle set a white paper cup and white bag on the table.

"Don't know. Lots of frayed nerves these days. Lots of rumors." Outside, my cousin Molly dashed by, an olive green messenger bag over her shoulder, keys in hand. "Michelle, make whatever Molly drinks. Please. To go."

"Double mocha." She tamped ground espresso into the filter basket.

"You must know everyone in town by their drinks," I said, and she flashed me a grin. "Does thinking about it that way remind you who came in Saturday, around the same time as Gerry Martin?"

Her eyes darkened. She turned back to the shiny machine, and pulled the lever, the *whoosh* and *hiss* of steam cutting off conversation. No doubt she hated being pestered—I wasn't the only one asking questions. Or maybe she didn't want to tell me.

The door opened and a gaggle of customers saved her from my quizzing. For now.

No lights were on in the real estate office when I walked up to the door. I rapped on the glass.

"Delivery," I said when Molly emerged from the back room and unlocked the front door. "Don't get used to it."

"Thanks, cuz." She popped the lid on her coffee and sniffed deeply, the joy of hot chocolate for grown-ups lighting up her face.

"Hey, a coupla questions. How well do you know Dave Barber? He's closer to our dads' ages than ours." And Molly was several years younger than me.

"Get those lights, would you?" She pointed to the switch by the front door and punched on the front desk computer as I closed the door behind me. "Him, I hardly know. His daughter was in my class. Smart, nice. One older brother, one younger. All good kids. But I wasn't close friends with any of them."

"Where did they live?"

She thought for a moment. "You know that old farmhouse up behind the cemetery, where kids used to go hang out?"

To drink and make out. I grunted agreement.

"I think it came from Dave's family. They sold it when they split up."

I sipped my latte. "Wonder where Dave lives now."

"Oh, right by me. Two houses down." Molly was renting a guest house above a garage in the upper part of town. And that put Dave Barber not two hundred feet from the River Road trailhead. He could easily have seen Martin Saturday morning.

Or seen who'd been following the man.

"You said two questions?" Molly sipped her mocha.

"Yeah. I ran into the Drakes at the bakery. I wonder how their house hunt is going."

"I bet they're working with someone else. Happens more than you think. Buyers get anxious, so they go looking with another agent, as if we aren't all using the same databases listing the same properties."

"Is every property on that database—what did you call it? MLS?"

176

"If it's listed for sale, yes. But there are private deals. Say your mother wanted to sell her house and already had a buyer."

"Yeah-h-h." I set my cup on the desk.

"Just—for example. They'd figure out the terms, then get a lawyer to write up a contract for deed. Or she'd come to us and we'd handle the paperwork for a flat fee. No official listing involved."

"Okay. I heard Rebecca owns rentals. What if she wanted to sell one of those?" That was three questions. Oh well.

"She owns tons of property, residential and commercial." Molly switched screens, clicking through files too quickly for me to follow.

A couple of minutes later, she gave me the news. "We've got listings for a couple of townhouses she owns near the golf course. Rentals she remodeled to flip. But I found something else you should see." She drew a slender file folder out from the bottom of a tall stack and slid it across the desk. I sat and read.

"Criminy." My dark eyes met her green ones. "Where did you find this?"

"After you asked about them, I dug out the Drakes' file. Finances aren't an issue—they plan to pay cash from a vacation property they sold back East. But there was a note about civil judgments, so I dug a little further. And found that."

I read the printouts, newspaper accounts of a year-long fraud investigation into Grant Drake, his companies, and his sons. No charges had been filed, but a dozen investors had brought civil suits against him. After the first multimillion-dollar jury verdict, he'd quickly settled with the other plaintiffs.

"They make him sound like Bernie Madoff, Junior," Molly said.

I closed the file. "You're one smart investigator."

She tossed her strawberry curls. "Runs in the family."

Twenty-One

That had to be why Ann Drake looked so nervous when I asked who handled the contracts and money, I thought as I jiggled the key in the Merc's front door.

Did the other board members know her husband's history? Did he actually have any financial responsibility for the festival?

The tricky part would be finding out without spreading unfounded rumors.

Upstairs, I sipped the last of my latte and let the caffeine course through me. The restless night combined with this morning's find on the road gave me a double dose of jitters. Add Molly's discovery to the mix, and I felt like I'd stuck an immersion blender in my gut.

Coffee might not help, but on the other hand, I needed the jolt.

Too bad I never caught Gabby alone. She probably knew Martin better than anyone around, except Rebecca.

I bit into my pastry and relaxed. Layers of buttery dough have that effect on me. As they melted on my tongue, they melted my cares.

Momentarily, anyway. I had calls to make. A high school classmate trimmed trees. He was already at work—I could hear his partner's chain saw in the background—but he promised to get my road cleared before I got home and move the downed trees at the big house. Then I called Bob to report on the weather damage.

A minute later, the printer in Pondera rang to say our labels were ready. We'd been chomping at the bit to get my mother's new pestos on the shelves, and Ray's kraut was selling so well that I'd penciled in time to can a double batch before tourist season hit full stride.

"I'll be back in an hour, hour and a half tops," I told Tracy moments after we declared ourselves open for business. Her full navy skirt and blue-and-white sailor top with a yellow tie were an advertisement for thrift store treasure hunting—and proof that she and Lou Mary had more in common than Tracy wanted to admit.

Maybe that was the problem, I mused as I dashed out to my Subaru. Though Tracy had just hit thirty-five, her ambitions didn't include being a sales clerk at sixty-five. But it's good work. The retail ladies keep Jewel Bay humming.

I grabbed the door handle. It didn't open. I never lock my car. Nobody here does. I fished out my keys and hit the clicker.

Still locked.

I made an exasperated noise and glanced around, then let out a cackle. I'd been trying to get into someone else's green Subaru. Mine was two spots away. Clearly my attention was being pulled in too many directions.

The printer's wife, who ran the office, was in a chatty mood, and I was way behind schedule when I drove back through Pondera, the Subaru's back end crammed with boxes of shiny labels, each branded with the logos my sister had created. I stopped at a light on Main Street, near the glass shop. Last winter, the shopkeeper, an extraordinary glass artist, had rescued me from my mother's wrath with handblown martini glasses to replace one I'd broken. We'd started carrying her glassware in the Merc, where it was a big hit.

The dashboard clock said I didn't have time to drop in, but I did wonder what she might suggest for a wedding gift. Did you buy your mother a wedding gift? Where was the etiquette guide? My sister sure didn't have a copy, and I felt a bit unmoored myself. I had no idea what my brother might think, out in the wilderness tracking wolves and their new pups. Until last winter, the likelihood of him revealing anything remotely like a confidence had been slim, but he'd changed.

We'd all changed. When she'd told us about their engagement, my mother had said that they hadn't decided where to live. Bill spent a fair amount of time at the Orchard, but he had his own home on a river slough north of Jewel Bay. What it lacked in family history, it made up with the riverfront and bird watching.

Come on, turn, I silently urged the light. Then I realized that the bank was on the next corner.

The light changed. Ahead, a car pulled out and I zoomed into the empty spot. Dashed down the street before I could change my mind.

What are you doing, Erin? She's a perfect stranger.

Sometimes you luck out. The sign outside the first office, its door open, read PAMELA BARBER, LOAN OFFICER.

I introduced myself and told her that Ned Redaway remembered her fondly. "And your ex-husband's name came up."

She sighed deeply, an attractive woman with a full figure, her short silver-streaked hair beautifully cut.

"Let me guess. I heard about Gerry Martin's death. Poor man. That raises problems for the Jazz Festival, and gives Ned an excuse to drum up old stories about Dave." She didn't say "again," but I heard it in her tone. She closed her door.

"That's about the size of it," I said.

"You'll understand why I'm going to ask you to keep this quiet. As quiet as you can. I don't know what Dave is up to now, but we were married twenty-four years, and I don't want something that never happened to be used against him."

Curious.

Pamela perched on the edge of the credenza, arms folded. "Senior year, spring prom. Eileen Redaway and I were in charge. We were always in charge of social events, starting in kindergarten." A small, memory-laden smile.

"Ned said Homecoming. That's in the fall."

She shook her head. "Prom. First weekend in May. I was starting to show and I wanted to get through graduation without anyone knowing I was pregnant, except Dave. And Eileen."

"Are you saying Dave didn't take the money? That you did?"

One hand gripped the other, her knuckles pale against her navy pencil skirt. "I needed maternity clothes, diapers, baby clothes, a crib. Everything."

"Your parents—"

"Didn't know and weren't going to help me. When I finally told them, the day before Dave and I got married, they hit the roof. Now that I have three kids, I understand how disappointed they were, but…" Her voice trailed off.

"You would have let your best friend take the blame?"

"No. Of course not. If Eileen had ever been accused, I would have admitted it. She knew the truth, no matter what her father thinks. Ned never accused Dave publicly, but I knew what he thought." She reached out and touched the edge of her desk, a deep reddish-brown. "It was wrong, and if I have to admit it, I will. Three hundred dollars seemed like a fortune back then."

But it wasn't much now. I couldn't imagine her losing this job, more than thirty years later, if the truth came out.

"What does this have to do with Dave, after all this time?" she asked. "You're not suggesting he stole from the festival?"

"No, but something's going on. And there are rumors of money missing from a promotional campaign the merchants ran a few years back. Any reason why Dave would suddenly have had money for new guitars, speakers, all the gear?" The kit and caboodle, in Ned speak.

"Dave would never steal. He never knew what I did, and he'd have been furious. I can hardly believe I did something so stupid." She slid into the brown leather chair behind her desk. "Here's the scoop. Our younger son decided to enlist. We weren't happy, but it's what he always wanted. I urged him to let me invest his college fund, for later, but he insisted we take half, since we'd squirreled away every spare nickel for the kids and never had money for ourselves."

"That's a generous child."

"We weren't good at marriage, but we raised great kids." Elbows balanced on the arms of her chair, she clasped her hands. "Dave used his share to buy the musical gear we'd never been able to afford."

"And you?"

She spread her hands, indicating the room. "I went to college. The finance and accounting classes got me this."

"Good for you," I said. "I wonder how this year's senior class fund is doing."

She caught my meaning in a flash, her eyes glinting. "I'll call the principal with a donation. About Dave ... That festival means so much to him."

"It means a lot to a lot of people," I said. Pamela Barber had cleared up some confusion. But I wasn't sure yet where this road led.

I was late. Not to mention ravenous. I punched in my mother's number, fingers mentally crossed. Thank heavens, the stars were in alignment. She was finishing an early lunch with Bill at the Jewel Inn, and would happily pop over to the Merc to spell Tracy.

That gave me time to find a little food for thought.

I'd rounded the corner when what to my wondering eyes should appear but Rebecca Whitman, standing outside a three-story sandstone mansion with a curved front porch and a mansard roof. The historic home now housed the valley's most prominent law firm.

Beside her stood a man and woman. Her hands moved and pointed as if she was giving directions.

To Ann and Grant Drake.

I tucked into an open spot down the block, behind yet another Subaru, and hoped they came this way. Slumped out of view, I kept my eyes on the mirrors. Curious indeed. Yes, they were friends, but friends don't usually go see lawyers together.

Rebecca's Subaru zipped by me, followed by the Drakes' black BMW. Connecticut plates. I'd have to take Landon over to the Harbor condos to walk the parking lots with his list and his fat pencil.

Traffic was quiet on this side street, so I hung back as we drove north. Rebecca's car had disappeared from sight. A Suburban the size of my living room got between the Drakes and me, but I kept them in my sights as we neared a major intersection. The Suburban turned. Ahead, the Drakes parked behind Rebecca, no doubt aiming for the Irish pub in the old redbrick railroad warehouse. I made an unsignaled hard right, and the car behind me honked in displeasure.

The luck of the Irish was with me. The threesome had already been seated, at a table by the far window. I took a seat at the bar. If I could see them, they could see me, but their attention lay on the large piece of paper Grant unrolled. A map, or a plat? The Drakes had been hunting for property, though I had no reason to think Rebecca was selling anything they might want. But sometimes an owner didn't know she was selling until an offer she couldn't refuse came along.

The pubsters were better cooks than proofreaders. The "coned beef fritters" were tasty deep fried bites of corned beef, served with Thousand Island dressing and a cup of tasty cole slaw.

Grant Drake had rolled up the mysterious map when their orders came, but now Ann unfurled it again. In the mirror, I watched her point at one spot, then another, glancing at Grant as she spoke. The scene had the air of a woman taking charge.

I tossed cash on the bar and strolled over. "Hey. Who's left in Jewel Bay if we're all over here?"

Ann tossed her napkin over the page, but not before I got a glimpse of lines and squares and tiny type. *Planning world domination over Guinness and corned beef?*

Grant sat rigid, his face pale. Rebecca, usually so calm and in control, caught her lower lip between her teeth.

What had I interrupted? And did it have anything to do with the festival or Gerry Martin's death?

Curiouser and curiouser.

Twenty-Two

$\mathcal{I}$ sat in my car, hand on the ignition, thinking. If Rebecca was selling property to the Drakes for their piece of the Montana dream, had she planned to sell Gerry Martin property as well? Or create a joint venture on a parcel she already owned?

One more stop, and then I could go back to Jewel Bay.

In the music shop. Rocco's white-boy dreadlocks swung as he talked. "Yeah, man. Don't get many chances to outfit a whole studio, 'specially a class A project. Sound booths, multiple boards. Woofers and tweeters up the wazoo."

"Bummer. Losing a big sale must have hurt."

"Yeah." He wacked the palm of his hand with a tuning fork. "We'll make up for it. Sold a brand-new J-200 to a guy in the beginning guitar class yesterday. That's a few thou. And a gal over in Lakeside's buying her husband a set of keyboards that'll send me and my lady to Hawaii for a week next winter."

I didn't know his lady, but with the Rasta hair and full sleeve tattoos, he'd be a sight on a beach.

"So, where was this studio going to be, anyway?" I gave a seed rattle a quick shake.

"On the lake. The woman who was fronting the project had a place she wanted to remodel. The house was too big for Martin—single guy, on the road a lot. But bands could stay there and walk out the back door to the studio. Big old metal building. Needed a ton of work and sound-proofing, but like I said, they had the budget for it."

Bingo. Now to figure out what property Rebecca had planned to use. Knowing that would help me identify the killer, I was sure. But I had another question first. "Was she buying gear for the festival from you, too?"

"Nah. They use the Playhouse gear indoors. And when they're outside, I rent to 'em. Better deal all around."

So the brochures and catalogs in Rebecca's office had been for the studio, not the festival.

"There was some kind of complication," Rocco went on. "I don't know what, but the guy reneged. I never met him, but I heard he was pretty demanding."

"Demanding how? On stage?"

"In everything. Wanted it all exactly right, but you know, there's lots of right ways to do things—depends what sound you're after."

The shop's long wall held more guitars than I'd ever seen in my life. I stopped in front of a guitar so gorgeous it made my fingers itch, and I barely know a bass from a mandolin. "What is that?"

"1964 Gibson ES 330. One of the finest hollow-bodies ever made," Rocco said in a reverent tone. "Rolled neck, Adirondack spruce. The reproductions are nice, but this is the real deal."

An image slid into place in my brain. "Doesn't Sam Kraus play one like this?"

"Well, he did. Jennifer brought it in on consignment."

Selling guitars? *At least I have my music*, he'd said, in a voice consoled by the thought. Not the voice of a man hawking his treasures.

I reached for the tag tied to a peg, and my eyes widened. "Can she get that much for it?"

Rocco pooched out his lips and raised one shoulder. "If she's lucky, right buyer comes along. It's a long shot."

"Is this guitar one Dave Barber might lust after?"

"Doubt it. He's got one real similar. He came in with his kid a coupla years ago, upgraded everything. It was fun—the kid buying guitars and mics for the old man, paying him back for his raising."

Just as Pamela Barber had said.

"'Course, a music guy can never have too many guitars," Rocco added. "Like Adam and his skis and kayaks."

Every obsession has its equivalent. Woe to anyone who counted my spatulas. "Thanks, Rocco. See you at the festival?"

"I'm enjoying being in the audience. But I'm running the sound Saturday for the finale in the park."

"Great. See you then." The triangle hung over the door rang crisply behind me.

"Oh! A foal." I craned my neck to watch the baby, a day or two old, struggle to her feet. Her mother, a handsome bay, stood close by. Behind them in the pasture, half a dozen other horses grazed on the newly green grass.

As I drove, I considered what I'd learned in Pondera. First, that professional printers are worth far more than their weight in paper and ink.

Second, that Ned Redaway had drawn the wrong conclusions all those years ago about his daughter's friends. I tended to believe Pamela

Barber. She hadn't sugar-coated their marriage, or her own teenage crime, but she hadn't blasted Dave, either. So many exes do that, and it always makes me cringe.

From her perspective, Dave was trying to create the career he'd never had, or at least the fun. Bringing in more international artists—promoting the festival's brand and expanding its reach, in business speak—brought him a little closer to the limelight, even if he didn't get center stage.

Nothing to kill over. What was I missing?

I rounded the last curve and the mountains seemed to jump out at me, carved from ice and snow and set against the crystal sky. *Dang*, it was good to be home.

What about the Drakes and Rebecca Whitman? Surely there was nothing suspicious about her selling them property for their new house. With so little undeveloped lake frontage, Molly's explanation of a private deal made sense. Cutting out the middlemen and women could easily be to everyone's advantage.

And Rebecca liked to be in the middle of her deals. She'd wanted an active part in Gerry Martin's studio, working with Chuck the Builder and Rocco the Music Man.

I slowed in front of the Playhouse for two kids crossing the street, one carrying a trumpet case, the other a bumpy black duffle shaped loosely like a sax.

Jewel Bay was alive with the sound of music.

"Darling, at long last." My mother's eyes twinkled as she zoomed in to kiss my cheek.

"Uh-oh. Did they kill each other? Is there blood?"

"What? Oh, no." She waved a hand. "It's a big change, but she'll get used to it."

She meant Tracy, settling into her role as part-time sales clerk and full-time chocolatier, feeling displaced by the presence of another woman, but I hoped my mother's prophecy held equally true of my sister.

"Hey, sorry for the short notice, and for being so late. Go ahead and get cooking. I've got an urgent call to make."

"Roasted Tomato Pesto." She made it sound like ambrosia. I'd had a bite of her sample batch—it tasted that good, too.

"The new labels are super-spiff," I called as I started up the stairs. "You'll swoon."

"My little business queen," she said and disappeared into the kitchen.

"Their vintages have done well," the wine buyer at SavClub said a few minutes later, after I'd wound my way through the voice mail system to her. "Especially the dry cherry. But Jennifer doesn't get that these aren't a national product. National distribution is doomed to fail."

"Why? Because no one expects fine wine from Montana?"

"They're regional and seasonal."

I rubbed the corner of my eye with a finger. "So what makes a wine regional? I mean, Champagne and Asti grow in specific regions, but people drink them worldwide. Their regions have become a mark of distinction."

She launched into a mini lecture on wine varieties, *terroir*, history, and tradition—all highly sophisticated and largely incomprehensible. But she made abundantly clear that national distribution of Monte Verde wines was not an option at SavClub.

"She's threatening to go to the competition," the buyer continued, "and I'm half ready to let her. Overreach can kill the brand."

I thanked her and hung up, irritated. I'd gone out on a limb for Jennifer, getting her in the door at SavClub. If her actions damaged my credibility, I'd be seriously peeved.

Talking wine gave me another idea. Did I dare sneak out again? I wouldn't go far.

I swung downstairs to make nice. My mother, clad in her vegetable print bib-front apron and the red Keds she calls her cooking shoes, had the kitchen smelling like my version of heaven: plum tomatoes roasting, pine nuts cooling, the air redolent with fresh thyme and garlic. She blew me a kiss. All was forgiven.

On the shop floor, Tracy huddled deep in conversation with a cocoa-maniac, debating the merits of seventy-two, eighty, and ninety percent cocoa solids, single-origin or blends, and other delectable details that make the passionate chocolate lover drool.

I love experts.

Lou Mary stood by Luci's soap and lotion display, studying the products.

"Don't look so worried," I said. "You're learning faster than I'd expected."

She glanced up. "What? Oh, no. This is fun." She waved a hand at the display, then reached for a tester bottle of lotion. I caught a whiff of lavender.

So what was worrying her? "I'm counting on it. I'm running to the liquor store. Back in two shakes."

Few villagers seem to enjoy life more than Donna Lawson, and not just because she enjoys tasting her own products. Or because liquor stores can be lucrative.

"I'll say this much, because it's you, Erin: it's not gossip if it's for a good cause." Surrounded by cases of wine and spirits in the closet-like back office, she peered over her glasses. Donna is the only woman I know who makes rhinestone-studded cat eyes look stylish.

"Works for me."

"Jennifer came to me last fall begging for help. I know all the distributors, so I made a few calls. We sent out sample bottles, took the product to trade shows. But…" She opened her hands in a *no go* gesture.

"Let me guess. Regional and seasonal. A novelty wine." That last bit I'd heard from a few of my customers, but in a specialty market with a sideline in gifts, that wasn't a bad thing.

"I prefer the term *niche*." She drew it out, rhyming with *sheesh*. "We got nibbles from two distributors, but their debt load sank the deals. Jennifer simply could not understand."

But I did. A classic Catch-22. You struggle and get into debt, which keeps you from expanding the business, and mires you deeper in debt. Why would any distributor voluntarily take on a supplier it couldn't count on to stay afloat? Even on the Merc's small scale, taking on a vendor is expensive. I have to be sure the vendor is committed, and that the market will justify my expense of time, space, signage, and more. Tracy and I had tussled over that last winter, when I said no to an oil and vinegar maker she championed.

"Did Sam get it?"

Donna sat back, arms folded. "Don't know. She came in alone. Even when she came asking for an investment."

Which was a puzzle. I had no idea what careers they'd had in California, before they traded their backyard vines for a Montana hillside full of fruit. But wouldn't Sam want to be fully involved in financing the future of his dream?

"You turned her down, too. Same reason?"

"I have no desire to buy into a winery. I'd rather buy and sell the fruits of someone else's labors."

Speaking of labors… "Gotta run. Thanks for the insight." A much nicer word than *gossip*. Halfway out, I remembered my other questions, and poked my head back in.

"Donna, you remember an incident a few years ago, when the merchants put together a promotion campaign and ran out of money? The Chamber ended up taking over."

She rolled her eyes. "Billboard company jerked us around. Nearly doubled the prices they'd quoted."

"So there was no question about embezzlement?"

She adjusted her rhinestone glasses. "At first, yes, but when we got the invoices and called the company, we could see what had happened. I know Ned suspected Dave Barber, and he should have gotten a quote in writing, but it wasn't his fault. Chamber hired an ad agency and it's been smooth sailing."

"Great. You were on the festival board for a while, right? Who is the treasurer?"

"Marv Alden. Good choice—he was the money guy for a big oil company for years."

"Not Grant Drake?"

"No. Grant joined the board when I was president. He said he was through counting other people's money. But he and Ann are great fundraisers, a good role for someone who doesn't live here." As she should know—she was the best fundraiser in town.

"Barber okay to work with?"

Her dark eyes narrowed slightly. A trick of the light on her lenses, or a hint of distaste? "He wants what he wants. But I suppose we all do, don't we?"

"That's the truth. Hey, do you still have that yummy J. Lohr Cab?" I bought two bottles. Donna had given me information worth paying for.

On my way back to the Merc, I wondered what Jennifer had wanted from Gerry Martin that Friday night when she chased after him. An investment? Had he hit the big-time, financially?

Had she been angling for an endorsement of their winery? A buyer for that pricey guitar? Or, despite Sam's reluctance to consider the possibility, had his wife been looking for love in all the wrong places?

Twenty-Three

$\mathcal{I}$ breathed a sigh of relief, happy to be back in the Merc. Lou Mary cocked her head toward a tall figure standing by our drinks display, a bag of our custom-blended Cowboy Roast in his hand.

"Good stuff," Tanner said at my approach. "I'd like to ship a case of coffee back for my employees. Huckleberry jam, too, and those pemmican bars."

"Blackfeet Naturals. Made on the reservation from grass-fed buffalo."

"Got time for a walk?"

So much for my plan to spend the afternoon cocooned in my office, catching up on details. But I relished the chance to get to know Tanner better.

Lou Mary made shooing motions with her hands, and Tracy handed us each a truffle. A double chocolate Kahlua gesture of friendship.

"Adam pop into work?" I said as we ambled up Front Street. "What did you think of the base camp?"

"Yep. The camp is amazing." Tanner ducked to avoid a hanging flowerpot. "Reminds me of the lodge in the Northwoods where we spent the summer we were sixteen, the summer before … before I got sick. We always loved running around outdoors, but that's when the wilderness bug bit Adam good."

I knew the story. A high school coach feared the two boys were headed for trouble, and got them summer jobs as camp counselors in training— unpaid interns. But when they got home, Tanner's latest foster parents had moved without leaving a trace, and the social workers struggled to find a placement for a teenage boy. So he'd moved into Adam's family's basement, across the hall from the quarrelsome Cain and Abel.

And then, leukemia struck.

What had it been like, sick and alone at sixteen? Memories of the pain and anger I'd carried after my father died flooded through my body, hot and swollen.

I'd made the turn toward the River Road without thinking. I paused, Tanner halting beside me.

"It's okay," he said. "Seeing a man fall to his death was shocking, but I'm not going to let it stop me from taking a walk with a beautiful woman on a beautiful day."

Though it's not a stretch to call me cute, beautiful is pure BS. But who cares?

At the trailhead, I ran a hand over the top of the gate, where some-one had hung a bouquet of silk flowers, a tiny plastic guitar tied into the ribbon.

Who left it here? I peered in for clues, but saw none.

A sign of remorse? Maybe. Or a sign that Jewel Bay would remem-ber Gerry Martin for more than the manner of his death?

The trail had leveled out when Tanner spoke. "Thank you for let-ting Adam come back to Minnesota with me."

"He doesn't need my permission."

"But he wants it. Not permission exactly, but your blessing. I want it, too."

Blast him for being so nice.

And so important to the guy who was so important to me. I couldn't entirely squelch my fear. Would Adam go back to Minneapolis and get sucked into running Tanner's company while he was in treatment? Then, because Adam did own half of it, end up staying?

He didn't own anything out here, except a good chunk of my heart.

A gray squirrel skittered across the trail. It's a slippery slope, trying to hold on to another person. That old line about loving someone enough to let them go makes a great poster in a college dorm room, but it's hard to put into practice.

So I did the chicken thing and changed the subject. "Did he find out if the assistant camp manager can start work earlier?"

"Not yet. And the wrangler fell in love with a guy from Australia and skedaddled. So he's got to find someone to handle the horses, or cancel the pack trip."

"The pack trip's the reason half the kids come."

"Erin." His somber tone pricked my ears. "Adam's not worried about the camp. He's worried about you."

"Me? I'll be fine. It's only a few weeks." I reached out and plucked an early leaf off a paper birch. "It's you we're concerned about."

The tall man beside me came to a stop. "I went into foster care at eight, after my mom died. Some years, I saw my dad once or twice, some years not at all. When I see you with your family, and how you've welcomed me, it gives me hope. And you put up with my goofball buddy. That says a lot."

I wasn't going to tell him he'd thrown a monkey wrench into my life. I was going to work it out. I sniffed back a tear and hugged him.

When we got to the spot where Gerry Martin had plunged to his death, we saw that the yellow barricade had been moved to the side of the trail, to keep the looky-loos from the same fate. Martin seemed an unlikely man to get distracted by the scenery, the amazing Wild Mile where the river runs through the rapids, curves sharply, and races past the village into the bay.

If you aren't careful, you could lose your footing—and your life.

"Tanner, did you notice what kind of shoes Gerry Martin was wearing?"

He ran his fingers up the side of his face, eyes closed. I clenched my jaw, sorry to have asked, but hoping he'd dredge up a useful memory.

After a long moment, he opened his eyes, staring into the distance. "The body was pretty beat up. One foot was bare. When we came back on the raft, one of the EMTs found his boot."

"What kind of boot? Hiking boot, cowboy boot?"

"Ankle boot. Black. Lots of guys wear them instead of dress shoes."

City boots. The kind Martin had worn on stage Friday night. The kind you might wear to the airport—easy to slip off and back on.

My hunch had been right: Gerry Martin hadn't meant to take a hike.

So who had been with him? Who had pushed him, whether with malice aforethought or in the heat of the moment?

Mortification finally overcame my curiosity, and I came to my senses. "Tanner, I am so sorry. You are the last person I should be quizzing about another man's death."

He draped one arm over my shoulder. "No worries, Little Miss Murphy. I'm not leaving this planet quite yet. Not without a hell of a fight."

"That way." I pointed my thumb left. "A little more."

Despite the Merc's open front door, Tracy couldn't hear me. With one hand, she gripped the top of the pony wall separating the display window from the shop. In the other, she held a heavy black music stand. She needed to move it two inches, to avoid crushing a box of Candy's pink marshmallows.

"Got it," I called. Inside, Tracy added sheet music, then climbed down the step stool and came out to join me. We'd borrowed old clarinets, a dented bugle, even a plastic ukulele for our tribute to the festival. Nothing the sun could damage.

Only a hurricane could touch Candy's marshmallows.

The other window held our DIY picnic baskets. So popular a couple of other village joints now offered them. I didn't mind—one shop with a new offering is a gimmick. Two or three make a trend, and trends make money.

"How's Lou Mary coming along?" I asked as we surveyed Tracy's handiwork.

Tracy grunted. "She can almost tell truffles from fudge. For her next trick, maybe she'll figure out the difference between black cap preserves and raspberry."

"We'll make a foodie out of her yet." Funny to hear a woman who washed down grocery store maple bars with Diet Coke grouse about another woman's lack of taste, but we all have our blind spots. "She's got a good eye. She can help with the displays."

"That's my job."

Tracy's insecurity was starting to wear on me. "We're all in this together, Trace. Lou Mary rearranging the pottery isn't going to cost you a job. Hiring her means you can do the job you wanted, as the resident chocolatier."

Her jaw quivered and she nodded rapidly, then swept inside, her long skirt swooshing behind her.

I followed more slowly. After our heart-to-heart about Adam, Tanner and I had kept on walking, saying nothing more about chemo or

Minneapolis. He had never mentioned giving half the business to Adam, or leaving him the rest in his will, though he had to know I knew.

But our walk had given me an idea.

I ignored the siren call of fresh Roasted Tomato Pesto and followed my thoughts upstairs. I sank into my chair, leaned forward, elbows on my knees.

My thinking pose.

It made sense that Tanner turned to Adam in time of distress. He trusted Adam more than anyone. The feeling was mutual—or almost. I liked to think Adam trusted me that deeply.

Adam could run a camp like clockwork. He could run a recreation program for kids. Run a bar tab, or a half-marathon.

But a textile and clothing company with a million moving parts?

No. I didn't think that's what Tanner needed from Adam. That would be like asking a leopard to become a zebra.

I sat back, arms crossed. Bad metaphor, but it got to the heart of the matter: We all have our skills. Tanner might wish for a business partner he trusted like he trusted Adam. But asking Adam to take over if Tanner couldn't keep on would be like me asking Nick or Chiara to take over the Merc.

Or my mother, who'd loved the Merc so much she'd nearly run it into the ground. Molly had other dreams, and her little brother Henry hadn't finished school yet. My other cousins had their own lives. For better or worse, I was the one with the bone-deep attachment to this pile of bricks.

Tanner could no more move out here for treatment and run his business from a distance than I could pick up and move to Minneapolis.

But there was one thing I could do.

I grabbed my phone while the computer warmed up. Sent Adam a text: I HAVE A PLAN. LOVE YOU.

Right now, I needed to update our Facebook page, schedule a few Tweets, and add the latest products to our e-commerce site. My fingers flew across the keys, pausing when my phone let out a short buzz. A text from Adam: GOOD PLAN. I smiled.

Updates done, I opened the Spreadsheet of Suspicion. Dashed downstairs for a refreshing cold drink. My mother had set out samples of her Roasted Tomato Pesto and Kalamata Olive Tapenade. It would be cruel to tempt the customers with the aromas and not let them sample the goods. Not to mention missing a business opportunity. A happy tongue and tummy send *Buy! Buy!* signals to the brain.

I slathered samples on crackers piled high on a napkin, snatched my water, and scooted upstairs.

Sat at the desk and pondered the clues and questions surrounding Gerry Martin's death.

First question: Was it murder? I thought so, and Ike Hoover agreed. Tanner had seen a shove, not a slip and fall during a heated confrontation. Not to mention that days later, no one had come forward confessing to an argument gone wrong.

I entered Y for yes.

Who? Big question. Nearly everyone upset with Martin had a reason to be in or near the village between nine thirty, when Michelle sold him coffee, and ten-ish, when Adam and Tanner clambered up the rocks to his body.

The body. Gerry Martin. You can know how old a guy was when he made his first recording and his first stage appearance. How many Grammy nominations, how many wins. How many gold and platinum albums he'd earned, how many songs had appeared in movies.

You can know everything someone wants you to know, and still not know what drove them.

I thought over what I knew. He'd first come to Jewel Bay a few years ago, at Rebecca's urging. He'd become a festival regular, leading to plans to open a recording studio and a sort of B&B for bands. But he'd dropped the idea. Why? Because his relationship with Rebecca was ending? Or was that a chicken and egg thing? Or because Barber, who'd made himself a major figure in the festival organization, had wanted him gone?

And would his decision to drop the studio plans and quit the festival have angered someone enough to shove him off a cliff?

Anyone besides Rebecca?

Suspect everyone, I reminded myself, and made a note in the Motive column where it intersected the row labeled with her name.

The next question was Martin's shoes. I typed in *city boots*. Pulled up the photos from Derek D'Orazi's phone. Doesn't matter how sharp and clear the photos are if the object is blurry and imprecise. And these were. Because of a struggle, or because the dirt could not hold an impression? In other spots along the trail, dense, heavy soil held moisture from Friday's rains, but in this spot, the soil was thin and slippery.

Deadly.

I stared at the footprints again. Mostly large, from work boots or sturdy shoes, worn by the EMTs and firemen. On closer look, I saw a few undefined, barely discernible prints that could have been Martin's, or my imagination. A few partials, vaguely like running shoes. No surprise—dozens of people walk and run the trail every day.

That was a call for forensics experts. I had no idea how they study footprints, what databases they consult, how they match a pattern to a shoe. But most of us change shoes regularly. My sister and I have identical spring green Mary Janes, in the same size, and nearly every woman who works at Le Panier or the bistro wears cherry red rubber clogs. Shoes aren't one-of-a-kind, unlike fingerprints or DNA.

Which reminded me of the paper cup. Le Panier was hardly alone in using plain white paper cups. I'd seen the same ones yesterday at Perk Up.

I added a column for the cup to the spreadsheet and put a question mark in the top row, Martin's row. As a clue, the cup was too generic to be much help. At least to me. Like the footprints, I left it to the professionals.

One last addition, to the Gabby Drake row: *Push? Innocent—meaning Ann and music—or ???*

I stood to stretch as best I could in a room barely eight by ten with an angled ceiling. My grandfather had tucked this space under the eaves in the days when everyone in this end of the valley bought groceries at the Merc, and a trip to Pondera was a major outing. He'd used extra planking from the Orchard house, cut and milled nearby, for the floors. No wonder I loved the place. It was my heritage.

Back to work, Erin. That spreadsheet isn't going to finish itself.

I hadn't been able to identify who Martin might have run into Saturday morning at Le Panier, but I could make a few guesses. Most of my suspects, as it turned out. Rebecca lived and worked in the village. Barber lived within spitting distance of the trailhead. Either of them could easily have seen Martin, and taken the opportunity to confront him.

Sam. Ike put him high on the list. He claimed an alibi but admitted he couldn't prove it—not even his own wife could testify that he'd been home, working on the compressor-cooler thingie all that morning.

The Drakes. They were staying close by. Any of the three of them was a possibility.

I sighed and rolled my chair back. My list was too long. How could I rule anyone in or out?

"Think sideways," I'd once heard a speaker on creative problem solving counsel. I tipped my ear toward my shoulder. Not what the expert had in mind, but it couldn't hurt. I desperately needed a new perspective.

Which made me think of Perspective, Rebecca's gallery. A good name, though much of the art did little for me emotionally. Odd as it had been to see her in Pondera, it had been stranger to see her cozy up with the Drakes.

Why were they out here? And what project had gotten them so jazzed over lunch?

"Erin? I got your text. You've got orders for me to pack?"

I swiveled toward the door. Straight from her after-school training run, Zayda George wore hot-pink-and-purple stretch capris with lime-green-and-turquoise runners. Long gone the silver eyebrow stud the teenager had worn last winter, a detail that nearly did her in. She'd tied back her white-blond hair, inherited from the Icelandic half of her family. Mottled purple guitar picks hung from her ears.

A festival fashion trend that had escaped me.

"Hey, great to see you. When's graduation? Three weeks?"

"Two," she said, sounding both excited and nervous.

I grabbed a file folder full of printouts and led the way to the basement. Once a repository for disorganized Christmas decorations and antique spiderwebs, it now held the key to the future.

Or so all the small-business gurus say. When those gurus urge e-commerce, they forget to tell you you're going to need a system.

But if there's one thing I'm good at it, it's working out a system.

So far, I had a long table with slots underneath for flat boxes in a range of sizes, a giant roll of bubble wrap with its own cutter mounted on one end. I had shelves loaded with the products we ship most often—jams and jellies, pestos and sauces, and dried pasta. With any luck, we'd be doing enough mail-order traffic in our drink line, Luci's soaps, and Ray's products to fill another set of shelves by summer's end. And I had two teenagers who came in after school and on Saturdays, trading off when Zayda had a track meet or Dylan had a theater rehearsal.

And I had nearly a dozen new orders, plus three cartons for Tanner. Once orders picked up—this summer, if all went well—we might have a dedicated iPad and printer in the basement for orders and packing slips.

Zayda taped boxes while I pulled the first orders, all gift packs of Montana preserves.

"I hear you and Dylan both got into film school. Congrats."

"Yeah." The tape made a shrieky-stretchy sound as she yanked the dispenser across a cardboard seam. "Thanks."

We worked in silence. She set the three boxes on the table, laid a square of bubble wrap in each one, and positioned the cardboard divider. I slid in the jars, double-checking the packing slips, then peeled off the shipping labels. Zayda sealed the boxes, I added labels, and we stacked them at the end of the table. The business gurus also forgot to say don't set up your packing and shipping station in the basement, but we had no other option. I consider box-lugging part of my workout routine.

"Erin," she finally said, as she stacked the next batch of box flats on the table. "How did you know Adam is The One?"

An out-of-the-blue question, until I remembered that Dylan's mother worried about the kids' eloping. *Tread carefully, Erin.*

"By dating a lot of guys who weren't." I checked off the items on the next packing slip. Some lucky soul was getting an Italian feast in a box.

"But did you think they were? And then find out they were douche-canoes?"

I capped the stinky marker and looked her straight on.

"Dylan thinks it's stupid to go to the same school, take the same classes, and pay for two dorm rooms. To share the bathroom sink with strangers when we already know we want to be together." Her words spilled over each other like water rushing over the boulders in the Jewel River. "He thinks we should get married. This summer."

"What do you think?"

Her dark Greek eyes filled and she clung to the edge of the table. I snared a stool and rolled it toward her.

"Sit," I ordered, and she sat.

It would be easy to say that if she was sure, she wouldn't be asking, but that wouldn't be fair. "Zayda, you're both young. Which is a terrible thing to say, I know. But it's true. And you are going to get your heart broken, whether in a relationship, or a job, or some other part of life. You can't protect yourself from that."

She sniffed, eyes on me.

"You know Polly Paulson and Bunny Burns?" I continued. "They're twins—Paulette and Bernadette Easter. We went all the way through school together. Bunny married our classmate Rob Burns and Polly married Pat Paulson, who was a year ahead of us, in a double wedding six months after graduation."

"They're still married," she said.

"Yep. And I'd be surprised if they don't go to the grave married." I picked up the marker again. "And none of them has ever lived anywhere but Jewel Bay. Polly works in the drug store and Pat drives the Coca-Cola truck. Rob and Bunny bought the brewery his dad started. It's the life they chose, and I think they're happy. But it's not the life you've talked about, traveling the world making movies."

"You sound like my mother." She made air quotes. "*Keep your options open.*"

"More like keep your heart open. Can you do what you want with your life if you and Dylan tie the knot now?" The ticking wall clock caught my attention. "Oh, pooh. We've gotta get these to the post office. Tanner's boxes can wait."

We zipped the last few packages together and loaded them into my car. I tossed her my keys.

"Erin." Zayda sniffed and wiped her nose on her long sleeve. "Thanks."

I held up a hand in acknowledgment and watched her drive off.

Telling other people what to do is easy. Running my own life? Not so much.

Twenty-Four

I grabbed another bottle of mineral water and sank onto a red stool. Too many thoughts, too many emotions, too many of them not my own.

My mother stood on the other side of the stainless steel counter, her garden print apron slightly wilted, her olive skin flushed from the kitchen heat and steam.

"Smells great, Mom."

"Thank you, Erin. I find few things more satisfying than sending a new creation out into the world. A tad bit terrifying, too."

My mother, terrified? Wonders never cease.

"What's bothering you, darling? Not the investigation?"

I ached to tell her. Because I wasn't entirely sure what to do about Adam. I knew my heart, and I thought I knew his. And unlike young Zayda, I knew what I wanted.

But I didn't know how to get from here to *there*.

I put on a smile. Not the time or place, even though she'd asked. I didn't want to interfere with her happiness.

"Um, yeah. Kinda. There's so much I don't know yet. Gerry Martin's relationship with Rebecca Whitman, for one."

"Rebecca's not easy to get to know," my mother said. "But she loves Jewel Bay."

The cold bubbles tickled my throat. "Seems like she's planted herself pretty deep, snatching up property."

"Not to mention propping up a few businesses, in return for a stake. When Ned made noises last summer about cutting back, she approached him about buying a controlling share of the bar. He sent her packing, but that's what gave him the idea to offer me the building."

And he'd started training his grandson to take over. My mother had become Ned's landlord, but she kept her fingers out of his business. Except for remodeling the women's room into a room women didn't mind using, and making a few other improvements that Ned liked to call "all that la-di-dah." But he said it with a twinkle in his eye.

How, I wondered, had Rebecca's investments played in to her arrangements with Gerry Martin? Had that been what he meant when he accused her of "false pretenses"? Terms of the deal that weren't what he'd expected?

Or because she'd lost the position that gave her the ability to boost his brand?

"Is she difficult to work with?" I asked.

"Better to say she drives a hard bargain. I'm sure that's part of her success. And successful women sometimes trigger resentment."

"From men and women."

"I'm afraid that's true. Darling, why don't you bring the boys by for dinner tonight? You and I can have a little talk."

"Can't. I do need to come over—there's a few things stashed in the house that I've been meaning to take off your hands. But we promised

Tanner a boat ride and a picnic on the dock. Spare me some of that new pesto?"

She set a jar, not yet labeled, on the counter. "Lou Mary seems to be settling in well."

"She seemed worried earlier, but she's doing great. You never did say why you wanted me to hire her, but you were right."

"Excuse me." A woman's voice broke in and I swiveled toward a plump woman about my age standing by the meat cooler. "You work here, right? A friend recommended your meat."

"All local." I slid off the stool. Lou Mary was helping a customer at the sidewalk produce cart, and I didn't see Tracy. "Local pigs and cows, local butcher."

We stood at the cooler, discussing cuts, how the sausage was flavored, and our wild game offerings. She chose several varieties, and I followed her to the front counter.

I filled her shopping bag and took her credit card. "When's your baby due?" The moment the words were out, I wished I could take them back.

"I'm not pregnant," she said. "Just fat."

"What are you planning to serve with all that beautiful meat?" Lou Mary asked, trailing her own customer through the front door. "We have fresh pasta and sauces. And asparagus so tender you can practically run it under hot water and it's done."

Bless the woman, she bought a pound of asparagus, fresh linguine, and basil pesto, and accepted a free trial-size bar of lavender soap.

"I can't believe I did that," I said when the door closed behind the woman's ample rear end. "I so know better. Thanks for the rescue."

"I've stuck my foot in my mouth so many times," Lou Mary said, "I have scars on my ankles. Part of the territory."

"That's some consolation. Things going okay?"

"Oh, yes. Honestly, I never knew how many interesting products the Merc carries. I'm going to try that special sauerkraut tonight with a pork roast."

"And Tracy?"

She put a hand on my arm, her turquoise and carnelian ring so large I wondered how she got it on and off. "She's a lovely young woman, reassessing her life, like you are. It's natural, at your age."

"You're quite remarkable, you know that?"

She laughed, a deep, throaty, ex-smoker's laugh. The door to the back hall opened and Tracy emerged, smoothing her skirt.

"What's so funny?"

"Only me making an idiot of myself with a customer," I said.

"Oh." Tracy let out a breathy grunt and rolled her eyes, her enameled cat earrings swaying. I thought of the guitar pick earring so out of place, but not clearly evidence. "Happens to me at least once a day, rain or shine."

Lou Mary gave me a wink.

"Erin, half the people who've been in here this week say the sheriff thinks Sam killed Gerry Martin," Tracy said. "That Martin was flirting with Jennifer, and Sam snapped. I can't believe it."

"Jennifer *is* very attractive," Lou Mary said. "A runner's legs."

"I agree—I can't picture Sam as a killer. But Martin rubbed a lot of people the wrong way."

The front door opened and we all straightened, expecting a customer, though not the one who jumped over the threshold, feet rattling in his hand-me-down brown cowboy boots.

"Auntie Erin! Mommy says you can give me a marshmallow for an afternoon snack."

"You bet." Candy's specialty does have its fans, Landon among them. I handed my nephew his treat and gave my staff an apologetic look. "Mind if we step out for a few minutes? I can't get far—Zayda took my car."

My two very different employees gave me nearly identical smiles.

"Are you investigating?" Lou Mary whispered.

My turn to wink.

∞

"You can let go of my hand now, Auntie," Landon said. "We're not on the street anymore."

I let him loose. He dashed to the Playhouse door and tugged on the handle, but it didn't budge. Before I could help him, the door opened from the inside, and a tall man in his sixties, guitar in hand, beamed down.

"Welcome, little man." He flashed me a grin I couldn't help but return. "And you, pretty lady."

"Why, thank you, kind sir."

"Jackson Mississippi Boyd, at your service."

Landon's eyes widened, then he started jumping up and down. "Mississippi! I've got Mississippi!"

After I explained the game to our new friend, he invited Landon to sit with him and play a song or two while he waited for his sound check.

"We came to town to see, That old tattooed lay-dee," the older man sang, Landon bouncing in his boots.

I leaned against a pillar, watching. Somewhere, maybe back in Mississippi, Jackson Boyd had raised children, or sang songs with happy grandchildren.

"Isn't he great? He's on the bill tonight. A mix of jazz and blues, old Southern style." Michelle the barista stood beside me, a plastic tub in her arms.

"I'm sorry I'll miss that. You need a hand?" She gave me the tub and brought in the last load. At the concession stand, I unpacked napkins,

210

straws, and stirrers while she set out paper cups. Those ubiquitous white paper cups.

Across the lobby, Landon sat with his new friend, the center of attention and lapping it up.

"What next?" I said, and Michelle pointed to the beer bottles waiting by the fridge.

Job done, I took a shot in the dark. "Michelle, you worked at Red's Friday night during Gerry Martin's last concert, didn't you?" Part-time barista, part-time bartender—the food and drink equivalent of the retail ladies.

She straightened, fingers gripping the neck of a wine bottle. "Yeahhh."

"So, Martin acted pretty upset that night, and I'm trying to figure out why."

"Ask Jenny Kraus, not me." Her empty hand flew toward her mouth, but she stopped it part way and started fiddling her hair, rubbing the back of her neck. Darned if she wasn't wearing guitar pick earrings, too—elongated black-and-gold picks.

"What did you see, Michelle? Or hear?"

She blinked rapidly, as if she could make this nightmare go away. What had her so nervous?

"I know what people are saying, that Sam suspected Jenny of fooling around on him with Martin, and he lost it. Sam, I mean. I can't believe that. I mean, I don't know what was up—if he broke it off and she was begging him to take her back. Martin, I mean. Or—or—I don't know, Erin. Every break, Jenny was after him, trying to get him to talk to her. But that's all I know. And Sam—he would never."

Behind me, a chorus of musicians and crew joined for the final lines: *"What we liked best was upon her chest, the shores of Waikiki!"*

When I turned back to Michelle, she was dumping coffee beans into a grinder, brows furrowed, lips pursed. I rested my hand on the counter. Why her observations had been difficult to reveal, I didn't know, but I wasn't going to push her. "Thanks. 'Preciate it."

"Auntie, he's fun!" Landon said. "I gotta pee." He clattered off toward the men's room.

"Thank you," I told Jackson Mississippi Boyd. "He'll be talking about you for weeks."

"He's a pistol. Says you're like a grown-up Hank the Cow Dog, sniffing around Gerry Martin's death."

My mouth fell open. "Where did he hear that? Not from me."

"Little pitchers have big ears. Are you? Investigating?"

"Unofficially. Did you know Martin?"

His black eyes narrowed and he poked his cheek with his tongue. "Our paths crossed a few times this past year, on the club circuit."

"And?"

The tongue moved to the other side. "An SOB. Unofficially."

"Not talking about me, I hope," a wiry man with a wispy red goatee said.

"Leo Patrick! Haven't seen you in a month of Sundays." Boyd enveloped the younger man in a bear hug. They released each other and Boyd made introductions. "You heard about Gerry Martin, I s'pose. Fell off a cliff. Or more likely, got himself shoved off. That's why the performance schedule's all cattywampus."

So, speculation was spreading, despite official silence.

"Yeah. Bummer." Patrick wrinkled his nose and sighed heavily. To me, he said, "Jackson's right. The guy could play, but he didn't think anybody else could."

"Believed his own press?"

"When somebody hits the big-time young, like he did, it can be hard living up to all the potential everyone claims to see," Patrick added. "I'm kinda glad nobody thought I had any talent when I started."

"Peaked early and he knew it." Boyd rested his hands on top of his guitar case. "That's why he was such a pain in the a—sorry."

My nephew was back, waiting impatiently for his new friend. I pulled cash out of my pocket. "Landon, will you buy Mr. Boyd a Coke or an iced tea? As our thanks for teaching you a new song." One guaranteed to stick in my ears for days. "And whatever Mr. Patrick would like."

"That's kind of you," Boyd replied, though the other man declined. "Iced tea, son. No lemon, lotsa sugar."

Landon headed for the concession stand. I had one more question for Boyd and his friend. "Did either of you hear anything about plans Martin had to build a recording studio in the area?"

"Izzat what he was talking about?" Boyd said. "Last winter, where were we? Blues festival in Tallahassee. He was bragging about a studio, saying we were all gonna wanna come play and stay. Some woman footing the bill. We got here, and I didn't hear one peep about it. Bet she figured out he weren't a big draw no more, and got out while she could."

That made things clear as Mississippi mud. Who broke with who? Were those the false pretenses?

And had they led to murder?

"Everybody's talking about recording," Patrick said. "Heard a board member say they're this close to bringing in a big name next year for a live concert album. Wants students to record with him, go on tour."

News to me. The artist Dave Barber had hoped to recruit?

Landon returned with Boyd's iced tea.

"Thank you, little man." The musician crouched and held out his hand. "It's sure been a pleasure to meet you. You come by and sing with me again, you hear?"

We thanked both men and wished them good luck this week. They'd given me a few more pieces of the puzzle. If only I knew what picture they made.

"Em-EYE-ess-ess-EYE-ess-ess-EYE-PEEPEE-EYE," Landon chanted as we strolled out the Playhouse door. Saturday's close call fresh in my mind's eye, I grabbed his hand. "Auntie, I've got twenty-seven states already."

"At this rate, you'll have all fifty by the Fourth of July."

"Forty-nine." His voice drooped. "I'll never get Hawaii."

In the gallery, Landon allowed his mother to hug him, then ran to the back room for his Fifty States Coloring Book. He wanted to finish it in time to show off at the kindergarteners' end-of-school party.

I stroked the soft leather tri-fold bag.

"Sorry I made such a fuss the other day," Chiara said. "About Mom and all."

"What? A Murphy girl overreacting? That's never happened before."

One corner of her lips twitched, and our eyes met.

"Mom wants Nick to walk her down the aisle." I swung the bag over my shoulder, then bumped it around with my elbow and hip to see how it fit the curves. "I don't know the chemo schedule yet. Or if Adam can be here."

"Little sis, if you want Adam to be sure you want him to come back, 'fess up. Shoot straight. Choose your metaphor, but speak your mind. Expecting him to know without you coming clean is the road to disappointment."

I hugged myself, rocking back on one foot. The bag slipped over my hip and hit me in the tail. Loaded with all my gear, it might do some damage.

In my Seattle days, every man I dated had been more fascinated by his work than by me. I responded by diving into my own work as deeply. If instead, I'd played the field and gone out on the town every weekend, would I have a teensy bit better understanding of the opposite sex?

It was no sure thing. I hung the bag back on its tree branch hook. Because as wonderful as they are, men just aren't like other people.

Twenty-Five

Adam eased the boat into the Pinskys' floating dock like an old salt. His steady hand on the tiller and his balance on the waves gave him a confidence I found most attractive.

Not to mention his shapely legs and firm backside.

Last summer, Bob had handed Adam the helm on a test run, and quickly pronounced that we could take the power boat out anytime we wanted—as long as we replaced any beer we drank.

Line at the ready, Tanner jumped on to the dock, ready to crouch and tie off. Adam cut the engine, and for a moment, all I heard were the waves lapping the gravel shore.

And the osprey shrieking in a tall tree, high above us.

I closed my eyes. The waves rocked the boat gently, like a lullaby.

"All ashore," Adam called, in a teasing tone. I stood and took the hand he held out, then stepped on to the long gray dock.

"I can't believe that shoreline," Tanner said. "I thought I knew lakes, but this is gorgeous. And those cliffs by the park and the public boat launch. Wow."

I shuddered. Adam squeezed my hand.

The dock led to a stone patio and an area Liz called "the outdoor kitchen." The only cooking I'd ever seen anyone do there was char a slab of beef or grill a hunk of salmon, exactly what I was about to do.

Adam fired up the grill while I got out the salads and fish, complete with Ray's best marinade. Thank goodness for take-out, the perfect side dish for a busy day investigating.

In minutes, we were seated around a swanky glass and metal table, toasting a glorious evening, despite a hint of May chill. Clear skies to the west. Tonight's concert was indoors, at the Playhouse, and long before the murder, I'd given the Merc's tickets to our produce suppliers as a thank-you. But I didn't want rain on anyone's parade.

"So I'm good to head back with you next week," Adam was saying. "Just need to make sure the kitchen boss finishes up her orders so she can get the base camp stocked. And nail down my assistant. And hire a new wrangler."

"It's not like you're going to the moon, man. You can text, and e-mail. Or call."

Adam leaned back in his chair, beer bottle in hand. "I admit, I did not appreciate what a pain hiring is back when I was one of those college kids who'd drop a job in a flash if a friend got a permit to float the Smith, or needed a fourth for a week in the wilderness. Notice, shmotice."

Not exactly like needing a fourth at bridge. My appetite for the outdoors didn't match Adam's, but I couldn't see either of us curling up with Hoyle in our golden years.

"This salmon is terrific, Erin. You and your family are spoiling me with good food."

"I'll send a care package with your staff gifts. Although you might not have much appetite." Cancer, the unwanted guest who won't take a hint and go away. "Not that you do now."

"No worries." He speared a couple of farfalle—bow ties—dressed with basil pesto, tomatoes, and pine nuts. "I'll never be too sick for your mother's pasta."

We ate and drank, chatting about hiking and music, Minnesota and Montana. Adam and Tanner cleared the table while I packed up the leftovers. Adam set the basket on the slate counter and wrapped his arms around me.

"I'm going to miss you," he said in a low voice.

"I know," I whispered as I worked. "But you need to go. He needs you. And I'll—"

His breath was warm on my ear. "I was hoping—"

"Hey, you two, take a load of this sunset."

We grabbed our beers and strolled down the dock to watch the colors. A few light clouds had moved in, those long, stretched-out clouds that so often tint the western sky in glorious shades of purple and orange. I sat between the guys, feet safely above the chilly water.

I'll be here when you get back, I hadn't gotten to say. What had Adam left unsaid? Something like *I was hoping you'd say you need me, too*? But he knew that, didn't he? I smiled up at him. He slid his arm behind my back and tucked the top of my head beneath his chin, then shifted his gaze to the horizon.

He knew.

Wednesday morning dawned uneventfully, always cause for celebration. I celebrated with a double latte and a croissant. I'd worked off the calories in advance, walking into town—the guys had driven me home the night before and my car was parked out back, wherever Zayda had left it. The birds didn't seem to mind me singing along.

I was busy brewing chai for our daily sample when Tracy arrived, bleary-eyed, her outfit lacking the usual panache. She plunked her breakfast on the counter.

"Feels like I never left. I made truffles till ten p.m."

"A cup and a half," I sang out, then stuck the scoop back in the canister. "A cup and three-quarters."

She waited patiently, amused. I finished with the spices and reached for the water pitcher. "Making dreams come true takes work, and risk," I said. "But you'll get there."

Her eyes turned serious. "Thanks."

Mid-morning, I decided to follow up on Molly's intel and my questions about the festival board. I found my car in the next block up Back Street, between the antique shop and Rebecca's gallery. Zayda must have run into parking trouble when she came back from the post office. Festival events did bring folks back into town early, for dinner before the concert. I hopped in and zoomed up the highway.

"He's on the phone." Marv Alden's wife stood inside the heavy wooden door, a dark finish I couldn't identify. "Is he expecting you?"

"Erin! To what do we owe the pleasure?" Alden appeared at his wife's shoulder. To her, he said, "Crisis averted. They'll honor the contract."

"I was hoping we could chat about Gerry Martin."

He ran his fingers over his smooth head. "Popular subject this morning. I'm late for a meeting at the clubhouse. Ride down with me, and we'll talk on the way."

The Aldens lived near the golf course, in a small development of gracious homes with grand views. Wood, stone, and sky—the Montana dream.

He returned a moment later, jingling his keys, and gestured for me to follow. I assumed we were headed for the garage. Instead, he unlocked a small stone-and-stucco building I'd passed without noticing. Too small for a guest house. A potting shed, or a pottery studio, maybe.

Inside, a gleaming maroon-and-silver golf cart revealed him as a University of Montana grad with a passion for sport. I hopped on and off we zoomed.

"I was on the phone with a trio in Missoula," he said above the sounds of the whirring engine and the small wheels spinning on the asphalt. "They were scheduled to play with Martin in the finale Saturday night, along with a few other artists. They'd been hoping to cut a record, or whatever they're called these days, with him."

"Meaning record in his studio, or record with him?" I pointed at a squirrel darting into the road. "Watch out."

Alden slowed down, the squirrel sped up, and we drove on. "Both, I think. They wanted the boost his name would give them, and they wanted to use his fancy equipment and engineers, once he got up and running. So with him gone, they had questions."

"A lot of questions going around." I gripped the side rail as he aimed the cart down the hill. A twenty-seven hole golf course, a marina, and hundreds of homes lay between the highway and the lake, once farm country and wildlife paradise. Paradise not fully tamed—homeowners were well-advised to fence their roses and geraniums, and grow their herbs and tomatoes in pots on their patios, away from nipping deer.

"So you're responsible for keeping the artists on the schedule?" I asked. "Aren't you the treasurer?"

"And contracts manager." He slowed to make the big curve, then turned south toward the club's main entrance. "Dave's board chair, but he's hands-on."

"So you've been working closely with Grant Drake," I said.

He shot me a knowing look. "If you're wondering whether I know about Drake's past, I'll tell you what I told Ike Hoover. I researched every member of the board and all the staff before agreeing to join." He stopped for a twosome pulling carts across the road. "It's what I do.

What I did for forty-odd years. Grant and his wife are very well connected. We need them, for access to donors."

Ike knew. Interesting. "But you weren't worried about potential embezzlement?"

"I talked to them. Made sure he was insulated from the money. And increased our insurance limits. We have our problems, but money management isn't one of them."

That sounded reasonable and prudent. It didn't completely convince me that Grant Drake had nothing to do with Gerry Martin's murder. He was too connected—through his daughter, his work on the board, and Ann's friendship with Rebecca, who had her own tangled connections to the late, unlamented Martin.

"Speaking of management, curious that you fired your executive director on the eve of the festival."

"Rebecca? We didn't fire her. She and Dave argued, and she quit." He zipped into a parking slot next to the clubhouse.

Had she told me she'd been fired, or let me think that? "Over what?" I was almost afraid to ask.

Alden clasped his fist around the golf cart keys. "Let's say, the extent of the festival's future relationship with Gerry Martin. But we're big kids. Situations become heated sometimes. She didn't need to quit."

"This is a small town. It's hard to work with people you don't like." Or trust.

"Does everyone in town like you?"

A rhetorical question, I hoped. "Point taken. Par for the course."

He inclined his head, as if pleased that I understood. "You know, I think Rebecca's been good for the festival. But she's got to become more of a community player. Now, if you'll excuse me. Our sponsors need reassurance. I'm meeting the rep from the music school right now."

A few minutes later, I trekked between fairways, careful to keep to the cart path and watch for stray shots, all while projecting the Spreadsheet of Suspicion in my mind's eye.

Martin's death was a tragedy, but it would not stop the festival, thank goodness. Alden had a firm grip on the money. Barber rubbed me the wrong way, as his show-off moment had rubbed Martin, and he wasn't in the clear for the murder. He'd wanted Martin gone for his own reasons, which I was now fairly sure didn't involve money—at least not money in his pocket. If Jackson Mississippi Boyd and his buddy were to be believed, Barber's motivation could be as simple and as complicated as wanting to bring in bigger names, to pump up the festival. And boost his own chances for a moment in the spotlight.

Why had Rebecca lied? Had she expected the board to fire her? Or misunderstood?

Thinking about the board brought me back to Grant Drake. Alden knew his sins and didn't fear them. A town that depends so heavily on the arts needs to cultivate the avid supporters and put them to work. It helped that this one had a talented daughter he and his wife desperately wanted to succeed.

Could one of them have joined Martin for a quick walk? They were regulars at Le Panier, where Martin had gotten his cappuccino.

With her opera training, surely Ann had the acting skills to hide nearly anything, and Grant had pulled the wool over investors' eyes for years.

What about their bright-eyed daughter? I wasn't convinced that passionate, high-strung Gabby shared her parents' ambitions for her own career, but she'd been bold enough to sidestep Martin's plans for their set and play her own composition instead.

I could see her running after Martin, continuing the fight for control that she'd started on stage. I could see him unleashing a verbal putdown.

I could see her pushing back. When it came to picturing her pushing him off the cliff and not letting on, my visual screen went blank.

But when it comes to life, death, and money, you never know what people will do.

∞

I retrieved my car from the Aldens' driveway. As I neared the grocery store, a glint of sun on metal caught my eye.

"Stay," I commanded, but the driver of the silver Volvo ignored me. She zipped out of the parking lot and zipped in front of me.

"Criminy." I slammed on the brakes. My blue bag and everything else on the passenger seat went flying. My skull thumped against the head rest.

But I'd missed hitting the Volvo, and no one had hit me. "It's all good," I said out loud, trying to convince myself.

I drove down Hill Street, heart racing, and slipped the Subaru into my usual spot behind the Merc. My stuff had spilled all over the floor, so I went around to the passenger door, opened it, and picked up the bag. Beneath it lay a guitar pick earring. Brown streaks on black, like the one I'd found on the lane by my cabin. But that one lay upstairs on my desk.

A sense of fear and dread began a slow crawl up my spine.

Twenty-Six

It took two cups of hot chai to warm me up.

The earring lay on my desk next to the muddy twin I'd found Tuesday morning. Had my new find been in my bag, or my car?

And how had it gotten there?

Only one other person had been in my car recently, not counting the guys.

But I could not imagine a reason Zayda would have been in the woods near my house the night of the storm.

I grabbed my phone. My thumbs flew. LOSE AN EARRING IN MY CAR?

She must have been on her lunch break. Even seniors, even in the run up to graduation, weren't allowed to use their phones in class or passing periods.

DON'T THINK SO! she texted back.

I grabbed my bag and rifled through all the detritus I'd scooped up and stuffed in it. An empty CD jewel case. The cord for my iPod—I wondered where that had gone. Two tubes of lip balm. And a three-by-five card with a note in precise, blocky handwriting.

YOU HAVE YOUR DREAM. DON'T DESTROY MINE.

Whose dream? And how had the note gotten where I would find it?

I set the note on my desk next to the earrings. Had the same person lost both earrings during the storm, one on the road, the other in my car?

But why mess with my car? To scare me, to warn me off the case? It gave me the creeps, it did.

It's a natural reaction, when someone asks about an earring, to reach up and finger your own. I could not imagine the time, or patience, required to weave the earrings Tracy wore today, countless tiny yellow, blue, and red beads in an intricate chevron pattern.

"No clue," she said. "Guitar pick earrings are common. Did you ask at the Playhouse? And where did you find them? One's clean, one's filthy."

"That is where the guitarists are," I said, ignoring her last question.

But the note made the earrings more than an item for the Lost and Found box. I labeled another plastic bag.

At the sheriff's office, a patrol deputy I didn't know told me that Ike had gone to Missoula for the autopsy on Martin's body. "Shoulda been done by now, but they had a backlog. And Deputy Oakland is out on call. Dog poop dispute."

"That stinks."

That made him smile. I explained where I'd found the earrings and index card, and the possible link to Martin's murder. Head tilted, he listened, then reached for the bag. Read my notes. Slapped a chain of custody form on the desk and started to explain the drill.

"I'm familiar with it," I said and initialed where he pointed, acknowledging that I'd collected the evidence and transferred it to him.

"You'll be hearing from the undersheriff or Deputy Oakland," he said.

"I'm planning on it."

Then I climbed back in my trusty Subaru and headed for the hills. Well, the horse barn first. Hills later.

∞

The Lodge, as everyone calls Caldwell's Eagle Lake Lodge and Guest Ranch, is everything you'd expect in a Montana dude ranch, and more. I parked by the main building, a classic log structure with a floor-to-ceiling stone fireplace and a slate patio overlooking the lake. Guests stay in honest-to-goodness cabins, and Western touches surprise the eyes—an old stage coach kids can climb on, a buffalo skull in a garden bed. Not too rustic, not too manicured—it's all just right.

Thank goodness for something "just right."

Truth be told, I wasn't in the mood to ride. I'd have much rather stayed in my shop, playing with jam and soap. But after making a point of reminding Kim at the concert that we had a riding date, I couldn't very well cancel.

And this might be my only chance to convince her to stay. I wasn't doing it for Ike. I was doing it for all of us.

In high school, my grandparents bought me a horse and the Caldwells let me keep her here. These days, they let me ride whenever I want, and I always choose Ribbons, a sweet-tempered chestnut mare. When I reached the stables, she greeted me with a soft neigh and a roll of her neck.

"Hello, girl. Miss me?" I ran one hand down her mane, then scratched behind her ears and rubbed her nose. An eight-hundred-pound pussycat.

Kim was already inside the tack room, gathering her gear under the watchful eye of decades of Rodeo Queens, our official portraits hung on the wall. If I'd been her, I'd have made the chief wrangler take mine down, but she hadn't messed with tradition.

Or more likely, Caldwell pride kept her from acknowledging that she'd been outdone on horseback by upstart me and that it bugged the horsehair out of her.

Thank goodness we were past that, I thought, after we greeted each other. I knew now that losing the rodeo championship to me hadn't been the reason she'd broken off our friendship.

Fifteen years is a long time to misunderstand the woman you once considered your best friend.

A few minutes later, we rode out of the corral, Ribbons content to follow Chukkers, Kim's big bay, up the trail. The mare stepped easily around the soft muddy spots. Alongside the trail lay a fallen spruce, eighty or ninety feet long, the fresh saw cut stinging the air. The Lodge's crews must have spent hours cleaning up after the storm.

The horse's breath came smooth and steady as we climbed the switchbacks. The shadows were cool, and I was glad for my fleece and the slicker rolled up behind me. A few larch and aspen punctuated the dense dark green stands of pine, fir, and spruce, and I drank in the delicious spring smell.

Eventually, the trail broke out into a flat-rock clearing and a valley vista. We paused, still mounted.

"How could anybody see all this," Kim said, "and not believe in heaven?"

"You need to come home. To stay."

"And do what? Wrangle horses for a living? Spend my days shepherding guests? Make sure they have a good time and don't get kicked in the head by a colt or knocked off a sailboat into the lake?"

"You need to go back to the sheriff's department."

Chukkers stepped sideways, then forward, responding to Kim's slightest movement.

I barreled on. "You're a good cop, Kim. It's the work you were meant to do."

She stared at me for a long moment, then whirled her horse around and broke into a canter.

Ribbons craned her neck, asking me what to do. "Slow and steady, girl," I said, and we moseyed up the trail.

We found them at the stream, swollen with spring runoff. Chukkers drank thirstily, while Kim pitched pine cones into the water. I dismounted and let Ribbons join her buddy.

"Look, Kim, I know you think I don't know why you became a cop—"

"How do you know what I think?"

"So tell me."

"I thought for sure you'd be on Kyle's side, begging me to come home and take my place at the ranch. Since you gave up your life for your family business."

"Is that what you think? No, I came back to Jewel Bay and the Merc because it's what I wanted. I'm living my dream." Part of it, anyway. No point bringing up my quandary over Adam and Tanner. "You love horses, but you're not burning to run a guest lodge. Your passion is justice."

"And if I went back on the job, would that stop you from investigating? You scare me half to death. You got lucky, and now you think—"

"Is that what you think, when I succeed? That I got lucky?"

"Erin, don't pick a fight. You're smart and determined, especially when danger threatens what you love, whether it's people or this place. But that's not the same as training."

I sighed. She had a point. "See what I mean? You look back to when my dad died and you see a mistake, but it put you on the path you were supposed to take."

She let out a long breath and slouched on a giant boulder, folding her arms. "Things change."

227

In an instant, everything can change. A car hits a patch of ice on a bridge. A man tumbles down a rocky cliff. Or a woman sees the light strike the zipper on a friend's jacket.

And in that instant, I understood something else. Adam wouldn't be Mr. Right if he didn't take his commitments to his friends seriously. I loved that about him. Now I saw that Tanner had made his plans for the future not to force Adam to move back to Minneapolis and make T-shirts. But because he trusted Adam to manage a situation too big and daunting to figure out himself. Tanner had known instinctively that he had to focus his energy on recovering. On living. Not on making plans for what would happen if he died.

But he never meant for Adam to give up his life, any more than my mother had meant for me to give up mine when she asked me to come home and run the Merc. Any more than I meant to let Kim walk away from the career she loved.

I stood and took a step toward her. "Don't you dare stop being a cop. Don't you dare give that up because of some twisted idea that you owe me and my family your sacrifice."

Her mouth fell open and she shook her head. "You don't understand. I only became a cop because of what I did to your family."

"You didn't do anything to us. Don't you get that?" I was shouting and I didn't care. "The only person responsible for what happened to my father is the killer. You were a kid who misunderstood what you saw. And it was too painful, so you hid it instead of speaking up. You weren't being malicious. You were honestly torn. I don't blame you. None of us blames you."

Her blue eyes filled, her jaw on the verge of a quiver. "How can that be true? Your parents treated me like another daughter, and I—"

I knew what she was going to say, and I couldn't let her. "No. You did not betray us. I know you. You could never do that."

She slumped back against the rock and buried her face in her hands. She was sobbing now. I stepped closer, my hand on her arm.

"Kim, if you truly don't want to rejoin the department, don't do it for us. But I've seen you work. I know how good you are at it. If one good thing came from my father's death, it's you discovering your passion. At least, that's how it looks to me."

At the edge of the water, Ribbons let out a soft neigh, and I took my oldest, dearest friend in my arms while she cried.

∞

"I need to get to the Merc," I said, after we finished grooming the horses and stashing our tack.

"Five minutes won't hurt. Cookies and lemonade," Kim said. Like we were kids again.

"Five minutes. The Drakes baffle me," I said as we walked toward the Lodge. "They're pushy stage parents, hoping to create a brilliant career for their daughter, but what else are they after?"

"And did he join the board for purely charitable reasons, or is he working some other angle?" Kim said. I'd told her everything I'd learned on our ride back.

"Marv Alden seems confident that Grant can't get to the money or do the festival any harm. They're social climbers, determined to be important, whether it's New York society or the little town in the big woods."

Kim opened the side door and we walked in to the dining room. Kyle emerged from the kitchen with a fresh tray of Snickerdoodles. "Perfect timing," he called.

I poured a glass of iced tea spiked with lemonade. "Kyle, you know the Drakes, don't you? I think they stayed here Gabby's first year at the festival."

"She's blond, former singer." He drew a shape in the air with one hand. "He wants you to know he used to be important. One kid, more interested in her guitar than the horses or the pool."

"And here I thought you never stuck your nose out of the kitchen." I reached for a cookie.

"I'm trying to be more involved with the entire operation." He pulled out a peeled-log chair and sank on to the leather seat. "And rope my cousin in, too. But seeing the two of you together makes me think that's not going to happen."

Kim and I sat across the table. "What else can you tell us about the Drakes?"

"Not much." His lower lip jutted out as he considered the question. "Nice enough, in that 'we've made it' way. More status-conscious than most of the local rich boys, but that may change after they've been here a year or two."

Not uncommon. "Any tensions that you're aware of? Between them, or with anyone else?"

"Now that you mention it—" He sat forward, teasing tone gone. "We're doing some catering for the festival, and today I ran the lunches up to the Playhouse. The mother and daughter were in the lobby. I don't think they saw me. The kid was saying something like 'don't try to buy me a new teacher—I'll find my own.' Not sure that makes sense."

I shifted my jaw and tapped my teeth together, thinking. "Yeah. Yeah, it does. Thanks."

"Sure." He shook out his ball cap and ran a hand over his hair. "What's going on? You two can't be up to any good."

"Nothing," I said at the same moment as Kim pushed back her chair.

"Yeah," she said. "But I need to tell my dad first. Erin, thanks for the ride and the conversation. It means more to me than—well, I think you know."

230

Kyle watched her walk away, her boot heels ringing on the time-burnished floor. "Don't tell me. She's going back to sheriffing."

I curved my lips but kept my mouth closed.

His shoulders sagged. "I get it. The family biz isn't for everyone. Hey, Adam called, looking for a wrangler."

"He called here?"

"Sure. We hear from lots of kids wanting summer jobs—more than we can hire. That's cool, as long as he doesn't poach my kitchen crew. I'll admit, when he said he was leaving, I wondered if maybe you'd finally give me a chance. But then he said he'll be back mid summer." Kyle's chair legs scraped the floor. His wink didn't tell me whether he was serious or teasing.

But hearing that Adam said he'd be back soon eased a tension I hadn't known I carried.

I walked out the Lodge's front door. The white Monte Verde Winery van idled in the narrow drive, Sam stacking boxes of wine on a dolly.

"Fancy meeting you here," I called.

Had it only been two days since I'd seen him? A long two days, judging by the circles under his eyes, the skin the color of old grapes. His jaw sagged, too. "Sam, what's wrong?"

"You were right, Erin. They do think I killed Gerry Martin. It's all over town. He didn't just fall—he was pushed. They think I was jealous because of the attention he gave Jennifer. But he flirted with every woman. I knew it didn't mean anything."

"She's told them that, right?"

"I don't know what she's told them. We're barely speaking."

Jennifer's secrets weren't mine to tell, but sometimes you have to speak up. Be a buttinsky. "Sam, listen. You have to talk to her. For reasons that have nothing to do with Gerry Martin."

231

I told him what I'd learned from the wine buyer at SavClub and from Donna Lawson. He gripped the handle of the old red dolly.

"That makes sense of a few things," he said, sounding both strained and a little relieved. "Jenny always wants more. None of this 'living in the moment' stuff for her." One side of his mouth curved up, then his face turned sober again. "Her dad was always off chasing the next big thing. He lost his shirt over and over, robbing Peter to pay Paul, telling her mom not to worry, he had everything covered. But he never did."

"Sounds like she's fallen into the same trap."

"I thought we were living the dream, but it wasn't enough for her."

What could I say? She'd treated him the way her father had treated her mother.

"Thank you, Erin," he continued. "Now that I know what's going on, I can make things right."

He tilted the dolly back and rolled it toward the Lodge's front door, his stride as decisive as his words.

There are worse things than being a buttinsky.

Twenty-Seven

Gabby Drake looped her arm through mine and pulled me through the crowd surging toward the theater's inner doors. "I was hoping to find you."

I'd snuck into the Playhouse lobby late for the Wednesday night concert, hoping to avoid my friends and neighbors. All I wanted was to get lost in the music. The downside of being a buttinsky is spending more effort solving other people's problems than my own, and I needed to refill the well.

A young man wearing a student lanyard held the door for us, and Gabby flashed him her million-watt smile as she led me outside. The temperature had dropped several degrees at sunset, and the air held a damp, ominous chill.

"What's up?" I tried to step back to face her, but her clammy fingers gripped my elbow. The bright expression she'd given our doorman was gone. From my sideways angle, her dark eyes appeared even larger and rounder than normal, her customary navy blue eyeliner smeared. Traces of coral lipstick clung to the corner of her mouth, and the tangerine cardigan she'd tossed over her floral print dress was misbuttoned.

"Everyone in town says ... " She paused, then dropped my arm. "Everyone says you're investigating the—the murder, and that you—you know and see things other people don't."

She made it sound like I had ESP or other superpowers, but this was not the time to laugh it off. I met her gaze and held my tongue.

"They say you've solved crimes before the sheriff's people did. That you've gotten them to understand they were focused on the wrong man. On someone innocent."

"Gabby, what's going on?"

"I know that man didn't kill Gerry Martin. The drummer, I mean. Sam." She spoke so quickly I had to lean in close to hear. "I think—Erin, what would you do if you thought you knew who the killer was? But you couldn't stand it. Because if they did it, they did it for you?"

A couple dressed for a night out rushed past us and into the theater. I led Gabby to a bench on the edge of the garden, away from the door. Away from the ears, if not the eyes, of the patrol deputies roaming the village streets. I dug an unopened water bottle out of my blue bag and handed it to her.

She took half a dozen small sips. Her skin glinted with a touch of sweat, a deep flush riding the top of her cheekbones. Tracy would adore her shoulder-grazing beaded earrings. Ann would hate them.

"Now, start at the beginning and tell me what's got you so anxious."

Her breath had returned to normal, but her voice was thin and ragged. "My parents went to the ends of the earth for me. Literally. To an orphanage in the outback of China. You know, you never quite forget that. I mean, I don't remember it—I was fourteen months old. But when you're obviously Chinese and your parents aren't, everyone knows your story just by looking at you."

I'd come from a town where everyone knew my story, but I sensed that this was different.

"My mom gave up her career for me. And my dad closed his financial business so they could help me build my career."

So she didn't know about the legal trouble. She wouldn't hear about it from me.

"They don't think I know they got me into music school. I flubbed the audition, but my mom is an alum and understudied for a woman who's a major donor. I heard her on the phone, practically pleading. They let me fly out and repeat the audition. I found out from other kids that they never do that."

"You must feel pretty lucky."

"Yes, but I also feel terrible. They came out with me two years ago, when I got chosen to study guitar with Gerry. Last year, too. Now they're buying a house here." She fiddled with the cap on the water bottle.

"You're going back to school in the fall, then wherever music takes you. They're moving on to the next phase of their lives."

"They're buying the house so they can worm their way into the jazz world. You should hear them. Whenever they meet someone, they're all on about me, and how I've sung at this festival, and played with that artist. They never shut up."

"They're proud of you." They were overbearing control freaks.

"Like today. This amazing bass player is here. He tours with everybody, and I decided even though I'm kinda half dropping out, I'd go to his Master Class. She came. The Master Classes are for students, and *my mother* came. Afterwards, she wouldn't stop telling him how much I could learn from him and what a good backup singer I am."

And then they'd argued, as Kyle had heard.

"Isn't that what you want? A new teacher? A new mentor?"

She leaned forward, pointing her finger at her chest. "I want to earn this. Myself. Not get favors because my parents made a big donation so they could get five minutes to brag about me to some famous guy."

A suspicion darted through my brain. "Is that what happened with Gerry Martin? Is that how you became his protégée?"

Her narrow chin quivered, and a tear rolled down her cheek.

I put my hand on her bare knee. "Then tell them that you're grateful for everything they've done. That you need to choose your own path, but you'll always look to them for—"

"What if they killed him?"

"Your parents?" I leaned forward, lowering my voice. "Why—how?"

"Saturday morning." She rubbed a knuckle against the side of her long straight nose, and sniffed. "I went for a run. I saw them, talking to him. I could tell they were upset."

"He died up on the River Road," I said.

"My parents walk on the River Road every morning. They get their coffee and they go for a walk."

Would fastidious Ann Drake have dropped her cup, or tossed it in the bushes? I'd already dismissed the idea that she and Grant had gone up on the River Road with Martin and argued over Gabby's future and their role in it, but if Gabby thought it possible …

I've never pushed a man to his death down a cliff above a raging river, but I'm fairly sure that if I did, I wouldn't be worried about littering.

"Did you tell Undersheriff Hoover?"

Her jaw tightened, and she gave a quick shake no.

"You have to tell him."

At the very least, if Grant Drake's prints and DNA were in a nationwide database, because of that business in New York, Ike could run a comparison. It might not prove anything, but it would be evidence. But he'd need solid legal reasons to compel Ann to give him prints and a DNA sample. I'd learned that much from Kim.

Gabby's parents had been in Le Panier yesterday around eight—much earlier than the window of Gerry Martin's death. If they were the creatures of habit that Gabby insisted, wouldn't they have gotten their coffee and taken their walk at the same time Saturday as on Tuesday? Wouldn't someone have seen them?

And if they'd been late, wouldn't Michelle have remembered them?

"What time? Tell me exactly what you saw, and where they were."

"I can't say what time. I didn't sleep well. He upset me Friday night, ripping into me. I kinda deserved it, I know—it was his gig, and I played my own piece instead. I came running through town, in the street." She gestured toward Front Street, a few feet from our bench. She'd been headed back to their condo on the bay.

"And where were they?"

"Outside the bakery."

"Did they see you?"

"I don't think so. There were cars parked on that side of the street, and they were pretty intent on him. Gesturing and stuff."

"Did they have coffee cups?" I held my hand as if holding a paper cup.

"I don't know. They usually sit and enjoy their coffee. But Gerry?" She closed her eyes briefly. "I don't think so."

Then he hadn't gone inside the bakery yet. They could have waited for him, and gone on a walk together. Or they could have left him and gone about their business, whatever that was.

"Gabby, is there something else you're not telling me? Some reason…"

She whipped her face toward me, her full brows raised. "They wouldn't have meant it. But he was so angry. And so were they. All this week, they've been so secretive. I know they're hiding things from me."

"And you're sure it involves you and Martin?"

Her brows dropped, bending toward each other, and her shoulders sagged. "What else could it be?"

Just because you're self-centered doesn't mean everything isn't always about you, but I had my doubts this time.

"The house?" No surprise that Gabby thought the house was about her, too. "Your mother seemed pretty certain they'd found one, when she bought the pottery in my shop."

"On the lake, I think. An old orchard? Tearing down, or remodeling—I don't know. Erin, you can figure this out, can't you? I mean, it's my parents. They can't be—killers. But if—well, I don't want that other guy blamed if he didn't do it."

Her hands felt so small in mine, and she looked so young. "I don't know who killed your teacher, Gabby. For what it's worth, I don't think it was Sam or your parents. But I'll do everything I can to figure out who did."

Only after she'd air-kissed my cheek and dashed back in to the theater did I realize that, like nearly everyone else who'd known Gerry Martin, Gabby Drake hadn't actually expressed any sorrow over his death.

I emptied Gabby's water bottle on the nearest rose bush, then checked my phone. It had buzzed with a text during her tearful wail, and I'd ignored it.

HOME FROM THE HILLS, Adam wrote. SEE YOU AT RED'S AFTER THE SHOW?

Walking in now and climbing over half the row to get to my seat might not earn me too many dirty looks—this was festival world, not the Metropolitan Opera—but I'd fallen out of the musical mood.

Oh, pooh. I'd given the other ticket to Lou Mary, who would fret up one aisle and down the other if I didn't show. And I couldn't text her—she took great pride in not owning a cell phone.

The woman behind the ticket counter promised to give Lou Mary a note at half-time: *Sorry I couldn't stay—fill me in tomorrow!*

Then, head down and hands in my pockets, I marched through town and over the bridge, not stopping to watch the river meet the bay. I needed to think, and to move. And call Ike.

Another layer of clouds had rolled in, blocking the stars and moon-light. Solar-powered lights, the kind you stick in the ground where you need them, lit the trail that skirted the south side of the bay. Jewel Bay had been blessed for decades with foresighted people who preserved this greenbelt, built the nature trail, aka the River Road, and kept the Playhouse running. They established the shops and galleries and restaurants. They created the festivals that made the town so much fun, and brought tourists from near and far to fuel our economy.

Would I be able to continue that legacy? Would my children want to do the same?

I hoped I'd have the fortitude, when the time came, to let them do what they wanted, with encouragement but without pressure. As my parents had done.

Poor Gabby. Her parents had made her the center of their world, and now she struggled to make the world turn on her own.

And she couldn't imagine them focused on anything other than her. But I was getting my own reminder these days about letting go of our parents, seeing how their lives continue on, independent of their children. They don't stop changing and growing—they pick up passions once set aside, move across the country, find new loves.

As it should be.

The light from the Harbor condos brightened this stretch, and my footsteps made soft thumps on the path. I ran my hand along a hedge of dwarf lilacs, and drank in their scent.

Had the Drakes argued with Martin on the street, then gone up to the River Road with him and continued the argument until it turned tragic, as Gabby feared?

Doubtful. One argument on the village sidewalk, I could buy. But stalking the man? Not the elegant Ann's style, despite her flair for the dramatic. And Grant Drake's misdeeds had been financial, not physical.

They doted on their daughter, and they would stand up for her. But push a man to his death and keep it a secret?

It didn't seem possible.

What about Gabby herself? Her confession of her fears seemed genuine. But a child that spoiled, that over-indulged, might think her parents would happily take the fall for her.

I heard movement behind me. Too much noise for a squirrel, although deer did occasionally meander through driveways and bound over the seawall to drink from the bay.

I glanced back but saw nothing. A cat, I decided, and strolled on.

What a day. My ride with Kim had been both energizing and draining. I could not recall seeing her sob like that since we were kids. Young kids, when we'd witnessed a horse break a leg. Her father had sent us home while he put it down. If she had cried when my father died, she'd kept it from me.

I hoped we were through keeping things from each other.

That thought led me to Sam. Could he confront his wife and get her to scale back their dreams to a mutually agreeable level? I crossed my fingers. I liked them. And their winery was a boon to the village.

I stepped into darkness—a missing light, or one out of order.

My musing returned to the brilliant idea I'd had earlier. Who better than me to help Tanner create a detailed business plan, one he could implement after he recovered his strength, or tailor to declining health? One that a future owner—Adam, an outside buyer, or a group of employees—could revise and adapt to fit their own needs. One that would keep the staff employed, the T-shirts rolling off the line, and Tanner's dream a reality.

From somewhere in the shrubbery came a rustling sound, then the crack of a branch. Before I could see what was making the noise, a hard object hit me in the middle of my back. I cried out, staggering forward, half bent.

The thing struck me again, this time from the side. The jolt knocked the breath of out of me, and I stepped sideways, struggling to regain my balance.

To keep myself from toppling into the bay.

My feet back under me, I spun toward my attacker. In the semi-darkness, I saw a shape about my height, and an arm ready to hurl a dagger at me. No, not a dagger—the missing solar light. I ducked. The light flew past me and splashed into the bay.

I wriggled my bag off my shoulder and grabbed the straps with both hands. I swung. The bag hit something—someone—who uttered a loud sound. Not quite a word, but clearly a cry of pain.

I drew back and let loose. Hit a second time. Heard a second cry.

Then footsteps, running away.

Leaving me alone in the dark, on the path above the bay. Me and my trusty blue bag.

Twenty-Eight

'm fine," I repeated. "And sit down. You're making me nervous."

"He didn't say anything?" Adam did not sit, rocking from one foot to the other in the Merc's courtyard. The guys were headed to Red's when they spotted me charging up the street, shaken and stirred. Our beers sat on the table. "Like 'stay out of it' or 'mind your own business'?"

"Not a word. I thought it was a cat. Until it tried to shove me into the bay."

"Shouldn't we call the sheriff?" Tanner asked.

"I already did," I said. "As soon as I got back to the bridge, where it's all lit up. They're going to barricade the path, put more reserve officers on patrol. The news will spread, and it will hurt the festival. But we don't know it's connected—I have no idea who came after me, or why."

Adam's brow darkened. "You know darned well why. Because someone knows you're investigating. How can you not see that?"

"I want to be strong."

"Do you want to be dead?"

"Hey!" Tanner held out his hands, separating kids on the playground. "Can they find that light and get fingerprints?"

"They'll search in the morning. The water's shallow there." Heat and fear stung my throat, but I was not going to cry. No one was going to scare me away.

"Don't encourage her," Adam said, and the lump in my throat swelled to the size of Texas. We'd been over this last winter, when I pursued another killer. Adam had sworn he wouldn't try to stop me, because he knew he couldn't, and because he loved my sense of justice. My determination to protect what mattered to me, even when it put me in harm's way.

Just like, I realized with a start, I loved his sense of adventure. His passion for plunging through rapids, for climbing rocks, for racing through snowy back country with boards strapped to his feet.

Tanner slammed his fist on the table, and I jumped. I hadn't touched my beer yet, and a swallow or two sloshed out of the glass.

He leaned in, intent on Adam. "Don't be an ass, Z. Don't you dare let her get away twice." I caught my breath. Tanner pivoted. "And you. A guy gets pushed off a cliff, and the killer's still out there. Everybody knows you're poking around, and you go for a walk in the dark by yourself?"

My eyes widened and my fingers covered my mouth.

"Hey, Adam, chow time." J.D.'s red head poked over the top of the fence. Adam and I burst out laughing. After a moment, so did Tanner, while J.D. stood on a picnic bench on Red's side of the fence, holding a basket of onion rings and another of waffle fries, a bottle of mustard in his apron pocket.

Fortified with beer, starch, and fat, we settled down to business. I told the guys what I'd learned from Gabby. "I don't think her parents killed Martin, but I'm convinced that they're hiding something."

"About Martin and the festival?" Adam asked.

"Maybe. At first I wondered if Grant Drake had his fingers in the cookie jar, but no one seems worried about that."

"Were they part of Barber's plan to bring in bigger names? That could help Gabby." Tanner bit into a fry.

"Doubt it. They saw Martin as her ticket to stardom." I picked up my beer glass. "I suspect they'll stay involved regardless because they enjoy music, and being big fish in a small pond. No, I think their secret relates to Rebecca and the building project none of them wanted me to know about."

"But that won't tell us who killed Martin," Adam said. "Though you might be the only one who cares."

Realization struck. "Oh my God. The Drakes. They're staying at the Harbor condos."

When I called Dispatch to report the attack, I hadn't talked to an officer. I hadn't told anyone what Gabby had told me. But it was time. I reached for my phone.

I already knew Dispatch would do nothing more than take a message and assure me that Undersheriff Hoover or a deputy would call me as soon as they were free. I texted Kim: URGENT. NEED IKE'S PERSONAL NUMBER. I laid the phone on the table, and the three of us eyed each other.

"I suppose it could have been a woman at the top of the cliff," Tanner said. "I can't say, one way or another. Gabby's small, but get a guy off balance, and it wouldn't take much force."

"But if my attacker and the killer are the same person, I'm not so sure it was her," I said. "I don't think she could have followed me in those stupid-high platform sandals. They're noisy, and impossible to run in, even for a kid."

"Is she in this with her mother? Call or text her at the condo, and say 'now's our chance'?" Adam asked.

"Too complicated," Tanner said. "Sherlock Holmes says the simplest explanation is usually the right one."

Adam and I stared at him.

"I watched all the old shows last time I was sick."

I reached over and squeezed his hand, then cradled my glass and leaned back, scrolling mentally through the unanswered questions. After all my hard work, I was back to square one, with nothing to show for it but a long list of suspects and a bruise on my back. Maybe it was time to stop.

"Wonder if Ike's found a witness, someone who saw who Martin ran into after he bought his coffee. Michelle swore she didn't remember," I said.

"The same Michelle who works for you?" Tanner asked Adam. "The one who has your drink ready before you give her your order? She doesn't miss a thing."

I squinted at my sweetie. "She works for you?"

"Yeah. She's the kitchen boss at base camp. She orders all the food, cooks when we're there, helps us get the supply packs ready for when we hit the trail. She trades for her kids' camp fees."

"She's got kids?" So much for knowing everything about everyone in a small town. "Plus she works in the bakery, tends bar, and takes on catering jobs? What's her husband do?"

"Single mom. Town may look prosperous," he said to Tanner, "but a lot of folks juggle two or three part-time jobs."

"I can see it could be hard for working folks to live here."

Adam nodded. "She rents one of the cottages at the winery. Cheap, but not cheap enough."

I stared at him. "Have you seen them? They're like the shack in our orchard, migrant housing built in the thirties when the cherry orchards were big business. That's no place for kids."

"You live rent-free on the lake in a designer cabin. Not everybody does."

"I know that. But if Michelle rents from Sam and Jennifer ... "

What had Michelle seen—or who? She'd come to Sam's defense. What if Sam had lied to me? What if he'd run into town for a part for that compressor-heater-fan he said he'd been fixing, seen Martin, and taken a deadly detour—and Michelle had seen him?

I'd been so sure Sam was innocent. But then, I'd been sure he and Jennifer were solid, and that the winery was slowly becoming a success.

Turned out, I didn't know half of what I thought I knew.

"No, you can't sleep in the closet all day." I backed out, on my knees, the next morning, Pumpkin in one arm, a long-missing black climbing sandal in the other hand. Thursdays are busy days at the Merc, and I needed comfy feet. "It's dark and stinky."

Which she loved.

Though Adam and I had gotten past our fear- and anger-fueled spat last night—the upside of talking through the investigation—I found myself feeling a little wobbly as I drove into town. A little wounded by his comment about my cabin and my lush life. Of course I knew I'd lucked out. I knew many villagers lived one paycheck away from nothing. That's why I give the Merc's unsold produce and other goods to the Food Bank, and created the Festa di Pasta as a fundraiser.

A lot of poverty hides behind the well-financed fun.

But I worried that Adam didn't feel the same attachment to Jewel Bay as I did. If he didn't, would he want to come back?

Would he want to stay?

Or was I being too sensitive? I'll admit, that happens every time a figure darts out of the shadows to whack me in the back with a pointy-ended metal object.

But replaying our conversation had given me an idea. One so vague that only a double shot of espresso had any chance of bringing it into focus.

∞

"Ah, so that's the secret to your energy. You sneak in a double shot when nobody's watching."

Michelle bounced to her feet. No customers clamored for coffee or nursed a morning macchiato. The kitchen, visible behind the front counter, stood strangely quiet.

"Don't get up." I poured myself water from the big jug. "I need to catch my breath before I think about coffee."

She sat, fingers tight on the white cup.

After I'd cooled down and watered up, I spoke. "You're in a tricky spot. I see that now. And I'm sorry if the truth makes things harder for you and your children."

She glanced at me sharply.

"Their lives seemed idyllic to me, too. Comparisons are danger-ous—judging our insides by other people's outsides never works. I thought they had it all: beautiful place on the lake, good marriage, suc-cessful business. Rental properties to help them through the dry spells."

"I don't know anything about that." She sounded tense, her thumb and forefinger pinching her collarbone.

My heart sank. Had I been wrong? "You saw Sam, didn't you? He lied about being stuck home all Saturday morning, making repairs.

He came into town to find out what was going on, and that's when you saw him confront Martin, and take him up to the trail?"

"What? No. I didn't see Sam." She stared at me, wide-eyed.

I stared back.

"What I saw—" She broke off, afraid to continue.

I leaned forward. "Tell me, Michelle. The sheriff suspects Sam, and half the people in town do, too. But if you know something…"

"I know Rebecca holds the mortgage, or whatever it is. And I know she got fed up with Jenny's broken promises of payment. And then I saw—" The espresso cup all but disappeared in her hands. "Erin, if they do what they say they're going to do with the property, where will we go?"

A piece of the puzzle clicked into place. The Carters had seen Jennifer leaving Martin's cottage Friday night when they returned to theirs. But I'd added up the facts wrong.

"You knew Sam and Jennifer were on the verge of losing the winery, and if they did, you'd need to move. So you didn't want anyone to know why Jennifer was pleading with Martin Friday night. It wasn't over an affair." My mother had said Rebecca was the money behind half a dozen local businesses, but until now, I hadn't imagined she'd been financing the winery. "She borrowed money from Rebecca and used the winery as collateral. Without Sam's knowledge."

"Jenny handles all the money," Michelle said. "We pay our rent to her. My son helped with the pruning last fall, and she tried to go back on paying him. Who renegotiates with a twelve-year-old? And I've heard other stuff."

So had I. Last summer, I'd overheard Jennifer worrying about a call from a banker. And it was all consistent with what Donna had told me. Except short-changing the boy—that was plain mean.

Michelle went on. "Our house is a dump, but the kids can roam for hours without me worrying. The school bus stops on the highway. And Sam is great with my son—he let him help when he fixed the leaky roof, and taught him how to scrape and paint the outside."

I had noticed one freshly painted cottage in the bunch. The one with the bike on the porch and the rusted red Subaru parked out front. Michelle was a true nest-builder.

"Then Jenny refused to give us credit on the rent. She's pretty hard on Sam, too, but I didn't believe the rumors that he was jealous over an affair."

"Let me guess. Sally Sourpuss never met a juicy rumor she didn't love to spread." I smiled in spite of myself. "So, when Jennifer got behind and couldn't catch up, Rebecca decided to take back the property, and convert it into Martin's recording studio." That fit with what I'd heard from Chuck the Builder, and from Rocco at the music shop. And Landon's new pal, Jackson Boyd. "She intended to remodel to create a retreat for him, and rent out the big house along with the studio. But why would Rebecca kill Martin?"

"Because Rebecca gets what she wants, one way or another. Jenny idolizes Rebecca for her success, but she couldn't pull it off. Or pull it together." Michelle stopped long enough to swallow back tears. "Erin, we can't afford to move. Every landlord wants first and last months' rent, and when they hear you have kids, they double the damage deposit. My son's growing out of his shoes every six months. My daughter wants piano lessons and hair that doesn't look like her mother cut it in the bathroom."

"I might be able to help you find a place. Tell me what you saw." I had to get her to confide in me before a customer came in and shattered the chance.

"Last week, Friday, I think it was. In the afternoon. Rebecca drove on to the property. Then this big fancy car came in behind her."

"Where were you? What were you doing?"

"In the vineyard, restretching the wires that Sam trains the vines on."

Good heavens. Was there any job this woman wouldn't do?

"Rebecca walked up the road with a couple, talking about what it would cost to regrade and put down new gravel. I was behind the pump house and they couldn't see me."

"Then what?"

"They started talking about the rentals. Eyesores, the woman called them. The man said they'd push them over as soon as they closed the deal. Clear out the trash, he said, and plant more vines. Trash, Erin. He meant *us*." Her fury was hard to miss.

"I'm sure he meant the buildings, Michelle. Not you. Not your family." My fingertips brushed her arm. "Who were they?"

"That's the worst part. They sit here and let me serve them coffee every morning. They don't even see me." She folded her arms and gripped her elbows. "I'm the help. I am invisible."

"The Drakes?" I said, my voice rising, my brain racing. It fit. They planned to build their dream house at the winery. It fit with spotting them and Rebecca leaving a law office in Pondera, where they'd drawn up a contract for deed. It fit the deal-making tone of their lunch, the changes they'd discussed to the roll of papers they'd been determined no one else see. Or at least, determined that I not see. Not a map or a plat, but the plans Chuck the Builder had drawn up for the studio deal, the deal Martin had nixed. No problem. Rebecca had a better deal waiting in the wings.

Maybe Martin hadn't pulled out after all. Maybe she'd changed her mind. Maybe *those* were the false pretenses, the plans he'd derided Friday night in the courtyard.

Maybe they'd walked on the River Road Saturday morning, and argued, and ...

Gabby had said her parents found the perfect property. They'd be tearing down and remodeling. That could apply to a hundred different projects, a hundred different properties. But it made sense of the puzzle. The Drakes' secret, one they'd kept from their daughter, was that they were buying a piece of property whose owners didn't know it was for sale. That they were helping hard-driving Rebecca push a hard-working couple off their land, displace their renters, and kill their dream.

I unclenched my jaw and focused on Michelle. "Did you hear anything else?"

"Not right then. The Drakes left. Jenny came home a few minutes later." She looked up. Two women stood out front, debating whether to come in. "I took the wire and clippers back to the maintenance shed. The big back doors to the winery were open and Jenny and Rebecca were standing inside. Jenny said"—she rolled her eyes up, remembering—"she said, 'You were our last hope. I can't believe you'd throw us out after all our hard work. For a washed-up musician's dream.'"

"She didn't know the studio deal with Martin was dead? She didn't know Rebecca had another buyer?"

Michelle slid her chair back. "No. And Rebecca didn't tell her. She just said, 'That's business.'"

The door opened and the two women entered.

"Michelle." I spoke quietly as the barista retied her apron. "I don't know what will happen to the property. But we'll work this out."

The look on her pale face said she trusted me. She stepped behind the counter and greeted the women eyeing the pastries.

Call Ike, my inner voice said, but I put it on hold. I sat at the tile-topped table, working things out. Whether Gerry Martin had backed out of the deal or Rebecca had driven him out, I didn't know. Jennifer had pleaded with Rebecca for more time, and she'd pleaded with Martin not to go ahead with the studio plan. Sam had said she'd driven in early Friday evening, leaving him to bring in the gear, so she could talk to someone. Later, she'd asked if *I'd* seen Martin. I'd bet my lucky red boots she had already gone to beg Rebecca for leniency, in vain.

She hadn't known Rebecca had another buyer already lined up. And Barber—he'd hammered on Rebecca to get his way, not knowing that Martin had dumped her and he wasn't likely to return to the festival.

No wonder she quit.

No wonder Martin had decided to leave early.

Had Rebecca played Martin against the Drakes, trying to get the best deal? Had she seen him Saturday morning, followed him up the River Road, and pushed him to his death?

When my mother said Rebecca had a reputation for driving a hard bargain, she hadn't known the half of it.

Behind me, the cash register beeped. "I'll bring your lattes out," Michelle said, and the two women settled at a table on the stone patio. The espresso machine hissed.

Michelle set a paper cup in front of me, hot and steaming. "On the house. For listening."

"Thanks," I said and watched her bump the door open with her hip, hands full of lattes and plates of rhubarb crumb cake.

What about the paper cup I'd found on the trail? According to Michelle, Rebecca had not stopped in here. If the cup hadn't been the killer's, was it Martin's?

Or a piece of trash, waiting to be cleared out, like the shacks at Monte Verde Winery?

One person's trash is another person's home.

Twenty-Nine

$\mathcal{I}$ had never seriously suspected Rebecca of Martin's murder. Had talked myself out of thinking it could be her.

But we see what we want to see. And conversely, we close our eyes to truths we'd rather ignore.

I SHOULDN'T, BUT HERE YOU GO, Kim's reply text this morning had said, and I used Ike Hoover's personal cell number. Bless him, he did not ask how I'd gotten it. I told him everything I'd learned from Gabby and Michelle, and how it all fit together. How it all pointed to Rebecca. I even confessed my sleight-of-hand with Derek the EMT's phone.

"I bet those other tracks, the ones so hard to see, were her sneakers," I said.

"Hmm," he'd said, then warned me to keep my distance from Rebecca's gallery and apartment. He'd gather his officers and take her into custody. "She had motive and could have made the opportunity. Crime lab says the cup you found was Martin's, but Oakland found a second cup a few feet down the cliff—nearly broke his neck getting it. And I've sent the other evidence you found for testing. I'm guessing the prints on the earrings, the note, and the light you were attacked with will all match."

And belong to the killer.

He didn't say "Good job, Erin," or "Amateurs to the rescue." But he did clear his throat. "Deputy Caldwell will be back on the job the first of June, thanks to you."

I gave Michelle an update on the investigation, and a special request. While I waited, I thought about Jennifer, willing to sacrifice her marriage for the prestige and promise of success the winery represented.

Suddenly, desperately, I needed to talk to Adam. To tell him how much I loved him. To confess my fear that he would go back to Minnesota and stay, because living without me back there was easier than living with my recklessness here. To confess that I would go with him if I needed to, to be together.

But he and Tanner were taking the kayaks out on the lake—one last, gentle adventure.

And I had a delivery to make.

Inside the Merc, the big white lights glowed. I knocked on the glass and waved at Tracy, busy rearranging the window display. I gestured across the street. She nodded and reached for a picnic basket.

In the middle of the street, genius struck. I spun around and dashed back to the Merc, unlocking the door long enough to stick my head in. "I know you want to be more than a sales clerk. How's this sound? 'Tracy McCann, Chocolatier and Creative Director'?"

She beamed.

Across the street, the surprises kept coming. My mother opened Snowberry's door and waved me in.

I handed Chiara her favorite drink—Michelle had known exactly what it was. "Sorry, Mom—I didn't know you were here."

"I'm glad you popped in," my mother said. "Your sister and I have some things to clear up, and I hope you can help."

Uh-oh.

"You know I adored your father," Mom said. "I loved being married. It's a compliment to him that I want that kind of relationship again—nothing says a good marriage has to be a once-in-a-lifetime thing. I can't explain why knowing that his death was unsolved held me back, but it did. And now all that's behind us. Erin, you could not be more supportive. Thank you. But Chiara, if you have a problem with this, then we need to work it out. Because I am marrying Bill. And I want your support."

Chiara made the noise Sandburg makes when Pumpkin sits on his ottoman. "Oh, Mom. I'm so sorry. I've been such a wreck. But Jason wanted to wait to say anything, because—well, you know."

Because Landon was six, and when people asked if she was going to have another baby, she always said no, he was more than enough, but I'd known that every miscarriage had broken her heart a little.

"It's early, eight weeks, but I have a good feeling this time." She patted her flat belly.

"Oh, darling." Mom wrapped her arms around my sister, visibly relieved. The Italian earth mother—and grandmother. "I should have guessed. Those hormones can be a bitch."

Finally, an explanation that made sense for why my sister had been acting all weird. I didn't mind that she hadn't said a peep. I was too happy. And I understood.

But I had one more mystery to clear up, an idea Molly had inadvertently planted. "Mom, are you selling the Orchard?"

She kept one arm around Chiara's shoulder as she faced me. "Oh, Erin. I don't know. Bill loves the property, and he's become part of our traditions." She waved one manicured hand and brushed against the driftwood rack that held those magnificent bags. A deer hide satchel fell to the floor, and the rack rocked back and forth. "But we're getting older, and it is a lot of work."

"I have another idea." I told my womenfolk my plan, conceived in the last thirty seconds, and watched their faces change.

"Erin, that's perfect," Chiara said. My mother beamed, speechless.

"Speaking of perfect." I reached out and plucked the origami leather bag off the wooden rack. I hadn't told them about last night's attack, or how I'd defended myself. Later. "I think it's time I bought a new bag."

The Merc rocked, from opening till noon. We were too busy to pay any attention to the goings-on up the street, the sheriff's rigs clustered around Rebecca's building.

Tracy and Lou Mary worked together beautifully, and I loved working with them. Loved knowing all my problems were solved, and I could focus on the Merc.

But even bosses need to eat, so after my staff took their lunch breaks, it was my turn. I decided to surprise the guys with a picnic at the state park. I filled one of our baskets with their faves, including a celebratory bottle of Monte Verde wine.

The state park is another gem of Jewel Bay. Two minutes from the village, on the lakeshore, it's got hiking trails, camping spots, and a gravel beach.

Adam's Xterra, its roof racks empty, stood alone in the upper parking lot. I stuck the Subaru next to it, grabbed the basket, and headed for the rocks above the lake.

Colored specks bobbed on the sparkling water. From a distance, little bobbing boats all look alike, and I had no binoculars. I set the basket down and waved with both arms.

I heard her before I saw her, and I almost heard her too late.

Before I could turn, a shove sent me staggering forward. My knee dipped in a lunge, my foot catching hold on the layered rock. I thanked my stars for the shoes Pumpkin had helped me find this morning, and their thick tread.

I spun toward my attacker, my center of gravity now lower than hers, grabbing her right arm and letting the momentum propel me forward, away from the edge of the rock, though not away from danger. Her left hand snapped out and snared my right arm.

We were face to face on the ledge, our fate in each other's hands, and I, for one, was terrified.

Jennifer.

Not Dave Barber. Not Sam. Not the Drakes, despite the proximity of their Harbor condo to the site of Martin's murder and of the attack on me. Not Rebecca, now in the sheriff's custody.

"It was you," I said, finally seeing the full picture. "You pushed Gerry Martin off the River Road. You attacked me last night with the solar light. You misled Sam about the winery's finances. You borrowed money from Rebecca without telling him. Without letting him know you'd mortgaged his dream."

"Dreams mean nothing," Jennifer said, face twisted with a pain she'd brought upon herself. "I dared to dream, and look where it got me."

"Dreams are everything," I said. "They keep us going. But we can't use them to hurt the people we love."

Her fingers tightened on my arm. "You don't know anything about it."

"I know you pleaded with Gerry Martin to drop the plans for the studio, hoping that if Rebecca lost her chance to turn the winery into another business, she'd renegotiate your loan. I think you followed him Saturday morning, up to the River Road. And you pushed him."

"He promised to help me, but he made a fool of me instead." Her eyes were damp and feverish, and she was sweating more than a runner should have.

"I know Rebecca lost patience with your promises and found another buyer. But you didn't find out until too late." *Keep talking*, I told myself, hoping to inch away from the precipice. If I could get to the basket, I could whack her with the bottle. "You tried to scare me off by coming to the cabin Monday night, but you got trapped by the storm. You lost one of your guitar pick earrings on my road."

She grunted, and tightened her grip.

"I don't know why you were in my car," I said, my eyes boring into hers. "You lost the other one there. Oh, no—you left it there on purpose, with the note saying not to destroy your dream. I didn't find it for a few days."

For a second, Jennifer's grip loosened and I managed a tiny step to my left. Over her shoulder, the sunlight danced on the blue waves. The boats I'd spotted earlier were out of sight.

"Your car? No, it was Rebecca's. I wanted her to know she needed to talk to me. To give me another chance." Her mouth fell open. "*Ohh.*"

"That's right. We drive the same kind of car, even the same color. And when the village is crowded, we sometimes park close to each other, on Back Street."

The horror and hopelessness of it all finally hit her. But instead of deflating, she clenched her jaw and straightened her back.

258

"No one can prove any of that," she said, "without you. There won't be anyone left to prove a thing."

She wrenched my arm and I lost my balance. My foot landed hard and my ankle buckled, pain shooting up my leg. Below me, the rocks rose into view, and the waves crashed against the cliff. A stunted spruce jutted into thin air—one of those brave trees that take root in the vertical nooks and crannies. My family calls them Montana bonsai. Brave, but not sturdy enough to hold me.

I tightened my grip on Jennifer's arms. Reached deep inside for my own brave roots, and pushed back, hard. Somehow I managed to scrabble to my feet, holding her as we twisted and tugged.

Her back foot slipped, and she fell to one knee, our arms still clasped. Her other leg dangled over the ledge. I was close enough to peer over, but I didn't dare, knowing what was below. It's like trying to avoid a rock when you're on a bike. You fill your brain with that damned rock, and you smack right into it.

"Let me go," she said. "Let me fall."

It was tempting. She'd killed a man. She deserved punishment, but not like this. Letting her plunge to her death would harm too many other people, including me.

"Jennifer, *no*," I said. "You don't want to die. You have to pay for what you've done, but you don't have to pay with your life."

I tightened my grip, inhaled, and leaned back. *An inch, then another...*

Then another pair of hands reached out. Adam grabbed her arm above where I held it, then circled his other arm around her back. Together, we hauled her up over the ledge, inch by inch, until the three of us lay shivering on the sunbaked rock.

"Where did you—" I gasped. "How did you—we need to—"

"They're on their way. We'd paddled close to shore, then we saw you struggling. We learned our lesson after last week—we packed a

259

phone in a waterproof bag. Tanner called for help, and I climbed up the cliff." Adam held Jennifer's hands behind her back. Fingers trembling, I pulled the cord out of my new hoodie and wrapped it around her wrists. She moaned. I jerked the cord tighter.

"I was wrong," I told him. In the distance, a siren neared. "I know you love Jewel Bay as much as I do. I know you want to be here. I know—"

"Erin, how could you have ever thought I wanted to be anywhere else, with anyone but you?"

And there, on the rocks, the waves lapping at the shore, the sun shining so gloriously, I knew it was true.

Thirty

Who named the Saturday shindig the GuitarBQ?" Tanner sat on the blanket on the concert lawn, a full plate in one hand, a beer in the other. "You?"

"I wish," I said. "It's a brilliant end to the festival."

"Speaking of brilliant," Adam said. "Mr. Manufacturing Genius showed me the business plan you created for him. It is so far beyond anything he could ever have put together."

Tanner mimed throwing his corn-on-the-cob at his best buddy.

"He helped. So did his bookkeeper, and the purchasing manager." I picked up a potato chip. "But you seriously need to hire a CFO. That's Chief Financial Officer," I said to Adam.

"Ah, but the best candidate wouldn't take the job," Tanner said.

"I've got my hands full with the Merc, plus working with Sam Kraus to get the winery's books in order." With Jennifer under arrest for murder, two counts of assault, trespass, and who knew what else, Rebecca had agreed to a refinancing plan that would allow Sam to keep the winery. My uncle Joe, a successful winemaker in California, would tour Monte Verde when he came up for my mother's wedding in a few weeks, and offer his advice.

Free of suspicion, Rebecca appeared to finally understand the connections between the people and places who make up Jewel Bay, who make it a community. At my urging, she'd persuaded the Drakes to invest in Monte Verde, enabling Sam to remodel the farmhand cottages. That created more security for Michelle and the other renters, as well as for Sam and the lenders and investors.

Rebecca had also agreed to take the townhouse she rented to Lou Mary off the market, at least long enough for my sales clerk to save up the down payment. My mother had learned of the listing when she dropped into the real estate office to ask Molly about selling the Orchard. In classic Murphy girl fashion, she'd figured out a way to help Lou Mary, by getting her a job at the Merc.

I'd convinced Ann that Molly would scour every inch of the lakeshore to find them their own dream property. After all, they already had the dishes.

I'd relayed to Ned Redaway what Pamela Barber had told me. Contrary to Ned's misbelief, and my own, I understood now that Dave wasn't driven by greed or money. What he wanted was a chance to be a star. It didn't need to be on the big stage, tempting as that was. Being the man who helped bring stellar music and a bit of prosperity to his home town was enough for him.

And I'd talked to Marv Alden and Donna Lawson about recruiting a professional recording engineer to build a studio in Jewel Bay. Chuck the Builder and Rocco the Music Man had agreed to lend their expertise.

One mystery remained: Who left the memorial bouquet on the gate at the trailhead? My money was on Gabby, but I might never find out. In a small town, gestures like that deepen the bonds that keep us here.

We finished our barbecue sandwiches, and I stood. "It's time."

We didn't bother hiding our glee as we strolled down to meet my family. Landon led the parade, Chiara and Jason close behind. Fresca and Bill followed, hand in hand.

They crossed the bridge and reached the park. Landon stopped. Heidi sat in the passenger seat of a gleaming black Mustang convertible, and Reg Robbins, wearing the loudest, largest Hawaiian shirt I'd ever seen, stood beside the driver's door.

Landon's mouth opened and closed several times, like a fish gasping for air. He jumped up and down, pointing at the license plate.

"Hawaii! I got Hawaii!"

How Reg managed to keep the registration current while keeping the car in Montana, I didn't want to know. All that mattered at the moment was that he'd agreed when Jason asked him to drive the Mustang into town tonight so Landon could check the most elusive state off his list.

After the hugs, and after Reg promised father and son a ride, we reclaimed our seats on the lawn for the finale.

"I almost don't want to leave," Tanner said. The glint in his eye mirrored the dampness in my own.

"Just be sure you come back."

The concert was a rousing success, each guest artist playing a short set. Pearl Django made my heart dance, and Jackson Mississippi Boyd got the crowd singing.

Gabby Drake replaced Gerry Martin in the finale, and bewitched us all. Her parents sat a few rows in front of us, beaming. Whether she would follow their plan, I didn't know. But when I saw the gigantic beaded hoops in her ears, I had a feeling Gabby had a plan of her own.

So did I.

This time, it was Tanner lugging the cooler full of sparkling wine and the box of secret ingredients to the Orchard. With the Merc open Sundays now, we'd had to rush to make the weekly gathering of family and friends.

"When I first started my company," Tanner explained to my mother as he set out bottles of bitters and a special liqueur, "my cash flow ran backwards. I tended bar at a fancy restaurant to pay the bills. The chef loved putting on elaborate wine dinners, and I got to create special cocktails. This one is for you, as my thanks for your amazing hospitality."

"What's it made with?" she said, ever the inquisitive cook.

"Typically, I use cava, the Spanish sparkling wine. The taste is flatter than French champagne, so it lets the other flavors through." He dropped a sugar cube in each flute, and added the bitters and liqueur. "But since we're at your place, I'm using Prosecco."

"What's the liqueur?" I asked.

"The drink the Romans invaded Spain for." He poured in the wine, then handed a glass to my mother and another to me. I managed to suppress my sneeze, and took a sip.

"Oh, my gosh," I said. "It tastes like a kiss."

"Tanner," my mother said, "this is divine. What do you call it?"

Tanner beamed and raised his glass in a toast, first to my mother, then to me. "The Italian Princess."

My sister arrived, toting a rhubarb custard pie. Both she and Jason beamed.

"How are you feeling?" I asked.

"So much better, now that I've told you. No matter what happens"—she hugged me tight—"I hate having secrets from you."

Before we ate, I asked Adam to take a walk with me in the orchard.

At the foot of my favorite tree, the one that held my tree house, I stopped and turned to face him. In a nest I couldn't see, in one of the cherry trees, a baby bird chirped.

Without one itty bitty trace of nerves or doubt, I pulled the small, black box out of my pocket.

"Adam Zimmerman," I said, looking into my true love's black-coffee eyes, "will you marry me?"

A dark curl flopped onto his forehead. He took the box and opened it. He raised his eyes to mine, a hint of a smile tugging at his lips.

Without a word, he slid the sparkling ring out of its slot and reached for my left hand.

And though I am a Murphy girl through and through, I have no words for what happened next.

THE END

The Jewel Bay Jazz Festival and Workshop Guide to Food and Drink

*Courtesy of the Merc, bringing you
the finest of Montana's food and drink since 1910.*

At the Merc

The Merc's jam maker processes her jams and jellies for long life and shipping, but this freezer jam version captures all the ripeness of late spring!

Strawberry-Rhubarb Freezer Jam

4 cups fresh strawberries, stemmed (2 quarts)

2 cups sliced rhubarb

2 tablespoons lemon juice

1 box fruit pectin

¼ teaspoon butter (to reduce foaming)

5½ cups sugar

Prepare 8 ounce jars and lids or plastic freezer containers before cooking.

Place fruit, lemon juice, and pectin in a large pot and mix well, crushing the berries as you mix. Add butter and cook, stirring constantly, and bring to a rolling boil. Stir in the sugar and mix well. Bring back to a boil, boiling for 1 minute, stirring constantly. Remove from heat; skim off foam.

Ladle into jars, leaving ½ inch of headroom. Seal. Let cool at room temperature until the jam is set, about 24 hours, then freeze.

Makes five or six 8-ounce jars.

Join the villagers for a courtyard concert!

Grilled Caprese Kabobs

Plan on two kabobs per person, as an appetizer. Choose cheese balls in their own herb marinade for an extra burst of flavor.

For each kabob:

3 small tomatoes, cherry or grape

2 fresh mozzarella balls, herbed or plain

3 fresh basil leaves

olive oil, if you're using plain cheese

salt and pepper

Balsamic vinegar

a metal or bamboo skewer (soak bamboo skewers first)

Heat your grill. Use a perforated grill sheet, if you have one.

Thread the skewers, starting with a tomato, a basil leaf, a cheese ball, another basil leaf, and so on, until you've threaded three tomatoes and two cheese balls, with a leaf between each. If your basil leaves are large, fold in half. If you're using water-packed cheese, brush with olive oil.

Lay on the grill or grill sheet and close the grill lid. Grill 2–3 minutes, until the tomatoes are soft and the cheese begins to melt. Don't let your cheese fall off! Remove from grill and place skewers on serving plate. Season with salt and pepper if you'd like and drizzle with balsamic vinegar. Enjoy!

Gorgonzola Stuffed Dates

Plan on three dates per person, as an appetizer.

½ pound Medjool dates (18–20)

½ cup blue cheese, Gorgonzola, or goat cheese

3 ounces thinly sliced prosciutto

2–3 tablespoons balsamic vinegar

Preheat the oven to 350 degrees. Line a baking sheet with parchment paper.

Pit the dates by making a slit along one side and popping out the pit. Stuff the opening with cheese. Cut prosciutto into 2-inch-wide ribbons, about 4 inches long. Wrap each stuffed date with prosciutto.

Place wrapped dates on the baking sheet. Drizzle with balsamic vinegar. Bake 7–10 minutes, then turn dates and bake for another 7–10 minutes, until the prosciutto is slightly crisp.

Remove from oven and place dates on a platter. Serve immediately.

At home with Erin

Enchiladas with Ray's Red Chile Sauce

Make your own sauce—this recipe has a rich, complex flavor that is not too hot—or follow Erin's lead and use a good jarred sauce. This sauce freezes beautifully and can be used in burritos, tamales, tortilla soup, or other recipes.

The Sauce

2 ounces dried Ancho chiles

2 ounces dried Guajillo chiles

2–3 ounces dried California chiles

½ large or 1 medium white or yellow onion, coarsely chopped

3 cloves garlic, smashed with the side of a knife blade

1 large carrot, coarsely chopped

½–1 orange, sliced, including the peel (if the peel is thick, use half of it)

4–6 cups chicken or vegetable stock

1 teaspoon ground cumin

1 teaspoon dried oregano, crushed in your hands

1 teaspoon kosher salt, or more to taste

1 tablespoon masa harina (corn flour) or very finely ground cornmeal

½ lime, juiced (2–3 tablespoons of juice)

Using kitchen scissors and optional gloves, stem and seed the chiles.

Heat a large skillet on high and quickly dry roast the chiles, in batches, 1–2 minutes, to darken the skin; do not burn.

Place the peppers, onion, garlic, carrot, and orange in a large pot, and cover with the stock. Cover pot and bring to a rolling boil, then turn off the heat and let mixture sit about 30 minutes.

Ladle 2–3 cups of liquid and vegetables, about half and half, into a blender. Puree about 3 minutes and place in another pot or a non-staining bowl. Repeat with additional batches till complete.

Return sauce to pan and add the cumin, oregano, and salt. In a small bowl, make a slurry of the corn flour and about ¼ cup of the chile puree, to prevent clumping, then add to pot and stir in. Add lime juice. Bring to a boil, then reduce heat and simmer for 30 minutes, stirring occasionally and tasting to adjust the seasoning.

The Enchiladas
8 corn tortillas, 8-inch diameter
oil
sauce
1 pound beef (stew meat), slow cooked until it can be shredded with a fork, OR 1 pound chicken breast, cooked and shredded, OR 1 pound black beans, cooked (or one 16-ounce can)
2 ounces diced green chiles, fresh or canned
2 cups cheddar cheese, grated
10–12 green onions, chopped
½ cup cilantro, chopped (optional)
sour cream (optional)
fresh tomatoes, chopped (optional)

Preheat oven to 350 degrees.

Lightly oil the tortillas on each side and warm them in the oven to prevent cracking—you can warm them while the oven is preheating.

Mix your beef, chicken, or beans with the green chiles, and if you'd like, a few green onions and cilantro.

Pour ½ cup (about a ladleful) of sauce in the bottom of a 9x13 baking pan. Place a warmed tortilla on a plate. In the center, place about ¼ cup filling and a tablespoon of cheese. Roll up tightly and place in the baking dish. Repeat with the remaining tortillas.

Ladle more sauce over the top of the tortillas and sprinkle with cheddar. Bake about 15 minutes, until cheese melts. Serve with chopped onions and cilantro, and optional sour cream and tomatoes.

Unbaked enchiladas freeze beautifully in the pan. To serve, thaw and bake 15 to 20 minutes, or until thoroughly heated and the cheese is melted.

Fresca's picnic feast

Any picnic is better with a bottle of something sparkly. Erin and her family are enjoying a bottle of Brut Rosé Anna De Codorníu, a cava or Spanish sparkling wine, a blend of Pinot Noir and Chardonnay grapes. It's surprisingly affordable, and the pink bottle will get all your neighbors wondering what exotic drink you've discovered!

Tortellini Salad

16 ounces dried tortellini (tri-color is prettiest)

1 to 1½ cup marinated artichoke hearts, lightly drained and chopped

2 cups chopped tomatoes (grape or cherry tomatoes hold their shape and stay firm)

½ cup green onions, chopped

2 tablespoons capers

1 cup Parmesan, shredded

1 cup hard or Genoa salami, stacked and cut in strips (optional)

2 tablespoons chopped parsley or basil

¼ cup olive oil OR oil from the artichoke marinade

salt and fresh ground pepper

chopped bell pepper, any color (optional)

Cook pasta as directed; rinse with cold water and drain, stirring to release steam and stop pasta cooking.

In a large bowl, combine the artichoke hearts, tomatoes, green onions, capers, Parmesan, salami, and fresh herbs. Stir in the oil and mix well. Season with salt and pepper to taste.

Serves 8. Keeps several days.

Green Bean and Potato Salad

1 pound small, thin-skinned potatoes

¼ cup olive oil

1 tablespoon white wine vinegar

kosher salt and fresh ground black pepper

½ pound green beans—the French *haricots verts* work best

2 tablespoons minced onion

dried dill

caraway seeds

Bring 2 quarts of salted water to a boil and add the potatoes; cook until tender when pierced with a fork, about 20–25 minutes. Drain and rinse with cold water to stop the cooking. When cool, peel and dice. Toss with oil, vinegar, salt, and pepper

Boil 1–2 quarts of water and cook the green beans briefly, 2–3 minutes. Make sure they don't lose their color. Drain and rinse; when cool enough to handle, cut on the diagonal in 2-inch pieces.

Add beans to seasoned potatoes, stir in onions, and mix. Sprinkle with dill and caraway.

Serves 6.

At the Orchard with the Murphy Clan

Omelet Muffins

For a Sunday family gathering, Fresca bakes two muffin pans of these eggy morsels. This recipe serves 2–3 people. Use any veggies and cheese you have on hand; the bacon is optional.

3 or 4 strips of bacon

3 eggs

¼ cup milk

½ teaspoon vegetable oil (such as canola)

½ teaspoon baking powder

2 green onions

¼ to ½ bell pepper, diced

1 tablespoon fresh parsley or other herbs, chopped

¼ to ½ cup cheddar or other firm cheese, shredded

salt and pepper

cooking spray

salsa or sriracha (optional)

Preheat oven to 350 degrees. Cover a baking sheet with parchment paper and lay out the bacon. Bake for 20 minutes; flip the strips and bake another 5–10 minutes. Remove from tray onto paper towels and let cool until you can break or snip into bite-sized pieces.

Chop the vegetables and grate the cheese. Crack eggs into a small bowl; add the oil and baking soda and stir with a fork or small whisk until fully mixed. Season with salt and pepper.

Spray muffin tins lightly with cooking spray (or wipe with oil or butter, if you prefer). Divide bacon and vegetables into the cups; add the cheese. Pour in the egg batter. Don't fill to the top; they will puff up beautifully, and may spill over if too full.

Bake 20–25 minutes. Insert a knife or a tester stick to check for doneness; it should come out clean. Muffins will pop out neatly. Eat immediately.

Serves 2–3.

The classic Bellini
For each drink:
2 ounces white peach puree
3½ ounces chilled Prosecco or other sparkling wine

To make the peach puree:
In a blender, puree one white peach, including the skin, ½ teaspoon fresh lemon juice, and 2–3 ice cubes

Place the puree in the bottom of the flute. Add the Prosecco.

Rhubarb Custard Pie
The pie dough:
2½ cups unbleached all-purpose flour
2 tablespoons sugar
½ teaspoon salt
1 cup (2 sticks) cold unsalted butter, cut into ¼-inch cubes
6 tablespoons cold water (more, if you live in a dry climate)

To make the dough by hand, stir together the flour, sugar, and salt in a large bowl. Using a pastry cutter or two knives, cut the butter into the flour mixture until the texture resembles coarse cornmeal, with butter pieces no larger than small peas. Add the water and mix with a fork just until the dough pulls together.

To make the dough in a food processor, place the flour, sugar, and salt in the large bowl. Add the butter and pulse to blend, then mix on low speed until the texture resembles coarse cornmeal, with the butter pieces no larger than small peas. Add the water and mix just until the dough pulls together, or "gathers."

Place dough on a sheet of waxed paper or parchment paper, or a lightly floured cutting board. Shape into a ball and divide in half. Flatten each ball into a disk. Flatten it with your hands or the rolling pin, then top with another piece of waxed paper and begin rolling from the center. Turn the paper or cutting board so you can roll it out evenly, to about 12 inches in diameter and ⅛ inch thick. Repeat with second disk.

Makes one 9-inch double crust or lattice top pie.

The filling:
1½ cups sugar
¼ cup all-purpose flour
¼ teaspoon ground nutmeg
dash salt
3 eggs
4 cups rhubarb, in 1-inch slices
2 tablespoons butter, cut in pieces

Preheat oven to 400 degrees.

Mix sugar, flour, nutmeg, and salt in a medium bowl. Beat the eggs until smooth, and add sugar and flour mixture. Stir in rhubarb.

Prepare the pie dough. Line a 9-inch pie plate with dough. Fill with rhubarb mixture. Dot with butter. Cover with top crust or lattice, and seal; if you're not using a lattice top, cut six to eight 1-inch slits to allow steam to escape. Some bakers sprinkle white sugar on top. Bake about 50 minutes, until golden.

The Spanish Princess, aka the Italian Princess
Who knew Tanner's special cocktail would prove him a romantic at heart? If opening sparkling wine daunts you, remember to twist the bottle, not the cork, and remove the cork slowly to avoid a pop and fizz.

For each cocktail:

one sugar cube

a dash of West Indian Orange Bitters

a dash of Aztec Chocolate Bitters

¼ to ½ ounce Licor 43

chilled Prosecco, cava, or other sparkling wine (avoid brut
   champagne; in this drink, it will be too dry)

a twist of orange peel (optional), cut with a channel knife

Place the sugar cube in the bottom of the flute. Add a dash of orange
and a dash of chocolate bitters. Add enough liqueur to cover the sugar
cube. Pour in the Prosecco, at an angle to avoid foam. Rub the twist
of orange peel over the rim, and drop it in. Stir to release more sweetness if you like, or just let the sugar cube dissolve.

   Salut!

Readers, it's a thrill to hear from you.

Drop me a line at Leslie@LeslieBudewitz.com, connect with me on Facebook at LeslieBudewitzAuthor, or join my seasonal mailing list for book news and more. (Sign up on my website, www.LeslieBudewitz .com.) Reader reviews and recommendations are a big boost to authors; if you've enjoyed my books, please tell your friends. A book is but marks on paper until you read those pages and make the story yours.

Thank you.

About the Author

Leslie Budewitz is passionate about food, great mysteries, and her native Montana, the setting for her national-bestselling Food Lovers' Village Mysteries. The first, *Death al Dente*, won the 2013 Agatha Award for Best First Novel. She also writes the Spice Shop Mysteries, set in Seattle's Pike Place Market. A practicing lawyer, Leslie is the first author to win Agatha Awards for both fiction and nonfiction. She is a past president of Sisters in Crime.

Leslie loves to cook, eat, hike, travel, garden, and paint—not necessarily in that order. She lives in Northwest Montana with her husband, Don Beans, a doctor of natural medicine and musician, and their cat, an avid bird-watcher.

Visit her online at www.LeslieBudewitz.com, where you can find maps of the village and surrounding area, recipes, and more.